SOMETHING FISHY

Shane Maloney is deputy director of the Brunswick Institute, a weatherboard think-tank financed by his wife (www.shanemaloney.com/the_brunswick_institute.html). His previous Murray Whelan novel, *The Brush Off*, was awarded the Ned Kelly Prize for best Crime Novel and shortlisted for the Vance Palmer Prize for fiction. He is also the author of *Stiff*, *The Big Ask* and *Nice Try*.

SOMETHING FISHY

SHANE MALONEY

CANONGATE

Edinburgh · New York · Melbourne

First published in 2002 by The Text Publishing Company,
Melbourne, Australia

First published in Great Britain in 2006 by Canongate Books,
14 High Street, Edinburgh, EH1 1TE

1

British Library Cataloguing-in-Publication Data
A catalogue record for this book is available on
request from the British Library

1 84195 810 7 (10-digit ISBN)
978 1 84195 810 1 (13-digit ISBN)

Typeset in Sabon by Palimpsest Book Production Limited,
Polmont, Stirlingshire
Printed and bound by Clays Ltd, St Ives plc

www.canongate.net

Politicians also have no leisure, because they are always aiming at something beyond political life itself, power and glory, or happiness.
Aristotle, *Ethics*

A fraction of a second, that's all it takes.

By my reckoning, Rodney Syce and Adrian Parish began their break-out from the Melbourne Remand Centre at precisely the moment I emerged from the trees in the Fitzroy Gardens and found Lyndal Luscombe sitting on the bench beside the birdbath fountain.

Her message said she'd wait there until six, hoping the Hon. Murray Whelan could make it. A personal matter. The Legislative Council usher must have liked that bit because he was even more inscrutable than usual when he passed me the note during the third reading of the Administrative Resources Amendment Bill (1994).

I got the note just after five-thirty, a welcome distraction from the drone of the Minister for Administrative Services. Rising from my place in the back row of the opposition benches, I bowed to the Speaker and sidled out of the chamber, hoping the party whip wouldn't notice I was gone.

Not that my presence in the upper house of the state legislature made a skerrick of difference, of course. Since our disastrous defeat at the last election, there were so few of us left in parliament that to describe the Victorian branch of the Australian Labor Party as an impotent rump would have seriously overstated both our size and influence.

I left Parliament House by the rear door, dodged a snaggle of peak-hour trams and made my way through Treasury Place, the pavement thick with homeward-bound public servants. Whatever it was, it must have been pretty important for Lyndal to summon me like this. Why not wait until parliament adjourned for dinner at seven, talk to me then? And why the gardens?

Oh Christ, I thought, picking up my pace as I entered the long avenue of overarching elms. She's in the gardens because of what borders them. The Freemasons Hospital. The Mercy. Medical suites and day-procedure centres and rows of Victorian terraces filled with specialists. She's been to a medico of some sort. Something's wrong and she wants to talk about it. Somewhere quiet, somewhere she'll have my full attention.

I came out of the trees and saw her before she saw me, bathed in a pool of late-afternoon sunshine, the light catching the chestnut hues in her hair. Her eyes were downcast and she was fiddling with the hem of her knit skirt where it ended just above her knees. Her lips were moving as if she were rehearsing lines. She definitely had something on her mind.

It was about then that the alarm must have gone off at the Remand Centre. Not that I could hear it, three kilometres away on the other side of the downtown grid. I was attending to my own, inner alarm bells. Don't panic, I told myself, wait until you hear what she has to say.

'Hi,' I said cheerfully, bending to plant a kiss on her cheek. Act natural, let her take her own sweet time.

Lyndal met my descending smile with a brisk, open-palmed slap. 'Don't you dare,' she warned. 'You filthy beast.'

I rocked back on my heels, jaw slack. What had I done to deserve this? It wasn't as though I hadn't tried to kiss her before. Or worse. And succeeded.

'What's got into you?' I said, hand pressed to my face.

Quickly glancing around, I checked that nobody was watching. Not exactly good for the parliamentary image, copping a biff from a woman, especially one as attractive as Lyndal. But the gardens were deserted. A mid-autumn chill was already rising from the lawns. A spill of white-clad nurses emerged from the Mercy Hospital across the road, but none of them looked our way. Cars rolled past, their drivers intent on making good time to the freeway.

'What's got into me?' said Lyndal. 'I'll tell you what's got into me. You have, Mr Sexpot. I'm pregnant.'

My jaw resumed the slack position. 'Pregnant?'

'Potted. Up the duff. Preggers. Bun in the oven. Expecting.'

Pressing both cheeks, I sank onto the seat beside her. 'Goodness,' I said.

Lyndal inched away. 'Goodness had nothing to do with it, pal.' Her counterfeit ire dissolved into a self-congratulatory grin.

'You're sure?'

'Sure as spermatozoa,' she nodded. 'And I've got the picture to prove it.' She fished in her handbag and thrust a

3

Polaroid at me. It looked like an underexposed satellite reconnaissance photograph of atmospheric turbulence over the South China Sea. 'She's the spitting image of you, don't you think?'

'She?' A grainy blob occupied the north-west quadrant of the photograph, a furball in a blizzard. 'How?' I said. 'I mean when?'

Lyndal's expression had become beatific, placid, wise. Christ, freshly duffed and she was already turning into the Earth Mother. 'By the usual method,' she said. 'Last January, during the summer holidays. One of those lazy afternoons with nothing better to do than.'

'Not that when,' I said. 'I mean, when's it due? I mean she.'

'Nine months from the time of conception, Murray,' she said patiently. 'Even you should be able to figure it out.'

My fingers did the sums. 'October.' But it was already April. 'How long have you known? And why didn't you say anything?'

'I wanted to be one hundred per cent sure that everything was okay before I told you.' She nodded towards the building beside the hospital. 'I've just seen the obstetrician. It's too early for amniocentesis but the ultrasound indicates a normal baby.'

'Normal?' I said, incredulous. 'With you for a mother? A sneaky minx who doesn't even bother to tell her poor dumb paramour that she's gone and got herself knocked up.'

Waves of relief broke over me, a treacly ocean of love and pleasure and pride. My feet executed a little jig. Slipping my forearm beneath Lyndal's thighs, I swung her legs up onto the bench and tilted her sideways so she sprawled on her back the length of the slatted seat. I dropped to my knees and gently pinned her shoulders.

'Under the circumstances,' I said, 'I don't see how you've got any choice but to marry me forthwith.'

She smirked back. 'Determined to make an honest woman of me, are you, Murray Whelan, MLC?'

Oh yes, indeed. I lowered my face to hers. She yielded, squirming beneath my caress, ripe and lush, letting her arms dangle. I laid a hand on her breast. 'Now that you mention it, I do detect a certain womanly fulsomeness.'

She smacked my hand away and swung her feet to the ground. 'Get up,' she commanded. 'You look ridiculous. Forty-two-year-old politician in a double-breasted suit, down on his knees, slobbering like a teenage Romeo.'

I stayed exactly where I was. 'Groping the tits of the fiercely independent thirty-five-year-old public policy analyst whose swelling belly is heavy with his love child.'

Lyndal tugged down her hem and smoothed her dress. 'Who are you calling heavy?' Her hands lingered on her abdomen for a moment longer than necessary as she adjusted the fall of her skirt. 'Let's go and have a celebratory drink. We've got things to talk about.'

I gave her my hands and let her haul me to my feet. 'Should you be drinking?' I tutted.

'Believe me, Murray,' she said. 'If it wasn't for drink, I wouldn't be in this condition.'

Hand in hand, we ambled towards the Hilton, the nearest licensed premises. 'This'll mean a lot of changes,' said Lyndal.

'About twenty a day for the first few months,' I agreed. 'There'll be crap everywhere. We'll need nappy service.

Lucky for you I already have some experience in these matters.'

'That's one of the things we need to talk about,' said Lyndal. 'How do you think Red will react to the news?'

Red was my thirteen-year-old son, the only good thing to come out of my marriage. After several years of Olympic-standard wrestling for custody with his mother, Wendy, I won the prime-parent medal when Red reached high-school age. Very convenient for Wendy, who had meanwhile plighted her imperious troth to a silvertail Sydney lawyer and spawned a brood of twins.

'Red adores you,' I said. 'He'll be just as pleased as I am.' An exaggeration, but only a slight one. Fact was, the two of them got along like a house on fire.

'He won't mind that his father has knocked up the babysitter?'

'That was a low blow. Red doesn't think of you like that.'

But it was a role she played well, tending to the home fires and riding herd on the lad's homework when duty compelled my attendance at an all-night sitting of parliament, a party meeting or a commitment in the constituency.

At a break in the traffic, we skipped across the road, hands still linked. The day was drawing to a close, the last beams of the sun slipping between the office towers of the central city, catching the filigree of cast-iron lacework on the rows of terrace houses that faced across the gardens. Had I looked over my shoulder, I might have noticed the police helicopter, a distant speck, still inaudible, coming fast out of the setting sun.

We entered East Melbourne, a district of well-heeled gentility, its appearance largely unchanged since the 1890s.

A block away, down a slight incline, lay the Hilton.

Conrad's pleasure-dome was a recent interloper, a tower of shit-brown bricks erected in the 1960s on the ruins of the Cliveden Mansions, an elegantly loopy late-Victorian lodging house for gentlemen bachelors. In place of four-poster beds and brass-potted aspidistras, the Hilton offered weekend-getaway packages and express checkout. Hardly our usual watering hole. But these were exceptional circumstances. Lyndal's news required immediate access to a flute of Moët.

'Anyway,' I said. 'You never complained about keeping an eye on Red from time to time.'

And she hadn't, of course. After all, we'd been shacked up together for the best part of a year. Informally at first, a matter of convenience. Then, after I sold the cramped little workman's terrace I shared with Red in Fitzroy and moved to a larger place in the electorate, officially.

We sauntered, our arms around each other's waists, our hips moulded together. 'If you're going to be a cry-baby,' she said, 'you'd better make the most of it before the real thing arrives.'

'Show me the picture again,' I said. 'I couldn't read the name-tag.'

Lyndal pulled the Polaroid from her bag and dangled it in front of my eyes. 'Lysistrata,' she said. 'See. Says it right there. Lysistrata Luscombe.'

I snatched it away and tilted it to the light. 'Lysistrata Luscombe-Whelan, don't you mean?' I said. 'A bit of a tongue-twister but it's got a certain ring. Wasn't Lysistrata that Greek chick who went on a sex strike? I hope you're not getting any ideas along those lines.'

To assure myself otherwise, I backed her against the

cast-iron fence rails of the nearest terrace, pressed my lips to her neck and began to work my way upwards. Lyndal squirmed against me in a gratifying manner. 'Get it while you can,' I whispered. 'Before your body is devastated by stretch marks and the ravages of childbirth.'

A car horn bleated in the distance, followed by screeching tyres and the faint metallic *clump* of a low-speed fender-bender. My head turned at the sound and Lyndal blew a raspberry in my ear. Snatching the Polaroid from my hand, she wriggled free.

I lurched after her, the two of us playing tiggy-tiggy-touchwood in the golden light. The only thing missing was a veil of gauze over the lens and a soundtrack of violins.

But it wasn't Mantovani and His Orchestra that surged in the background. It was the thunder of an approaching motor, a swelling chorus of sirens, the bass thump of a helicopter.

As we turned, wondering at the sudden ruckus, a powerful motorbike erupted from the gardens, its rider hunched low over the handlebars. A passenger straddled the pillion, the two helmeted figures clad in identical orange coveralls. Rocketing across the kerb, the bike cut the path of the oncoming traffic, then banked sharply to the right, coming our way.

A police car flashed past us, speeding to intercept, siren wailing, lights flashing. Cut off, the bike swerved and went into a skid, spilling its riders as it toppled over and skittered across the roadway. It came to rest against a parked van. The prowl car braked and two uniformed cops jumped out. Drawing sidearms, they crouched behind their open doors, bellowing for the riders to halt.

But the boiler-suited men were already back on their feet. One sprinted for the bike, the other hobbled to catch up. The cops were yelling, more sirens were converging, horns blared, tyres screeched. The first rider reached the bike, wrestled it upright and climbed aboard. His limping confederate struggled to cover the distance. A shot rang out. He was shooting at the cops. They returned fire. *Pam, pam, pam.*

We were thirty metres away. It didn't seem nearly enough. I caught Lyndal by the wrist and pushed at the front gate of the nearest terrace. The iron latch was down. I fumbled with it, letting go of her. *Pam, pam, pam.* Above the sound of the shots, the bike roared into action. My mind was clear but my fingers were putty. My legs turned liquid. The bike reared, front wheel spinning, then it burned rubber and shot forward, past the police car, up over the gutter and along the footpath, heading straight for us.

Lyndal pressed herself back against me as I finally managed to lift the latch. The gate sprang open and I stumbled through, reaching back to drag Lyndal with me. As I grabbed her elbow, the speeding motorcycle slammed into her, tearing her from my grasp and flinging her into the air like a doll.

Above the roar of the departing bike, I heard a crack as her head hit the stonework of the gatepost.

I dropped to my knees at her side, just in time to see the light go out of her eyes.

On the day the coroner's report was due to be released, I woke in darkness.

But not, it gradually came to me, total darkness. A faint, blood-tinged glow hovered at the edge of my consciousness. After a while, I rolled onto my side and turned my eyes towards it, the digital display on the clock-radio by my bed. For exactly eighteen minutes I stared at the numbers, counting them off. One minute for every month since the events in East Melbourne.

At 5 a.m., I threw back the bedclothes, planted my feet on the floor and cancelled the alarm just as the sting sounded for the news. The news could wait. As far as I was concerned, the whole world could fucking wait.

The house was cold and I cursed myself for having forgotten, yet again, to pre-set the timer on the central heating. Truth be told, the house was too big for just the two of us, much bigger than our old place in Fitzroy. But a member of parliament should live in his constituency and Fitzroy did not fall within the boundaries of Melbourne Upper, so a move was inevitable from the moment I was endorsed for the seat. Anyway, there were three of us when I bought the place. With more to come, I'd hoped.

I padded down the hall in slippers and bathrobe, straight into the kitchen without knocking on Red's door. Another ten minutes wasn't going to make any difference. And a growing lad needs all the sleep he can get. Thirty-six hours a day, minimum, if Red was any indication. I lit the gas, opened the blinds and stood at the window while I waited for the kettle to boil. Not that I could see anything. The October dawn was still an hour away.

In daylight, I would have seen a rectangle of dewy lawn, slightly overgrown and bordered with clumps of daffodils. Garden furniture, still sheathed in winter plastic. Drifts of japonica blossoms, turning to mush. My personal low-maintenance Gethsemane. And beyond the back fence, the rooftops of Melbourne's northern suburbs.

For more than thirty years, off and on, I'd lived and worked in this part of town, breathed its vapours, taken its temperature, counted its heads. I was a kid when my father took the licence on the Carter's Arms in Northcote. After university and a stint as a union official, I returned to run the office of the area's representative in the state legislature. A job which I now held in my own right, thanks to 69.52 per cent of its voters on a two-party preferred basis. It was my Province, to use the terminology, from the Ford factory in Broadmeadows to the Greek senior citizens home at Thornbury, in all its brick-veneer, blue-collar splendour.

Unfortunately, my election had coincided with the utter defeat of the Labor Party after a decade in office. The worm had turned and, for the past three years, my constituents had been punished for their traditional adherence to the party of social democracy. Their schools and hospitals had been closed, municipal councils abolished, a poll tax imposed.

About which, at that particular moment, I could not have given a tinker's. What did the voters of Melbourne Upper, asleep in their beds, know of loss?

Most days, I managed to keep a lid on my self-pity and heartache. But that particular morning, I felt entitled to the consolations of blame.

The kettle began to whistle. I poured boiling water over a tea-bag and carried the brew towards the bathroom. As I passed, I thumped on Red's door with a balled fist, threw it open and flicked the switch.

'Yes or no?' After a silent count of ten, I repeated the question. 'Yes or no?'

The lump on the bed shifted. Sock-clad feet emerged from the quilt accompanied by a compliant moan. 'Okay, okay.'

Exactly twenty-seven minutes later, we crossed the Yarra at the Punt Road bridge. The streets were almost deserted. As usual, Red hibernated the whole way, his school uniform stuffed into the backpack between his feet. He was fifteen now. His voice had deepened, fluff was sprouting on his upper lip and he would soon be taller than his father. But although no longer a cub, he was not yet the full grizzly. He was still my baby boy.

Over the river, I followed Alexandra Avenue along the bank, the ribbon of water veiled in a thinning mist. The sky was high and clear and the last of the stars were fading fast. A fair spring day was predicted. As we approached the boathouse, I shoved the *William Tell Overture* into the tape deck and cranked up the volume.

Red lunged for the eject button, swearing like a stevedore at a joke that was even more tired than he was. He fumbled for his bag as I nosed into the kerb. 'I've got play rehearsal after school, don't forget, and we're working on the maths challenge at Simon's place. Won't be home until eight-thirty.'

'Got everything you need?' I dug out a twenty. 'Rake the path and mow the lawn, I'll double it.'

'Weekend,' he yawned, feeding a tangle of limbs though the car door.

He was long and lanky, taller and thinner than I had been at fifteen. His teeth were straighter than mine, too, thanks to an orthodontic bill that would have financed a moon shot. But the similarities outweighed the differences. In the ways that mattered we were very alike.

As he closed the door, Red paused. 'That inquest thing,' he said. 'It's today, right?'

I nodded.

'Fucking coppers,' he said. 'Covering their arses.'

Other lads were already lowering sculls into the water and sorting equipment. Hoisting his backpack, Red shut the door and loped down the incline. When he reached the bottom, he looked back and raised his arm in farewell. He made his open palm into a clenched-fist salute. *Venceremos*, Comrade Dad.

I drove towards the city centre, following the course of the river.

I turned on the radio for the six o'clock bulletin. The

announcer's voice droned. Jury still out on O. J. Simpson. Federal election tipped for early in new year.

A butterscotch smudge was creeping upwards from the eastern horizon. Over the mist-shrouded river, beyond the tubular metal canopy of the tennis centre, lights were appearing in the office towers. A pod of joggers powered along the path beneath the newly mantled elms. This was the postcard view of Melbourne, the garden city on a river of bridges. It was a pretty sight at dawn, one that I enjoyed three times a week, thanks to Red. But the pleasure was qualified. My home town was changing fast. Not just the shape of the skyline but the spirit of the place.

Further downstream, a vast new casino was taking shape beside the Yarra. The plutocrats were at the helm and a veil of secrecy had descended over the processes of government. A cult of personality surrounded the Premier. The smirking bully was king and Fuck You was the official ideology. The public interest was a bankrupt notion in the heads of fools.

I switched off the radio, made an illegal U-turn and parked. Sculls began to appear from upstream. A quad, then a coxless four, their hulls half-concealed in mist, oars dipping rhythmically. Girls, I realised, their coach on a bicycle. Ducks rose as they skimmed past, flapped and settled. Then, a few minutes later, came an eight. Red's crew. Year Ten boys, C division, all knees and elbows, still settling into their stroke.

I stood beside the car and watched the boat glide past. Focused on his task, pumping away between Max Kline and Danny Chang, Red was oblivious to my presence. That was fine by me. Rowing was his thing, unprecedented in our branch of the Whelan family. But that's what you get when you send your son to a private school. Not that I had much choice. Not after they closed the local high school. Not with the senior bureaucrat in the education department being paid a cash bounty for every government school teacher fired or strong-armed into redundancy. Four thousand of them in two years.

So it was either have Red commute to an overcrowded classroom with a leaking roof and a demoralised teacher or bow to *force majeure* and go private. And it wasn't as if I was the only Labor politician to take his kid out of the public system. After all, it's only natural to want your child to enjoy the same privileges that you had. All the more if you never had them. And, Christ knows, it kept the boy's mother off my back, hectoring me long-distance about my paternal shortcomings.

Red had adjusted well to the change of schools. Some of his mates from Fitzroy High had also made the shift, which eased the transition. And he'd discovered rowing, an activity more benign than others available to his age group.

'Builds up the shoulders,' he argued, beefy delts being a self-evident good to the contemporary teenage male.

As I watched him pass, tending his oar, I suspected that the allure of the sport lay in the opportunity it provided for him to be both alone and part of a team. That, and a sort of aristocratic élan behind which a boy can conceal his adolescent uncertainties.

Flash motors were beginning to whoosh down the hill from the thicketed heights of Toorak. When Red's eight slid under the Swan Street bridge, I got back into my Magna Executive and joined the flow.

By six-thirty, I was pacing the treadmill in the gym at the City Baths, a towel around my neck, a newspaper draped across the console. I did my usual ten kilometres, going nowhere, reading as I went. The *Age*, the *Australian*, the *Herald Sun*, a summary of pending amendments to the Gaming and Betting Act, agenda papers for the Public Accounts and Estimates Committee. Anything to keep from thinking.

Lyndal had weaned me off cigarettes and making the effort to stay healthy had become a way of honouring her memory. But trudging along a rubber belt was never more than a chore and I still kept a packet of smokes in the glove-box of the car for moments of maximum stress. I finished my session with a couple of laps of the pool and a bowl of fibre in the chlorine-scented snack-bar, then crawled through the swell of rush-hour to Parliament House.

For all its neo-classical splendour, its colonnaded portico and gilded chambers, the House was feeling its age. A haughty Victorian dowager, it was inadequate to the demands of the late twentieth century. Behind the brass and marble, beyond the pedimented portals and wood-panelled halls, it was a rabbit warren of file-filled crannies and windowless cubicles. Only the biggest of the big chiefs warranted a private office and for opposition backbenchers like me, the lowest of the low, it offered a desk in a shared office in a permanently temporary outbuilding abutting the carpark.

The Henhouse, we called it. But despite its clapboard construction and nylon carpet, it met its obligations to protocol. The name-plate beside the plywood door listed me as 'The Honourable M. E. Whelan'.

The first to arrive, I turned on the lights as I walked along the corridor to my office. Twenty years of schooling and they put you on the day shift. I transferred the contents of my briefcase to the desk and hung up my overcoat. Aquascutum, a fortieth birthday present to myself, a bit the worse for wear. Like its owner.

Get a grip, I warned myself. Today would be hard, but there had been harder days. Much harder. Keep it in perspective, don't let them get to you. Lyndal's death was part of a big news story, a major episode in an unfinished saga. And with the cops keen to generate optimum coverage, it was inevitable the media would come after me when the report became public.

And what would I say? That I felt some sort of closure? Pig's arse I did.

Problem was, I couldn't say what I wanted to say. It wasn't just that it was impossible to express my feelings about Lyndal's death in a neat, five-second sound bite. If that was all they wanted, the platitudes could be found. I was a politician, after all. But what if I was quizzed about the subsequent events? If that happened, and if I didn't keep a tight rein on myself, the shit would really start to fly.

I sat down at my standard-issue, formica-veneer desk. Keep it moving, that was my watchword. Head down, tail up. In-tray to out-tray. The first item was a reminder letter from the state secretariat regarding the deadline for submissions to the party reorganisation review process. I stared down at it and yawned. The phone rang.

'Saw the light,' said a woman's voice. 'Thought it was you. Wondering how you're set today. Any chance of a favour?'

It was Della McLeish, administrative assistant to Jim Constantinides, leader of the opposition in the upper house, calling from Jim's office in the main building. Jim was the closest thing I had to a boss, so a request from Della carried a certain amount of weight. 'It's a last-minute stand-in job,' she explained. 'Out-of-town sitting of the Coastal Management Advisory Panel. Comes under Natural Resources, Moira Henley's brief. Moira's gone down with the flu and Jim feels we should show the flag.'

'It'll mean missing a day in parliament,' I said. 'And you know how much I enjoy sitting on the backbench with my thumb up my quoit. So what's the pay-off?'

'A chance to observe the democratic process,' said Della. 'And a free seafood lunch in beautiful San Remo.'

'I don't know anything about coastal management.'

'What's to know? The tide comes in, the tide goes out. Session starts at eleven, finishes at four. I'll send over the agenda papers, okay?'

'Might as well,' I said. 'And thanks, Del.'

'For what?'

'As if you don't know.'

San Remo was a hundred kilometres away. Good old Della had cooked up a reason to send me somewhere beyond the reach of journalists. Somewhere I wouldn't get my nose rubbed in it.

I was touched by the gesture. It reminded me that the Labor Party was a kind of family. Dysfunctional, certainly, but one to which I had belonged, man and boy, for almost thirty years.

I spent the next forty-five minutes drafting a speech opposing a forthcoming amendment to the Government Audit Act, a measure requiring that the Auditor-General carry out his duties with a bucket over his head. You do what you can. By the time I'd roughed up an outline, other MPs and staffers had begun to arrive for the day.

I found a half-dozen of them in the lunchroom, clustered around the coffee plunger, chewing the fat. The Honourable Kaye Clegg, Member for Melbourne West, had just returned from Sydney. She was talking about an event that happened there a year earlier, the murder of a Labor MP as he arrived home after a party branch meeting. The case was still unsolved.

'Word is, it was a professional hit by Vietnamese heavies,' she said, dunking a shortbread.

'At least somebody thought he was important enough to kill,' said Dennis 'Ivor' Biggun, the Member for Ballarat. 'Here in Victoria a Labor MP can't even get run over. People cross the street when they see us coming. What do you reckon, Murray?'

'I'm thinking of having a whip-around, see if I can raise enough for a contract on you-know-who.' I cocked my head in the direction of the Premier's office.

Ivor tossed a coin onto the table. 'Count me in.'

'Pay to have him whacked? I wouldn't give him the satisfaction,' said our deputy spokesperson on health.

Most of the others dredged change from purses and pockets, adding it to Ivor's ten cents. The total came to ninety-five cents.

'That's this party's problem in a nutshell,' sighed Kaye Clegg.

We drifted in a group to Parliament House for the weekly caucus meeting. A new leader had recently been installed, a thin-lipped automaton with television hair and the voter appeal of diphtheria. He gave us a half-hour lecture on the need to shake off our image as big spenders. I sat at the back and rested my eyes.

When I got back to the Henhouse, the agenda papers for the coastal management whatsit had arrived. I tossed them into my briefcase and rang my constituency office in Melbourne Upper. It had just gone nine-thirty, opening time. Ayisha, my eyeball on the ground, answered the phone.

'That cop, Detective Sergeant Meakes,' she reported. 'He rang a few minutes ago. Said to tell you that the coroner's findings'll be handed down mid-afternoon and the police media unit will issue a statement immediately afterwards. Said if you've got any questions, don't hesitate to call him.'

'Very thoughtful,' I said. 'Considering what the cops think about my questions. Anything else?'

'Three media calls, so far. "Today Tonight", the *Herald Sun* and ABC radio. You going to talk to them?'

'Think I should?'

'It might help,' she said.

'Do you really think I should allow myself to be made an object of pity because the cops can't do their job? Act like a politician who can't resist the chance to get his face on the news?'

'Maybe there's a chance it'll help, that's all I'm saying.'

'If only that was true, mate. But it's all bullshit. Call them back and tell them I'm not available.'

'That won't stop them looking for you.'

'They'll search in vain,' I said. 'I'll be in San Remo for the rest of the day.'

'San Remo? What's happening in San Remo?'

'Very little,' I said. 'I hope.'

An hour down the South-Eastern got me to the Bass Highway turn-off at Lang Lang, where the suburban sprawl finally gives way to the lush green of dairy farms, market gardens and wetlands. The forecast was holding and the only clouds in the powder-blue sky were thin shreds on the southern horizon. The highway forked again and Westernport Bay came into view, a verdigris slab fringed with mud-flats and tidal shoals.

Just before the bridge across the narrows to Phillip Island, I took the turn into San Remo. The venue for the day's meeting was a function room in a motel at the jetty end of Marine Parade. I found the place, parked out front and stood for a few minutes, breathing the ozone and contemplating the view.

At the public fish-cleaning benches on the foreshore reserve, a flock of seagulls squabbled over the innards of somebody's catch. Down at the jetty, commercial fishing boats were unloading tubs of whiting and school shark, fodder for the fish'n'chip shops of Melbourne. Near the war memorial, an elderly couple was sharing a thermos at a picnic table, squinting out at the water.

According to the paperwork from Della, the Coastal Management Advisory Panel had been established to provide input into government management of the state's coastline. A seaside location was chosen for its inaugural public meeting to facilitate the participation of what were called 'coastal resource user groups'.

It was just past eleven. I went into the motel lobby and followed the signs to the Cormorant Room. It had salmon-pink acrylic carpet, stackable furniture and wide windows that overlooked the Phillip Island bridge. The five-member panel was presiding from behind a long table on a platform facing a couple of dozen chairs, less than half of which were occupied.

I recognised one of the panel members as Alan Bunting, the National Party member for the Mallee, semi-desert country a long way from the wave-lapped littoral. A genial, slightly tubby thirty-year-old, he owed his seat in parliament to the depth of his father's pockets. The Nats were the junior partner in the ruling coalition, and Alan was very much a junior Nat.

The other familiar face belonged to the chairman, Dudley Wilson, a big bluff fellow in his sixties with bulldog jowls and tragic blow-dried hair. Wilson was the leading light of GoVic, a cabal of business identities and civic worthies that served as a kind of kitchen cabinet to the Premier. Slash-and-burn free-market ideologues to a man.

I wondered why a high-flyer like Wilson was chairing such a low-key advisory committee. Dudley Wilson didn't waste his attention on anything that didn't have a dollar in it.

The only other face I recognised belonged to the civil servant taking minutes. Her name was Gillian Zarek. During Labor's time in office, I'd worked with her briefly at Planning and Regional Development. Behind her butterball exterior, Gillian was sharp as a tack. She saw me at the door, gave me a wry smile and used her chins to indicate where I should sit.

I nodded hello to Alan Bunting, then sat and thumbed through the agenda papers. A bloke in a bargain-basement suit was making a submission on behalf of the Sporting Anglers Association, directing his words straight at Dudley Wilson.

'Last time I saw a face like that,' he was saying, 'it had a hook in it.'

Wishful thinking, I realised. He was, in fact, affirming the ongoing commitment of the recreational fishing sector to managed bio-diversity. It was already evident that the Coastal Management Advisory Panel was going to be an arid source of diversion.

Over the next ninety minutes, the bio-sustainable line-dangler was succeeded by speakers from the Surf Lifesaving Association, the Shipwreck Heritage Trust, Disability Access and a group opposed to the dumping of raw sewage into the Gippsland lake system. Proceedings drifted like the continents, the room was overheated and my attention soon wandered out the window.

The seagulls had quit the gutting-sink. They were perched on the railing of the bridge, grooming their plumage. An incoming tide inched across the mud-flats. A wet-suited sailboard rider tacked back and forth. A gaff-rigged couta boat sailed out of the marina at the tip of Phillip Island, then sailed back in. The customary Greeks bobbed for squid off the jetty.

At 12:45, Dudley Wilson announced the lunch adjournment.

Alan Bunting immediately pounced. 'Hello, Murray. You're doing duty for Moira Henley, so I've been given to understand. You'll be joining us for lunch, of course.'

He led me into a room where the official party was lining up, plates in hand, at a buffet table laid with platters of prawn salad, breadcrumbed calamari rings and a baked schnapper with a slice of pimento-stuffed olive over its oven-roasted eyeball.

'You know our chairman, of course,' Bunting said, manoeuvring me towards Dudley Wilson.

Wilson regarded me over his jowls. We'd once exchanged a brief handshake at some public event. Wilson nodded, remembering, and I nodded back. Then, casting a disdainful glance at the buffet, he pulled a mobile phone from his jacket pocket and walked away, dialling as he went.

Bunting introduced me to the other suits, a cross-section of the ruling demographic. An old boy, a wide boy and a bean counter. I made some tiny-talk over a plate of prawn salad, then slipped outside for a breath of air. I found Gillian Zarek sitting at a log picnic table on the foreshore, eating a sandwich from a paper bag. We exchanged hellos and agreed that the weather was indeed splendid for the time of year.

'So what's the story with Dudley Wilson?' I said. 'This is a bit downmarket for a big wheel like Dud, isn't it?'

Gillian wiped her fingers on a paper napkin, mock-dainty.

'Dudley Wilson is a well-known philanthropist, always atten-
tive to the voice of the community.'

A trio of pelicans wheeled overhead, wings spread, then
splashed down near the jetty.

'And that's a fine flight of pigs,' I said.

Gillian chortled. 'I could speculate, I suppose. But strictly
in a personal capacity.'

I ran fingertips across my lips, zipping them shut. Gillian
dropped her voice, although there was nobody within
hearing range.

'This public input stuff, it's just window-dressing,' she said.
'A couple more meetings like this, then the real agenda will
emerge. The privatisation of public assets along the coast.
Camping grounds, piers, lighthouses, they'll all be flogged to
commercial operators, turned into theme parks, resort hotels
and pay-per-view whale-watching towers. This panel will
recommend who gets what and how much they pay. As its
chairman, Dudley Wilson will be uniquely situated to
identify the easy-money opportunities.'

'Nice work if you can get it,' I said. The function of the
government, after all, was to transfer wealth from public to
private hands.

'Big cuts in the department's field staff are also on the
cards,' Gillian continued. 'Park rangers, fisheries officers and
so forth. They'll say it's more cost-effective to use contract
labour.'

'Flexible types who can be persuaded that jet-skis and
dolphins are a natural mix.'

Gillian balled her empty sandwich bag and flicked it into
a nearby litter bin. 'Exactly.'

We contemplated the prospect in morose silence. For the

moment, it was just speculation. In time, it would be a *fait accompli*. Either way, there was nothing we could do about it.

I left Gillian with the pelicans, took a turn down the jetty, then returned for the afternoon session. The panel was settling back into place, preparing to hear from the Friends of the Ninety Mile Beach. Alan Bunting beckoned me over. 'Forgot to mention,' he said. 'There's a bit of a boat trip afterwards. A tour of Seal Rocks in the Natural Resources launch. You're invited, of course. Privilege of rank and all that. Three-fifteen at the jetty, unless you have to hurry back for some union conclave at the Trades Hall.'

I indulged his little joke with a self-deprecating shrug. 'I'll check,' I said. 'Thanks for the invite.'

Frankly there was scant appeal in the prospect of being stuck on a boat with a bunch of government placemen, a young fogey and a corrupt henchman of the Premier. Seals, I thought as I took my seat, waving their flippers and bellowing. It'll be just like parliament.

Proceedings resumed, first with the beach lovers then the Charter Boat Operators Association. As the voices droned, my thoughts returned to the coroner's report. Not that I had any doubt about the verdict.

The facts of the case were simple. Two career criminals, Adrian Parish and Rodney Syce, used smuggled explosives to blast their way out of the Remand Centre, where they were being held for sentencing. Both were looking at major time— Parish for robbing a bank, Syce for an aggravated burglary in which he bashed an elderly man.

Their escape was well planned and aided from the outside. The bike was waiting nearby, a stolen Kawasaki racer, key in the ignition. Syce was the rider. Taking advantage of the rush-hour traffic, the pair made a daring and dangerous dash through the congested streets of the central city and under the tree canopy of the Fitzroy Gardens.

They might well have got away if not for a couple of rookie cops en route to the bingle outside the Hilton. Responding to the radio alert, the young cops intercepted the escapees as they emerged from the gardens. Parish died in hospital that evening, a police bullet in his lung.

The Kawasaki was found in a laneway in nearby Richmond. But the police dragnet closed on empty air. Syce had evaporated.

Lines of enquiry were pursued, screws applied, trees shaken. The bike was supplied by one of Parish's crim associates, a small-timer. On Parish's instructions, he put two pistols in the pannier. Only one gun was recovered, so the other was presumably taken by Syce. But as to Syce himself, Parish's mate didn't know him, had no idea where he'd gone or might be.

Initially, the police were confident. Syce wouldn't get far, they swore. He was no mastermind. He would leave a trail. It was just a matter of time before he was back in custody, facing the consequences. Cold comfort, they admitted, but the only kind they could promise.

But that wasn't what happened. Fuck all was what happened. Weeks, months, a year passed. Old leads petered out. New leads failed to emerge. Finally, someone senior decided to bring on the coronial hearing into Lyndal's death. The attendant publicity might refresh the memory of the public. Or prick a guilty conscience.

So Lyndal's inquest, which should have been the formal

administrative response to a death in a public place, became a desperate media stunt.

I played my part. I stood in the box and gave my eye-witness account. I was the grieving widower at press conferences and Coroner's Court door-stops, appealing for anybody with pertinent information to come forward.

The net outcome was a fat zero.

And now, months later, the slow-turning wheels of justice were grinding out the formal verdict. Again the media would turn its fleeting attention to Lyndal. Again the coals of memory would be fanned. Again the police would call for anyone with information to ring the Crime Stoppers hotline. Again they would present themselves as resolute and tireless. In fact, they were clueless, incapable even of tracking down a petty crim with no known associates in the state.

Useless bastards.

The last speaker of the day, a representative of the Abalone Industry Association, was finishing his presenta-tion. Sober of suit and careful with his words, he came across more like a lawyer than a man who made his living by scraping marine snails off submerged rocks, 'reminding the panel that the legal abalone catch is worth $50 million a year to this state. The ongoing sustainability of the industry depends on government willingness to tackle the issues confronting it.'

Dudley Wilson cleared his throat and peered down from the table. 'On behalf of the panel, I thank you for your input. Your views will be given every consideration when we are framing our recommendations.' He then declared the meeting adjourned until a date to be advised.

It was just on the dot of three o'clock. Unable to contain

the urge, I scurried out to the Magna and twiddled the radio dial across the hourly bulletins. French nuke Pacific atoll. Again. Princess Diana denies bonking rugger bugger. Government approves further casino expansion. No mention of the inquest.

I decided to take the boat ride after all. The temperature was holding nicely, the sky appeared benign and almost four hours of daylight remained. I shed my tie, traded my suit jacket for the sweatshirt in my gym bag, and headed for the jetty.

The Department of Natural Resources launch was moored at a landing near the berths of the commercial fishing fleet, motor idling, exhausts burbling at the waterline. It was a seven-metre fibreglass-hulled cabin cruiser with a covered cockpit and a small rear deck. A youngish bloke in a khaki windbreaker with DNR shoulder flashes was standing on the jetty, issuing life-jackets to Dudley Wilson and Alan Bunting.

Wilson had changed into boat shoes and a thigh-length navy-blue waterproof jacket with big flap pockets and cord piping. A regular outdoorsman, Dud. Must have cut quite a swell at the yacht club regatta. Bunting, still in his suit and tie, bulged from his bright yellow buoyancy vest like an animated grapefruit. I took a jacket and fastened it over my windcheater.

The three other panellists were coming along the jetty. Before they reached us, they were overtaken by a solidly built bloke of middle years in a DNR windbreaker. He spoke to them briefly, erasing the air with his hands and shrugging his shoulders. Then, leaving them milling uncertainly, he continued to where we stood beside the launch. He had

Popeye forearms, a pepper-and-salt buzz-cut and a face like a pontiac potato.

'Bill Sutherland,' he announced. 'DNR fisheries compliance. Sorry, gents. Trip's off.'

Wilson scowled. This smacked of disrespect, poor organisation. 'I'm Dudley Wilson,' he said. 'Chairman of the Coastal Management Advisory Panel. What's the problem?'

'Bottom line, Mr Wilson, operational priorities. Follow-up on tip-off re possible illegal activity.'

Commodore Wilson was dressed for seafaring and he wasn't about to be brushed off. 'What do you mean, illegal activity?'

'*Possible* illegal activity,' Sutherland repeated. 'Half an hour away. *Suspected* unlawful taking of abalone. Boat access only. And this is the only boat we've got in this part of the state. Long story short, got to gazump your sight-seeing trip. No choice. Sorry.'

He didn't look sorry at all. He looked like he could think of a hundred better uses for the departmental launch than ferrying freeloading pollies around Seal Rocks.

'Listen here,' said Wilson. 'This could be a very good opportunity to get a first-hand perspective on some of the issues being examined by our panel. What say we come along?'

Sutherland shook his head. 'No can do. Due respect, Mr Wilson, fisheries enforcement isn't a spectator sport.'

'Not spectators,' insisted Wilson. 'Official observers.'

Sutherland rubbed the back of his neck, not quite sure how to deal with Wilson's persistence.

'I'll make sure your superiors are made aware of your co-operation,' Wilson continued. Or the opposite, the implication was clear. 'We won't get in your way, I assure you.' He looked to Bunting and me to back him up. 'Isn't that right?'

Alan Bunting started to unfasten his life-jacket. 'I'm not sure about this, Dudley. There's probably regulations or something.'

'Suit yourself,' said Wilson. 'What about you, Whelan?'

As much as I disliked being co-opted by Wilson, I had to agree that reconnoitring abalone poachers sounded a lot more interesting than gawking at seals.

'Your decision,' Sutherland jumped aboard. 'But we haven't got all day.'

Wilson boarded. Bunting hesitated, then joined him. Me too. Sutherland took the console while the deck hand cast off the lines. Three minutes later, we were motoring down the main channel. When we cleared the sandbanks, Sutherland opened the throttle, veered east and let rip. The bow slapped the waves, raising plumes of spray.

We ran parallel to the shore, a kilometre or so out from a line of ragged cliffs and blunt headlands. The shelter of Westernport Bay lay behind us now. This was Bass Strait, a notorious stretch of water. Come a change of weather, it would rear up and throw huge waves against the coast, smashing a craft like ours to matchwood.

My innards were churning, rising and falling with the motion of the boat. Bunting, too, had gone a little green around the gills. Wilson was loving it. He stood at the stern, eyes narrowed, scanning the horizon. Captain Pugwash rides again. When spray swept his face, he wore it like a complimentary spritz of Old Spice.

Once we were well under way, the deckie took the helm and Sutherland joined us for a proper round of introductions.

He might not have been happy about running a passenger service, but he had enough professional sense not to waste an opportunity.

'One of the last viable abalone habitats in the world,' he declared, sweeping his arm along the line of coves and cliffs, his voice raised above the thrum of the engine. 'Shallow-water reefs, plenty of wave action. The abalone feed on specks of pulverised kelp.'

Wilson didn't want a natural history lesson. 'Tell us about these poachers,' he said.

'If that's what they are,' said Sutherland. 'Shore-based, most poaching. Less conspicuous that way. All you need's a snorkel and a lever to prise the buggers off the rocks. But our tip-off says these guys are diving off a boat, using breathing apparatus. Could be recreational, looking for an old wreck or something, forgot to hoist their blue-and-white. Could be not so innocent. Weather like this, chance to work a reef you can't get to from the land. Harvest as many abs as possible, take off before they're noticed.'

The wind bit through my pants and the sleeves of my sweatshirt. My stomach churned. An endless swell rippled towards us from the horizon and sludgy clouds were advancing from the west. The sky was the colour of a dirty sheep. I took deep, regular breaths and considered moving down into the cabin. Pride got the better of me. I didn't want to look like a wimp in front of Dudley Wilson.

'Lot of abalone poaching, is there?' I asked Sutherland.

'Enough,' he said. 'Used to be a cottage industry. Collect the public bag limit, ten a day, sell them to restaurants for cash. Huge demand in Asia these days. Big profits, professional crims.'

'I've never understood the appeal,' said Wilson. 'Underwater escargot, they call it. Tastes like shoe-leather to me. Give me a crayfish any day. Or a good feed of oysters.'

At the mention of food, my prawn salad lunch stood up and saluted. I clamped my jaws shut and breathed through my nose. Alan Bunting went a greener shade of pale.

'Can't be farmed,' said Sutherland. 'Unlike oysters. When it's gone, it's gone. California, Canada, Japan, nix. A high-value fish-stock…'

Fish-stock. The word conjured bouillabaisse. First the name, then the smell. My stomach lurched. 'So what's the drill if this lot are poaching,' I said quickly, chasing the subject elsewhere. 'You arrest them, or what?'

'Try,' said Sutherland. 'But if they resist, our options are limited. Like our means of self-defence. The minister's just taken away our sidearms.'

'Quite right, too,' said Wilson. 'Since when do fishing inspectors need to go armed? Let civil servants carry guns, who knows where it'll stop? Look at America.'

'With respect,' said Sutherland. 'For forty years officers of this department carried guns. Never once fired a shot.'

'So you're not going to miss them,' said Wilson.

'Good theory,' said Sutherland. 'Try standing on a rock platform, facing off some desperado with several grand of illegal ab in one hand and a diving knife in the other, nobody around for miles. Mere fact he knows you're armed can be a big help.'

Bunting took a deep breath and lurched into the conversation, obliged to support the decision of the minister, a fellow Nat. 'But you can call in the police, right?'

'True,' said Sutherland. 'Subject to operational availability.'

San Remo was far behind us, long vanished over the horizon. The next settlement on the coast, Inverloch, was fifty kilometres to the east. Five hundred metres away, the southern edge of the Australian continent was a line of abraded bluffs, sandstone cliffs rising to a wind-swept hinterland.

'And where exactly are the nearest police?' I asked.

'Wonthaggi,' said Sutherland.

Wonthaggi was somewhere inland. A three-cop town. Definitely no helicopter.

'Main strategy, deterrence. Patrolling. Maintaining a presence. Surveillance. Avoid confrontation until we've got full control of the situation.'

Sutherland resumed control of the helm and steered the launch closer inshore. The tide washed across a platform of pitted rock that extended outwards from the base of the cliffs, rising and falling like the breathing of some vast living creature.

We rounded a stubby headland and Sutherland dropped the motor into neutral, letting us drift across the mouth of a sheltered cove with a half-moon beach of crushed shells.

A boat was moored in the cove, a chunky beige-coloured craft, a box sitting on two fibreglass hulls. A wiry type in shorts, tennis shoes and a woollen sweater was emptying a bucket over the side. Fiftyish, grizzled, a short ponytail sticking out the back of his peaked cap. As soon as he saw us, he grabbed a hose that was running into the water and gave it a solid jerk.

'Shark-cat, twin 200-horsepower Yamaha outboards.' Sutherland raised binoculars. 'Registration number concealed with duct tape.'

34

It was about a hundred metres away. Bunting craned for a view. Wilson firmed his jaw, a representative of law and order. I wondered what the hell I was doing there.

A figure in a hooded wetsuit surfaced beside the shark-cat. He hurried aboard, hauling the hose up behind him. Ponytail was firing up the Yamahas.

As the shark-cat began to move, Sutherland opened the throttle.

As it gathered momentum, the shark-cat rose on hydroplanes, skimming the water. It raced for the far side of the cove, a Formula One shoebox.

The hooded diver ducked under the canopy, his shoulders hunched, no more than a black shape. Ponytail glanced back over his shoulder, his lugubrious weather-seamed face clearly visible. When the young DNR crewman emerged from the cabin with a video camera, he pulled down the bill of his hat and flipped us the bird.

We gave chase, heading to intercept. The shark-cat hugged the shore, taking advantage of its shallow draft. Sutherland swung the launch into deeper water, steering a curved course. As we chopped at the swell, the launch tilted and rocked. So did my stomach.

Whoah, I thought. Pass. Not today, thanks. Enough already. A surge of nausea lapped at my Plimsoll line, tasting of curdled mayonnaise and masticated crustacean. I wished I was anywhere else, as long as it wasn't moving.

Lunch wanted out. And it got what it wanted. A fountain of hot lava, it hurtled upwards. I lunged for the side and barfed into the briny. I retched again. Sour milk and corn flakes, this time.

Then, without warning, a stream of berley erupted from Dudley Wilson's mouth and hit Alan Bunting in the face. This was not how the Nats usually spoke to each other, except at woolshed dances. Aghast, Bunting staggered backwards, gagging. At that moment, the deck tilted as the launch banked, turning to intercept the shark-cat. Bunting, struggling to find his footing, skidded on Wilson's mess and toppled overboard.

He hit the water with a splash, then vanished in the churn of our wake. Wilson leaned over the side and finished parking the tiger. Bunting bobbed to the surface and raised an arm, as if attempting to hail a cab.

Sutherland was already on the case. The launch slewed around, circling back. My head throbbed and a bilious taste filled my mouth. Wilson wiped his mouth with the back of his hand, squared his jaw and resumed his Captain Queeg stance, as though nothing had happened. The deckie reached with a gaff and hooked Bunting as we came around. In short order, he was being manhandled up the stern ladder like a disconsolate dugong.

Wilson tried to help, but Bunting wasn't having it. 'B-back off,' he hyperventilated, snatching back his arm. His teeth were chattering and torrents streamed from his ruined suit and pooled around his sodden brogues. Unbuckling his life-vest with trembling fingers, he let the crewman lead him down into the cabin. 'Th-thanks, m-mate,' he said. 'Wh-what's your name?'

'Ian. Mind the step.'

The shark-cat was rounding the point, running for open water. 'That's torn it,' said Sutherland, his binoculars trained on the mocking V of its wake. 'Never get near them now.'

'But can't you radio...' started Wilson.

Sutherland lowered the field glasses. 'No point, pace they're travelling,' he said through clenched teeth. 'Didn't even get a chance to hail them. So if your stomach is now settled, Mr Wilson, I suggest you wait below while we try to find out what our thieving friends were up to.' He turned to me. 'You too.'

I followed Wilson down into the tiny cabin. Alan Bunting was already occupying most of the space. Stripped to his jocks, he towelled his pudgy, goose-pimpled flesh with ill-concealed irritation. The deckie, Ian, handed him a fluorescent orange wetsuit. 'This'll keep you warm until we get back.'

Bunting squeezed into it, looking daggers at Wilson. 'You might as well have pushed me,' he said.

'You've had a nasty shock,' said Wilson. 'But I hope you're not suggesting it was my fault.'

'You spewed in my face.'

'Not deliberately,' said Wilson. 'You're just not used to boats, that's all. No reason to be embarrassed.'

'*Embarrassed?*' He looked like a giant orange gum-drop.

I wedged myself into a seat and buried my face in my hands. I needed to wash out my mouth, but didn't dare move for fear of another up-chuck. The vibrations of the engine came up through the seat, compounding the movement of the boat. Bunting and Wilson bickered. Misery enveloped me.

We returned to the place where the shark-cat was parked when we first spotted it. Sutherland cut the engine and dropped anchor. Ian changed into a wetsuit and went over the side, snorkelled and flippered. He made a slow circuit, occasionally disappearing below the surface. When he climbed back aboard, he held up an abalone shell. The light caught its opalescent interior.

He and Sutherland conferred in an undertone at the stern, then Sutherland stuck his head into the cabin. 'How you feeling?' he asked Alan Bunting.

Bunting made a brave face. 'Sorry about this,' he said.

Sutherland nodded, then handed the crusted shell to Wilson. 'Hundreds of these down there. They were shucking them on board, probably stashing the meat in hidden compartments. Couple of grand's worth, just here. At it since dawn, different spots. Day's take, before we interrupted them, maybe ten thousand dollars.'

Wilson examined the palm-sized shell gravely, as if appraising an antique.

'Pity we had to abort before we IDed them,' said Sutherland. 'Top it off, I'll be carpeted for letting you lot come along.'

Wilson tried to hand back the shell.

'Keep it,' said Sutherland. 'Souvenir. Best get you back to San Remo ASAP.'

After we'd been under way for ten minutes, sipping sugary instant coffee from the launch thermos, Wilson broke our self-imposed silence. 'When this gets around, we'll be a laughing stock,' he said. 'Throwing up. Falling overboard.'

I slowly raised my head. 'Stuffing up a fisheries enforcement operation,' I croaked. 'The press are going to love it. Given any thought to your resignation letter, Mr Coastal Policy Chairman?'

Wilson narrowed his eyes and looked me over closely. 'This Sutherland.' He jerked his thumb upwards. 'You want him to lose his job?'

'The cuts you've got in mind,' I said. 'He'll probably lose it anyway.'

Wilson leaned forward and stuck his face in mine. For an awful moment, I could see the stream of spew flying from his rubbery gob. Worse, I could smell it. I flinched and turned away. Wilson gave a satisfied grunt and, dipping out of the cabin door, stood at the console talking to Sutherland.

'I don't think it's right,' whined Alan Bunting. 'Trying to make political capital out of a situation like this. I'll have to resign from the panel, too. And it wasn't my fault. If anyone's the injured party, I am.'

I didn't know where to begin to answer that one, so I didn't try. They mustn't have offered Politics 101 at agricultural college.

Wilson returned. 'He wants to talk to you,' he said.

I found Sutherland seated at the wheel, driving towards the low-slung sun, surveying the way ahead through oversized Sunaroids. 'Beautiful, isn't it?' he said.

I took a deep, stomach-settling breath of air and absorbed the view. It swept across a burnished sea from weathered sandstone cliffs at our starboard to pink-edged billows of cloud on the southern horizon. 'Magnificent,' I agreed.

'Like your job, Mr Whelan?' said Sutherland. 'Think it's worth doing?'

'Sometimes,' I said.

Sutherland tilted his head back, master of all he surveyed. 'Love mine,' he said. 'Pretty good at it too I reckon, all things considered. Less than fifty of us fish dogs, you know. More than seventeen hundred kilometres of coastline.'

'You've done a deal with Wilson,' I said. 'And I'm the fly in the ointment.'

Sutherland shrugged. 'What if that Bunting bloke had drowned?'

'No chance of that,' I said. 'Too buoyant. Completely empty head.'

'Tell that to the committee of enquiry, just before they transfer me to shore patrol ticketing dog owners for crapping on the beach. Thought you might understand. Being Labor.'

I heaved a defeated sigh. 'Yeah, all right,' I said. 'None of this happened. And if it did, I didn't see it. Just get me back on dry land pronto, okay?'

The light was fading when we cruised into the San Remo boat harbour. Up on the Phillip Island bridge, the coaches were bumper-to-bumper, packed with tourists bound for the twilight parade of penguins waddling ashore at the rookeries.

I hit the dock as soon as we tied up, glad to have something solid beneath my feet. Next time I got on a boat, I promised myself, it would be nothing smaller than the *Queen Mary*.

It was nearly six o'clock. I walked down the jetty, past the fishermen's co-operative and into the front bar of the Westernport Hotel. Three blokes in working clobber were nursing beers at the bar, swapping monotones. A bunch of bozos were playing pool, their banter lost in the plink-plink of the poker machines from the gaming lounge. 'Wheel of

Fortune' was showing on the box above the bar. I parked on a stool and ordered a Jameson's. 'Straight up,' I told the barman, a girl in a Jim Beam tee-shirt. 'Water on the side.'

I diluted the whiskey and sipped, letting it settle my stomach. When the television news began, I tipped the last of it down my throat and signalled for another.

The inquest story came after the first ad break. The state coroner, the newsreader reported, had found that Lyndal Luscombe, thirty-five, was murdered by convicted felon Rodney Syce during a break-out from the Melbourne Remand Centre.

Of course it was fucking murder. It was murder the instant that the motorbike slammed into Lyndal. You kill somebody while you're escaping from jail, it's murder. Not manslaughter. Not involuntary homicide. Not reckless driving. Not oops. Murder, plain and simple.

Lyndal's picture filled the screen, a full-length shot cropped from a portrait taken at her cousin's wedding in late '93. She was laughing, crinkling her nose at the camera like a naughty schoolkid.

'Despite an extensive search here and interstate, Syce remains at large,' continued the newsreader's voice.

The screen filled with a mug-shot. It showed a thick-lipped, round-faced man with a receding brow and dark, surly eyes. He looked like one of those guys who stand at road works, directing traffic with a lollipop sign. The sort of face you see, but don't register.

'Police are hopeful that the coroner's finding will result in new information that may lead them to Syce.'

Vision cut to a sleek, fortyish man in a fashionable suit and rimless glasses standing on the steps of the Coroner's

Court. A caption identified him as Detective Sergeant Damian Meakes. 'This man Syce is dangerous and absolutely desperate,' he said, leaning forward into the camera, one hand holding down his tie. 'Anyone who believes they might have seen him on the day of the escape or any time since, or has any other information, should contact the Syce Task Force or Crime Stoppers. Under no circumstances should members of the public approach him directly.'

And that was it. Sixty seconds, tops. My second whiskey was on the bar. I slammed it down neat and stomped out the door, fire raging in my belly.

The sea was purple with the last shreds of the day and the air was acrid with rotting seaweed and diesel fumes. I put the key in the ignition of the Magna and drove across the bridge to Phillip Island. I went past a tourist information booth and a flower farm, down streets with nautical names, following the road through the sand dunes to the rectangle of asphalt beside the Woolamai lifesaving club.

A half-dozen vehicles were parked overlooking the beach. Sedans, tradesmen's utilities and a panel van with roof-racks. Solitary men sat in two of the cars, gazing out at the monotonous pounding of the surf. Sad, lonely fucks like me, pining their lives away.

Should I ball my fist and bang on their windows, I wondered? Tear open my shirt and display the scar where my heart had been torn out? Defy them to outdo my wounds? Squat with them in the tufted dunes and howl like a stricken animal at the rising moon?

I lit a cigarette from my emergency pack in the glovebox and sat on the topmost plank of the wooden steps leading down to the sand, shoulders hunched against the deepening chill.

Aeons ago, I'd surfed here at Woolamai. Driven down with friends from university, spent a weekend catching the break that unfurled beyond the sandbank. But tonight the waves of Woolamai were not surfable, not by me anyway. They reared up, menacing black walls, their crests shredded by the wind, their glassy surface bursting open as they smashed against the shore.

The cigarette made my head spin. I gave it the flick and plodded down the steps to the empty beach, hands buried in my pockets. When I reached the edge of the water, I took off my shoes, stuffed my socks inside, hung them around my neck by the laces and rolled my pants to the knee.

Talk about a fucking wasteland. It wasn't supposed to be like this. We were going to have a daughter. There would be the father, the mother and the children. An affectionate, intelligent, playful, semi-blended family. We would adore each other. The big brother would cherish his little sister. She would worship him. The father would be a competent provider, the beloved butt of his children's teasing. The mother would outshine him and he would glory in her accomplishments. They would all live happily ever after.

Then had come a man on a Kawasaki racer.

The man of my dreams.

Rodney Syce was a light-fingered chancer with a tendency to lose his grip when things got slippery.

The third child of a Darwin construction worker, he was sent to live with elderly relatives in a one-silo town in Western Australia's wheat belt in 1974, after his mother was killed by flying debris during Cyclone Tracy. At fourteen, he was already in trouble with the law. Illegal use of a motor vehicle was the first entry in a ledger that grew to include breaking and entering, possession of stolen goods and trespass. The juvenile court gave him good behaviour bonds and suspended sentences.

I knew this because I'd made it my business to find out.

The cops had told me a certain amount, of course. In the beginning they were falling over themselves to keep me in the picture. Later, when the search became a long-haul operation, they were much less forthcoming. But by then, I'd started making my own enquiries.

Call it a kind of therapy. Or fuel for speculation in the absence of news. Information is currency, they say. I wasn't sure what the facts I was gathering could buy me. Not peace of mind, that's for sure.

I collected newspaper clippings and studied video footage. Read court transcripts. Talked to lawyers, journalists and jailbirds. Pulled what few strings I could still lay my hands on. Assembled a file. Sifted it. Pored over it deep into the night.

Height: 168 cm. Weight: 75 kg. Eyes: dark brown. Distinguishing marks: nil. Criminal history: extensive.

At seventeen, Rodney Syce quit school and headed for Queensland, and a string of short-lived rouseabout and labouring jobs on cattle stations. His first taste of jail came at nineteen, two months for assault and robbery after he rolled a drunk at the Cloncurry races. The magistrate was less exercised by the ninety-seven dollars lifted from the victim's wallet than the metal fence picket used on the back of his head.

Back on the outside, Syce fluctuated between low-wage jobs and petty crime. He worked in canneries, on a prawn trawler, down the Mt Isa mines where he was dismissed for pilfering from the employees' changeroom. Then came a two-year stretch in Boggo Road after he pushed a night watchman down a flight of stairs during a bungled factory break-in. On release, he took up with a gang of Brisbane car thieves. That ended when he bashed the employee of a dodgy panel-beater with a steering-wheel lock. She turned out to be the girlfriend of a local heavy. On the wrong side of both the cops and the crims, he hightailed it to Melbourne.

Within a month, he was back in custody. Disturbed during a daylight burg in South Yarra, he belted the householder, an eighty-two-year-old retired judge, with an antique inkstand. The old beak went down squeezing his heart-attack alarm. The ambulance arrived just as Syce was coming out the front door, making like he lived there. The paramedics, burly boys, sat on him until the cops arrived.

In his ten-year life of crime, Rodney Syce had generated enough paperwork for a psychological profile to emerge. In layman's terms, he was a gutless mongrel, a coward given to unprovoked outbursts of violence, a loner who had trouble maintaining relationships with other people.

Except in prison. There, Syce seemed to find the sort of society he craved. Quick to suss the pecking order, he found ways of attaching himself to a high-status inmate, some means of making himself useful to a top dog.

Someone like Adrian Parish. At fifty-three, Parish was king of the heap in remand. An armed robber and old-school all-rounder, he was a tiler by trade. He had a reputation for covering his tracks well and keeping his head down between jobs. He used violence only when he believed it was necessary. Shooting at coppers to avoid arrest, for example. And, although he'd been charged with dozens of offences, he had a knack for beating the rap. In a thirty-five-year career as a professional criminal, he'd served a mere eight years and seven months of jail time.

But Parish had run out of luck. An armoured-truck heist had turned to shit. Shots were fired. A guard had a coronary embolism and nearly died. Dye-bombs spoiled the cash. When fingerprint fragments were found in the burned-out getaway car, the driver rolled over. Parish was rousted from his marital bed at 5 a.m., charged with everything but indecent exposure, committed to the County Court for jury trial, found guilty and remanded for sentencing. The judge was poised to throw the book. The way things were going, Adrian Parish would be a very old man by the time he got out of prison.

But while he was waiting for sentence, Rodney Syce entered his orbit. And Rodney had qualities that Adrian appreciated. He could ride a motorbike and do what he was told.

The sands of Woolamai beach had turned to grey. The sky and the sea were seamless. The breaking waves advanced, line after line, roaring like distant artillery.

If I had a gun, I told myself, I'd kill Rodney Syce. Do it with my bare hands if necessary. If I ever found him, came face-to-face with him, saw him walking down the street.

But I knew that it was just as well I didn't have a gun. If I had a gun, I might already have taken revenge.

Three times I'd spotted Syce. The first was during the AFL grand final. The Eagles were thrashing the Cats. Late in the last quarter, Peter Matera darted from the pack and took a stab for goal. The ball went wide and sailed into the crowd. Fans rose, reaching to grab it. A camera tracked the action, magnifying the image on the electronic scoreboard. One of those who reached for the incoming pigskin was Rodney Syce.

I knew him as soon as I saw him. He had a beanie pulled down around his ears, a West Coast scarf swathing his neck. Probably figured he could pass unnoticed, one of thousands decked out in blue and yellow.

I came up out of my seat, fumbling for my mobile,

dashing down the stairs to the section of terrace where the ball had landed, jabbering at the task-force detective who picked up the phone. Then the full-time siren blew and the crowd was streaming for the exits, ninety-seven thousand people in motion.

Even before the last of the fans had dispersed, two dicks were sitting with me in the stadium's media centre, running the tape over and over, slow-motion and freeze-frame. Yes, they agreed, the guy did look a bit like Syce. It was possibly him. But within a week, it wasn't. The seat was bought with a credit card by a retired librarian from Warrandyte. The lead was scratched.

The second time I saw Syce, he was coming out of a service station on the Hume Highway near Wangaratta. It was Boxing Day and I was driving back after spending Christmas with Lyndal's parents at their orchard near Beechworth. It was their first Christmas without her, Red was in Sydney with Wendy, and I hadn't seen Lyndal's family since the funeral. We ate roast turkey on the screened veranda and sat not saying much in the listless afternoon heat and I slept on a trundle bed on the floor between two near strangers who would have been my brothers-in-law if not for Rodney Syce.

An hour into the trip home, I was filling the tank at a roadhouse pump when a man came out the gas-station door and got into a dust-covered Falcon. Wraparound sunglasses, stringy goatee, but Syce all right, no doubt in my mind. I bolted inside to the cashier. 'That guy just left, you know him?'

The cashier shook her head, I grabbed the phone and the Falcon was intercepted at roadblock just south of

Glenrowan. The driver came out with his hands in the air, babbling that he'd paid already, the cheque must have been held up in the Christmas mail. An unlicensed driver with $900 in outstanding speeding fines. A win of sorts, but not Rodney Syce. Not by a country mile.

After my third sighting, I had a house-call from Detective Sergeant Damian Meakes of the Syce Task Force.

I'd never warmed to Meakes. He seemed bloodless and far too style-conscious for a copper. Four-button suit and designer spectacles. Talked to me down his nose.

'A courtesy call, Mr Whelan,' he informed me. Courtesy my arse. He'd brought a social worker with him, a sincere young thing with spaniel eyes and a Masters in Hand-holding.

'Sightings of this kind aren't uncommon, Murray,' the Victim Liaison Officer reassured me earnestly. 'They're a recognised coping mechanism. A victim's way of dealing with feelings of helplessness and frustration. Even guilt.'

'Guilt?' I said. Syce was the guilty one. And so, I was beginning to think, were the rozzers. Guilty of gross fucking incompetence. 'First you let this prick escape, then you fail to catch him.'

'Your anger is perfectly understandable,' cooed the VLO.

'If I want my bumps read,' I told her, 'I'll find somebody better qualified than a cop shrink.'

There was no more counselling after that. I did, however, receive a phone call from the Chief Commissioner. One of the privileges of my parliamentary rank was to have the balm dispensed from the highest level. But it was the same old balm. The recapture of Rodney Syce, the CC assured me, remained an ongoing priority. But it was probable that he'd left the state, possibly even the country, so an arrest might be some time in coming. In the meantime, the chances of my lucking upon him were low. And I was helping nobody by cracking the shits with his officers.

I ate crow, right and proper. Thanked him for taking the time. Promised I wouldn't trouble the constabulary again, not unless I had substantial cause. Offered my assistance, should an appropriate occasion arise. That's when he pitched the idea of fast-tracking the inquest.

And now the inquest had come and gone, another milestone on the road to nowhere. Syce was the free man and I was a prisoner of self-pity and hunger for revenge, so bent out of shape that it sometimes took all my strength to keep hold of the things that made life worth living.

The surf raged and pounded. I let the icy tide wash over my feet, felt the tug into oblivion.

But this too solid flesh refused to melt. It stood there, barefoot in the freezing water, shivering. Get a fucking grip, I told myself.

Nothing could bring Lyndal back. It was time to stop wallowing in misery and dreams of revenge. Time to concentrate on the here and now. Count my whatnots.

For a year and a half, the folds of my wallet had held the ultrasound photograph of the embryo in Lyndal's belly. The girl-child with the joke name. Lysistrata Luscombe-Whelan. Had she been born, she'd be almost a year old, crawling around the kitchen, playing merry hell with the pots and pans.

I opened my wallet, took out the picture and touched it to my lips. I placed it gently on the swirling foam and watched the tide carry it away. As I waited for the moment when it disappeared into the embrace of the sea, the sharp clap of a breaker rang out. Above the far horizon, Venus was rising.

Then I was splashing forward, calf-deep, grabbing at the photograph, wiping it dry on my chest.

This wasn't over yet.

A soft rain was falling by the time I got home from San Remo. It continued to fall, in varying degrees of softness, for most of the next six weeks. In Melbourne we call it spring.

If the coronial circus provided any new leads, the police didn't share the fact with me. To the best of my knowledge, Rodney Syce remained no closer to capture than he was on the day he killed Lyndal.

From time to time, I bumped into Alan Bunting in the corridors of Parliament House. We did not speak of the sea. Red's eight came third in its heat at the rowing carnival. By early November it was still raining but the air grew a fraction warmer each day. I began to consider destinations for the summer break.

The Legislative Council of Victoria was designed by its colonial fathers as a brake on progress. It did the job well. As the spring session began to peter out, it sat for only two or three days a week. To fill the available time, the parliamentary party turned its energies to a new round of factional warfare.

The Australian Labor Party is composed of two main factions. Them and Us. Ideologically distinct only at their extremities, their function is the distribution of spoils. But fighting over the spoils of defeat was a ritual for which I could muster little enthusiasm. For the moment, I was content to lick my private wounds and leave the backstabbing to others.

Certain party obligations, however, remained inescapable. One of these was the annual Melbourne Upper fund-raising dinner and trivia quiz night. That year, it was held on the second Friday in November. As usual, the venue was La Luna, a restaurant near the Moonee Valley racetrack. Steaks and seafood a speciality.

La Luna's proprietor, Tony Melina, once fancied himself as something of a player and helped round up some stray Italian votes in the preselection contest for the local federal member. But that was years ago. Business had long since taken precedence over politics, and Tony's involvement in the party was ancient history. But he always gave us a discount price for the fund-raiser, so we stuck with La Luna. Whatever its faults, the Australian Labor Party has a great respect for tradition.

Starting as a check tablecloth and Chianti-bottle candlestick sort of place, La Luna had worked its way steadily upmarket, evolving into Tony's idea of contemporary Mediterranean. The wrought-iron torch sconces and bagged brickwork were superseded by murals in the manner of ancient Roman mosaics. Nymphs and satyrs now peeked from behind *trompe l'oeil* plasterwork. The floor space was expanded and a central bar installed, black marble with onyx inlays and overhead glassware racks. Messalina meets Maserati.

Tony's wife Rita pounced as I came though the door. 'Murray, you big hunk,' she said, offering her cheeks for a peck-peck. 'It's been ages. Getting too high and mighty for your old friends?'

Rita was petite, not yet forty, tight-packed and high-maintenance. She had a haystack of raven hair, sculpted nails and enough gold jewellery to drown a duck. She abducted my arm and dragged me to the bar. 'Your lot are upstairs, getting stuck into the nibbles,' she said. 'Have a quick drink with your auntie Rita before you go up.'

We perched knee-to-knee on tubular chrome barstools and the barman poured two glasses of white wine. Rita locked her big brown eyes onto mine and ran a hand down my arm. 'Still hurting, aren't you, baby?' Her hand settled on my knee.

I shrugged and hid behind my drink. 'Life goes on. And my boy keeps me busy.'

Rita nodded knowingly. 'He must be what, twelve, thirteen now?'

'Fifteen,' I said, glad to be off the hook. 'Doing okay at school. Couldn't ask for better. Yours?' I racked my memory. 'Carla and…'

'Lauren. Both fine. Carla's married now, threatening to make me a grandmother. Lauren's on the overseas trip, waitressing her way around Europe. Must be in the blood.'

'You were never a waitress, Rita,' I smiled. 'Your old man would never have stood for it.'

Rita's father Frank had a furniture emporium just down the street from the electorate office. Rococo, traditional and moderne. An immigrant success story, he had higher hopes for his only daughter than marriage to the boy from the fish'n'chip shop. But when his ambitions were thwarted by teenage passion and its unintended consequences, he copped it sweet. He bankrolled young Tony into the pizza business, but only on condition that his princess never knead the dough or sling the capricciosa.

'Maybe I should take it up,' sighed Rita. 'I need a career now that the chicks have flown from the nest and Tony's busy building an empire.'

She waved her drink with weary forbearance at the starched napery, floral centrepieces and mood lighting, as if fate had condemned her to sit by the fireplace like some shrivelled, black-clad nonna.

'Speaking of Tony,' I said. 'Is he about? I should say hello.'

A party of six were being led to their table by a waitress, a bit of a strudel, a fleshy blonde in her late twenties. One of the men made a joke and she laughed, a little too loud, too saucy. Rita's rings tightened around her wineglass and her lips thinned.

'Tony?' She raised her shoulders a millimetre, a gesture of utter indifference. 'He's around somewhere, handling something.' She lit a Marlboro Lite, exhaled a long stream of smoke and showed me her profile, also utterly indifferent. 'Handles everything around here, Tony does.'

Just then, rescue arrived in the form of Ayisha Celik, my electorate officer. Ayisha and I went back a good ten years, back to the time when she worked at the Turkish Welfare League and I took care of the electorate office in Melbourne Upper. Once upon a time I entertained certain delusions about my chances with the kohl-eyed Levantine looker, but Ayisha was long-since married to a Macedonian mother's boy and was now a mother of three herself.

Since her days at the TWL, Ayisha had worked for the Multicultural Resource Centre and, until the incoming government cut its funding, an advocacy organisation for self-help groups. Foster parents, women's shelters, recovering glue-sniffers, fur-allergic cat-fanciers, you name it. She also worked as Lyndal's campaign manager in the three-way preselection contest that sent me to parliament. She knew Melbourne Upper like the back of her hand. Me, I suspected, she knew even better.

'Started drinking already?' she said. 'Hello, Rita.'

Rita squeezed out a faint smile. 'Hello, Ayisha. Got everything you need?'

Ayisha laid a proprietary hand on my shoulder. 'Except an emcee,' she said. 'Our guest comedian hasn't shown up. Looks like you'll have to do the honours.'

'Duty calls.' I gave Rita a shrug, downed my drink and followed Ayisha's ever-broadening backside towards the stairs.

'What a classic,' said Ayisha over her shoulder. 'You know she's only here tonight because she knew you'd be coming. She had to satisfy her curiosity, get the gossip. Poor Murray, she'll be able to tell the other ladies-who-lunch, what that man needs is a…'

'You make me sound like a train wreck,' I said. 'What's the turn-up?'

'Thirty-two,' she said. 'Even fewer than last year. Frankly, I don't know why they bother. We'll be lucky to cover costs.'

'It's not the money, it's the participation,' I reminded her, as we started up the stairs. 'The only role left for rank-and-file Labor Party members is attending crappy fund-raisers that don't raise any funds.'

We found the party faithful seated at two long tables in the upstairs dining room, tucking into antipasto and forming themselves into teams for the trivia challenge.

The lighting was harsher than downstairs, there were no flowers and the tablecloths were paper. But Tony's special price included complimentary garlic bread and adequate quantities of wine and beer, so nobody was complaining.

I knew almost everybody in the room. They were the bedrock of the local membership. Handers-out of how-to-vote cards and veterans of a thousand pointless meetings. Sentimentalists and failed opportunists. A retired tool-maker and his librarian wife. Three schoolteachers and a nurse. A kid so young he thought the White Australia Policy was an ironic marketing push for a new laundry detergent. I shook a few hands, patted some cardiganed backs, kissed some cheeks. Then Ayisha handed me a list of questions.

'Good evening, friends and comrades.'

Jeers of amiable derision erupted.

'Let's begin with an easy one. For ten points, in what year was the shearers' strike that led to the foundation of the Australian Labor Party?'

'Point of procedure,' shouted somebody up the back.

By ten o'clock we were done. The questions were asked, the jokes shared, the raffle drawn, $235 raised for the collective coffers. For the thousandth time, the outrages of the current administration were reprised. I recited the party line that we'd fight our way back to power at the next election, but I didn't believe it and neither did the troops. Our last years in government were a shambles. We just had to take our lumps and wait for the tide to turn. In the meantime, all we could do was gnash our teeth, rend our garments and commiserate with each other over spaghetti con vongole and Caterers Blend coffee.

As soon as decency permitted, I split.

Back downstairs, the clamour of a hundred diners was bouncing off the walls. Staff flitted between tables, trays laden. There was no sign of Rita. I asked the barman if Tony was in. He pointed his bow tie towards the kitchen door. 'Office,' he said. 'Better knock.'

Beyond the kitchen was a greasy-floored alley stacked with drums of cooking oil and cartons of tinned tomatoes. 'Private,' said the peel-and-stick sign on the door past the staff washroom. I gave a brisk rap.

'Come,' came the command. If Tony was doing any handling, he was doing it very lightly.

I opened the door a fraction and peered though the gap. The office was a windowless cubicle, its every vertical surface layered with pieces of paper. Price lists, invoices, booking sheets, postcards, staff rosters, suppliers' phone numbers, fish identification charts, health department notices, a calendar with a scene of Mt Vesuvius. The horizontal surfaces were cluttered with ring-binders, ledgers, clipboards and phone books.

Tony was sitting at a desk that was pushed against the wall just inside the door, signing some documents. He finished with a flourish, looked up and gave me a broad smile. 'Hey,' he said, spreading his palms in greeting. 'Murray, my man, I was just gunna come up.'

'Sorry to disturb,' I said. 'Couldn't leave without saying

thanks. A friend in need and all that.'

Tony was a stocky, slightly paunchy Neapolitan with a van dyke beard and sleek black hair brushed back from a high receding brow. He wore a charcoal-grey polo shirt under a pale-lemon, crumpled-linen sports jacket, the cuffs pushed back to his hairy forearms, Miami Vice style. Give him a tunic and laurel crown, stick a bunch of grapes in one hand and a Pan pipe in the other, and he wouldn't have looked out of place amid his trattoria satyrs.

'Hey guys,' he said cheerfully. 'Meet Murray Whelan, our local MP. Labor, unfortunately, so knowing him ain't worth shit.'

I put my head around the door and found two other men in the room, one leaning against the filing cabinet, the other sunk in a worn-out armchair. They were observing Tony with amusement, like he was a novelty act, the genial wise guy. This, I imagined, was exactly the effect he was trying for.

The bloke at the filing cabinet was small and neat, well into his fifties. Thick-rimmed spectacles. Brown suit, bland tie. The total package suggested a clerical occupation. Accountancy or somesuch. 'This is Phil…' said Tony.

I nodded hello around the door and Phil nodded back. His eyes sideways behind his glasses, goldfish in a bowl.

'…and Jake Martyn.'

Tony delivered the name with the hint of a flourish. It was one I'd heard before. A name name.

Martyn was a culinary trend-setter, the proprietor of Gusto, a fashionable restaurant in seaside Lorne. A frequent mention in the epicure pages, he was the pioneer of the *dernier cri* in fine dining, a style eponymously called '*con gusto*'. Out with those finicky morsels of yesteryear, the smidgin of

scallop on a wasabi wafer, the flutter of quail over an infer-
ence of artichokes. In with the hearty mouthful, the
port-glazed porterhouse on a shitload of mashed spuds, the
pan-seared swordfish with a bottle of beer and a burp.

An embodiment of the pleasures of the table, he was a
barrel-chested, generous-gutted man in his early forties with
a round, cheerful face, robust shoulder-length hair the colour
of old oyster shells and an air of easy affability. He was
wearing a just-folks sweater and scuffed hiking boots, as
though making it plain he had no time for fussbudget fiddlers
with sea-urchin roe.

He came up out of his seat a fraction of an inch, gave me
a brief spray of charm and dropped back. 'G'day.'

His charm was the kind you can see coming but don't
resent. Through it I sensed that he recognised my name. I
was that guy whose girlfriend got killed and sometimes, when
people met me for the first time, they didn't quite know how
to respond to that fact. Whether to say something or not.
Martyn went for not, which was the way I preferred it.

'Ah,' said Tony. 'Here it is, at last.'

The waitress with the flirty laugh appeared beside me in
the doorway, a liqueur bottle in one hand, three snifters in
the other.

'I'll leave you to it,' I said. 'Thanks again, Tony.'

'We're finished here,' he said, slipping the signed form and
some other papers into a manilla envelope and handing it to
the accountant type. 'Stick around. Have a drink with us.
VSOP.'

The waitress squeezed past me and Tony rose to relieve
her of the bottle and glasses. In doing so, he found it impossible to avoid pressing against her. She squirmed free with

practised ease, but not before he managed to grind his groin against her rump.

'A tasty drop,' he smirked, sniffing the cork. 'Bring another glass, will you, honey?'

I stepped back to give the waitress plenty of exit room. She raised her eyebrows as she sidled past, and rolled her eyes.

'Not for me,' I said. 'Had a couple of beers upstairs and I'm driving. Don't want to end up blowing into a bag.' Or providing the pretext for a repeat demonstration of Tony's amatory technique. 'Nice meeting you, fellers.'

I went back through the kitchen, amused and wondering. Jake Martyn was a long way out of Tony Melina's league. Finding him at La Luna was like bumping into Coco Chanel in Woolworths. Whatever had lured him there, Tony was keen to impress. There was definitely business in the air. Was Tony trying to flog him something, I wondered?

Vice versa, as it turned out. And Tony paid far too much for it.

I drove down Mount Alexander Road in a thinning trickle of traffic, harness-racing enthusiasts home-bound from the track, then cut through North Melbourne to Dudley Street and parked behind Festival Hall.

The old boxing stadium was looking its age, a relic from the days of 'TV Ringside' and 'Rollerderby', a grimy shed redolent of hotdog water, cork-tipped cigarettes and extinct chewing gum. But, more than just a shrine to the gladiators of the glove, the House of Stoush was also a centre of excellence in the musical arts. Little Richard had played there. The Easybeats. George Thorogood and the Destroyers. The Clash. Dolly Parton.

Tonight, the bands were called Chocolate Starfish, Bum Crack and Toothbrush Messiah. The gig was a cut-price show for under-age punters, sponsored by a zit cream manufacturer. It had just finished and teenagers were pouring from the building, gathering in droopy-jeaned hordes at the kerbside and malingering around the kebab vendors and doughnut caravans. I double-parked across the road from the main entrance and scanned the crowd.

Red was standing with a cluster of kids beside the box-office window. His hair was gelled into a cockatoo crest, his shoulders were slouched and his clothes hung off his frame like a scarecrow. He merged, in short, with the crowd.

I recognised some of the gang, friends and classmates, male and female. They were full of beans, teasing and joking. Their weekend had already begun. I sat watching from the Magna. Red was looming over a smaller kid, listening intently. There seemed something self-conscious about his stance, as though he was making an effort to appear relaxed. His hands were thrust into the back pockets of his jeans and his hip was cocked in an attempt at nonchalance. Then the other kid turned a little and I saw that it was a girl. A wisp of a thing, a pixie-faced waif with chopped hair and cast-off clothes. Her arms were folded across her barely-there chest and she tilted her head sideways when she looked up at Red.

I couldn't place her among the usual suspects, the crowd from school. But, even from thirty metres away, it was plain that she was reaching parts of my boy that hadn't been reached before. Not, at least, to my knowledge.

Girls were nothing special in Red's circle of friends. They were peers, pals, members of the tribe. The boys and girls treated each other with the casual camaraderie of brothers and sisters. But this, if I was not mistaken, was something different. The lad was mooching like a man smitten. Was the young sap rising, I wondered? Was he feeling his oats? Or the unexpected sting of Cupid's dart?

The poor little bugger didn't know where to look. His gaze darted from the girl's shoes to his knees, alighted on her face for a moment, then moved back to his knees. The girl, too, seemed deliciously ill at ease. She tugged a thread from the shredded elbow of her tatterdemalion sweater and absently toyed with it.

A Landcruiser pulled into the kerb, blocking my view. A recent model, roof-racks, rear window plastered with surfwear stickers. Ripcurl. Balin. Hot Tuna. The driver stepped out and checked the crowd, standing in the angle of the open door. She was lean, crop-haired, a wading-bird with a cashmere shawl draped over her shoulders. It was just beginning to drizzle and, as she raised the shawl over her head, the flecked light caught a dark seam that ran down her cheek, hard against her ear, and crossed the angle of her jaw.

Urchin-girl saw the woman and waved, then detached herself from the gang, flapped her sleeve-ends in a collective goodbye and tripped to the Landcruiser. A boy I had seen before, maybe one of Red's classmates, straw-coloured dreadlocks, got into the front passenger seat. Red watched them drive away. He kept watching until the car turned the corner.

I tooted and he came, bringing a boy named Tarquin Curnow with him.

Tarquin and Red had been mates since kindergarten and their friendship had survived Red's years of exile interstate after my divorce from his mother. His parents, Faye and Leo, were my closest friends, family almost, pillars of strength and providers of casseroles in the dark days when I was fit for nothing. Back in Fitzroy, our houses were separated only by a cobbled lane and the boys spent so much time together whenever Red came to town that they might as well have been joined at the hip. After Red's permanent return to Melbourne, the boys went to Fitzroy High together. Now at different schools, they were still as thick as ever.

Adolescence had done wonders for Tark. Formerly a drip, he had transformed himself into a Goth. Spiky black hair, funeral weeds, fingerless gloves, high-laced Doc Martens. A pet rat, too, until the cat ate it. Purple candles and Nick Cave records. But Faye and Leo had drawn the line at the eyebrow piercing. And no tattoo, not yet.

Not that his parents were panicking that Tarquin was on the slippery slope to glue sniffing and satanic rituals. He was too smart for that. His maths were good enough to get him into an advanced studies program, his general aptitude test placed him in the top eight per cent for the state and he was vice-captain of the school debating team.

He and Red loped across the road and piled into the back seat of the car, like I was the chauffeur.

'Any good?' I said. 'The bands?'

'Wimpy pop,' declared Tarquin. 'Think they're alternative, but they're not.'

'He can't wait to get home,' said Red. 'Take the Marilyn Manson antidote.'

We drove past the market, windscreen wipers scraping the drizzle, and turned down Victoria Parade towards Fitzroy. The boys talked bands, names I'd never heard, until we were almost at the Curnows' place.

'Before I forget,' said Tark. 'Mum wants to know if you've decided about the holiday house.'

Faye Curnow had invited the two of us to spend part of the summer break at Lorne, a couple of hours west of town, in a rented beach house. I'd mentioned the idea to

Red, but we hadn't yet discussed it in detail.

'What do you reckon?' I asked Red. 'Any chance of an opening in your hectic social calendar for some time at the beach with your poor old dad?'

Red had been giving the matter some thought. 'I've got Christmas with Mum, so I'll be in Sydney until the twenty-seventh,' he said. 'We could go down to Lorne when I get back, take Tark with us. Then Faye and Leo can come down with Chloe after New Year when Faye's holidays start.' Chloe was Tarquin's nine-year-old sister. 'There's that non-residential rowing camp in mid-January, but I haven't made my mind up yet. Maybe we can stay at the beach longer, see how it goes.'

'With Jodie Prentice,' said Tarquin.

'Get stuffed,' said Red.

'Who's Jodie Prentice?' I said.

'A girl,' Tark informed me, authoritatively.

I glanced at the rear-view mirror. Tarquin clasped his hand to his breast, turned his gaze upwards and heaved a lovelorn sigh.

'Jeeze, you're an idiot,' said Red.

'This Jodie, she wouldn't have been the one you were putting the moves on, back there?' I said. 'Little Orphan Annie.'

'She's Matt Prentice's sister,' said Red, like I was supposed to recognise the name. And not notice that he was sidestepping the subject.

'The rasta?' I guessed.

'Surfer,' said Tarquin. 'He's in Year Eleven. She's in Year Nine. Their mother's an architect. Designs these ecological houses. They've got a place at Aireys Inlet, spend a lot of time there.'

I got the picture. Aireys Inlet was just along the coast from Lorne. A couple of weeks surfside would give Red ample chance to pitch his novice woo in the general direction of the elfin Jodie.

'That was her in the Landcruiser,' I said. 'The mother?'

'She's divorced,' said Red. 'Quite attractive, don't you think?'

'Fancy her, too, do you?' I said.

Red shook his head, despairing. 'It's known as sublimation, dad.'

'Actually,' I corrected him. 'It's called projection.'

By the standard measure, I was a man in the prime of life. My forties still lay before me, half of them anyway. I was moderately fit. I still had my own teeth, most of them. Secure employment, good pay, flexible hours, excellent pension plan. With the right lighting, not entirely repulsive. Hydraulic equipment in full working order.

So there were, of course, women after Lyndal. Three, to be precise. Brief encounters, regretted even before they began.

There was nothing wrong with the women. Except for the nut case, but she'd been so forceful as to represent a collapse of resistance rather than a lapse in judgment. Nor, with the passage of time, was fidelity to Lyndal's memory an issue. I missed her and thought about her every day, but nothing would bring her back. I nurtured no illusions about dedicating the rest of my life to the chaste remembrance of my lost lover.

Always pragmatic, Lyndal herself would have been the first to urge me to find a new squeeze. Although she might have had something to say about the randy desperation which led me to crack onto a half-sloshed twenty-four-year-old legal stenographer at the Lemon Tree by pretending to be a recently divorced commodities broker.

Problem was, I needed more than a hump. I needed what Lyndal had embodied. Passion plus compatibility. A shared bed, a shared world, a shared future. A combination it had taken me the best part of my life to find.

I'd met Lyndal during the '88 election campaign when she was doing some sort of voter-profiling work for the state secretariat, number-crunching the demographics in a raft of wobbly seats on the urban fringe. Taking the customers' measurements, she called it, so our wonks could tailor policy to a snug fit.

I loved it when she talked like that, her scepticism pitched midway between the earnest cant of the old guard and the blatant cynicism of the up-and-comers. I quite fancied other things about her, too. Eyes, lips, hips, those kinds of things. I planned to make my move at the election-night party, the victory knees-up. I left my lunge too late. It was three years later before I got a second shot, both of us on the rebound.

What I missed most about Lyndal, apart from the touch of her body, was her sharp eye for the nuances, her bedrock sense of justice and her bullshit detector.

And there's never a shortage of bullshit, not in my line of work. You don't even need to go looking for it. It seeks you out.

In early December parliament went into recess until the following March. I spent the next three weeks avoiding factional brawls, handling constituent matters, playing the minor dignitary at civic events and assisting with the disposal of free beer at end-of-year piss-ups. By then, the sky had begun to behave itself, the mercury was pulling its weight and summer appeared to have arrived. Like everybody else in Melbourne, I suspected a trick.

Christmas Eve was the last business day of the year. The only business of the day was to shut the electorate office for the four-week break.

At ten, I drove Red to the airport for his flight to Sydney. The baggage-handlers had turned on their customary peak-period go-slow and there was no danger that the flight would leave on time. I contrived to steer Red into the Mambo outlet.

'You'll be needing a surfboard,' I said. 'It can be your Christmas present.'

He beamed and picked out a three-fin thruster.

'Act surprised when your mother gives you a wetsuit,' I told him.

When I told Wendy that I planned to give Red a board for Christmas, she immediately suggested that she complete the package with a wetsuit. At first, I took the suggestion as her reminder of the deficiencies of my universe, like I was personally responsible for the water temperature in the southerly latitudes. As if to say that when he lived with her in Sydney, her son hadn't needed thermal insulation. Thinking the worse of my former wife was a reflex, but considering her previous form Wendy had been remarkably sympathetic about Lyndal, the whole mess, and since I was the victor in the custody war, I no longer had any true cause for resentment.

'And I got some of that fizzy bath stuff for her,' Red said. 'And this is for you. You can open it now, if you like.' He handed me an inexpertly wrapped object.

'A 48-piece socket set,' I said. 'This'll be really handy.'

'Get stuffed,' he said. 'At Christmas dinner, I mean.'

There was no point in Red schlepping the surfboard with him to Sydney, so I waved him off at the gate-lounge and carried it back through the terminal, a man in a business suit with a Balin thruster under his arm.

On the way to the electorate office, I stopped at AutoBarn in Tullamarine and bought a set of roof-racks for the Magna, then found a chain bookstore and picked up a present for Ayisha.

The electorate office was a shopfront in Bell Street, Coburg, near the municipal library. When there were no delivery trucks blocking the view from the back window, you could see all the way across the K-Mart carpark to St Eleptherios basilica and the dumpsters behind Vinnie Amato's fruit shop.

I arrived just after one o'clock and found Ayisha surrounded by bags of groceries, talking to her husband on the phone. 'Since when do Macedonians have roast turkey on December twenty-fifth?' she was saying. 'It's not even orthodox Christmas. And I'm a fucking Moslem, culturally speaking. You want it, you cook it.'

Reminded of lunch, I went into the kitchenette and scraped together a tub of low-fat cream cheese, a jar of kalamata olives, a packet of crispbread and the remnants of a bottle of chenin blanc. I waved the bottle in Ayisha's general direction. 'Fancy a quick one before you go? This won't be worth drinking by the time we get back.'

She gave me the thumbs-up and finished her call. I filled our glasses and handed her the present.

'*Lenin's Tomb: The Last Days of the Soviet Empire,*' she read, peeling back the wrapping. 'For the girl who has everything.'

In return, she presented me with a recent biography of the Prime Minister, 487 pages, hardbound. 'Take it to the beach,' she suggested. 'Bury your head in the sand.'

We toasted ourselves for having survived another year, then she gathered up her groceries and departed in the general direction of a month's holiday, leaving the locking-up to me.

The sign on the front door said the office would be open until two o'clock. Since it was unlikely that anyone would have urgent need of our services in the next half-hour, I figured I'd eat lunch then close up early.

Five minutes later, as I was brushing crispbread crumbs off my shirtfront and putting the olives back in the fridge, I heard the front door open and the buzzer on the reception desk ring.

It was Rita Melina. She was wearing pedal pushers, a loose blouse that hung to mid-thigh and big-framed Jackie O sunglasses. A glossy shopping bag with the logo of the Daimaru department store was slung over her shoulder.

'Happy Christmas, Rita,' I said.

'Maybe for some,' she said bluntly. 'Can you spare a few minutes, Murray? I need to talk to somebody official, but not too official, if you know what I mean.'

'I guess that just about fits my description, Rita,' I said. 'I'll be happy to help, if I can.'

I led her into my office. She drew up a chair, put her elbows on the desk and pushed her sunglasses up onto her hairdo. 'This is confidential, right?' she said.

I was about to make some kind of a joke, until I saw the look of flinty determination in her eyes. 'Up to a point,' I said. 'I'm a member of parliament, not a priest or a doctor. I couldn't conceal a crime, for example.'

'Say we were talking hypothetically?' she said. 'Or I was here on behalf of a friend?'

'Ms X, for example?' I said.

'Mrs X, actually,' said Rita.

'Ah, so,' I said. 'And what is the nature of Mrs X's hypothetical problem?'

'She's worried about something Mr X has done, or might have done, and she's wondering how she might raise her concerns with the appropriate authority.'

'And you're hoping I can provide some informal advice, steer you right,' I said. 'On behalf of Mrs X, that is?'

Rita flicked her wrist dismissively, dispensing with our tippy-toe pas-de-deux.

'I think we've established the ground rules, Murray,' she said. 'Tony's left me. Shot through. Not a word of goodbye, except for some half-baked message on the answering machine about having being called out of town urgently on business. I didn't believe a word of it, of course. He must think I'm an idiot.'

'Oh,' I said. 'I'm sorry to hear…'

She cut me off with another peremptory flap. 'I'm not here for marriage guidance counselling, Murray. Some sort of a bust-up between me and Tony has been on the cards for a while, ever since the girls left home. What's he expect me to do, sit around the house counting my wrinkles while some little gold-digger sinks her claws into him? Anyway, a few days ago I finally put my foot down. Told him I wasn't prepared to tolerate his womanising any longer. Told him that if he didn't get rid of that waitress, the one he's been slipping it to, I'd divorce him, take him to the cleaners.'

I sank deeper into my seat and wished that I'd locked the door while I still had the chance. 'Catholics don't get divorced, Rita,' I said. 'They stay together and fight to the death.'

Mrs X wasn't interested in my observations about matrimony. She took a pack of Marlboro Lites from her bag, fired one up with a disposable lighter and looked around for an ashtray.

'It's forbidden to smoke in government offices,' I said.

'Sunday night, I gave the prick twenty-four hours to make up his mind,' Rita exhaled. 'Next day, he goes to work, never comes home. Vanishes. So does mega-tits, his bit on the side. She quits without notice, moves out of her flat, tells the neighbours she's going on a long trip. So it's obvious what's happened. Tony's made his choice, taken off with this cow. And good riddance to him. Except for one thing. His passport's gone, too, along with a whole bunch of business papers he keeps locked in his den at home. Banking details and whatnot. The bastard's left me high and dry.'

I tipped the paperclips from a saucer and put it between us on the table. 'I can understand you being upset, Rita,' I said. 'But what you need is a lawyer, not a member of parliament.'

She held up her palm, not finished yet. 'I called Immigration, tried to find out if he's left the country in the last couple of days. They say they can't tell me. Some bullshit about the Privacy Act, even though I'm his wife. So naturally

75

I thought of you, thought that you'd be able to pull some strings, make some unofficial enquiries on my behalf, that sort of thing.'

As a former adviser to a Minister for Ethnic Affairs, I was not entirely unfamiliar with the labyrinthine back corridors of the federal Department of Immigration. So it was quite within the realm of possibility that I could find somebody who knew somebody who could get an informal peek at the information that Rita wanted. On the other hand, it is axiomatic that getting sucked into your constituents' marital disputes is a zero-sum game.

'I wish I could help, Rita. I really do. But Immigration's federal, I'm state. Different worlds. And frankly, I just don't have that sort of pull.'

'I thought you were my friend,' she said.

'I'm not a magician, Rita,' I said. 'Anyway, even if you confirm that Tony's left the country, what good does it do you?'

'Apart from wanting to know, one way or the other?' she said. 'Remember my friend, Mrs X?'

Here it comes, I thought. Whatever it is. Hell hath no fury like a woman stiffed by her spouse of twenty years.

'Mrs X is just a simple housewife,' said Rita. 'She knows nothing about her husband's business dealings. Never has. She's always been the home-maker, he's been the provider. A traditional marriage, strict demarcation. She's never had any reason to want it otherwise. After all, he's quite successful, business-wise. Starts out with a little pizza joint, builds it into a booming restaurant, branches out into the wholesale seafood line. Always some iron in the fire. Long as the bills get paid, Mrs X sees no reason to think twice about the situation.'

I nodded, letting her know that I could see where she was going. 'But now that Mr X has run out on her,' I said, 'maybe left the country, she's begun to worry that some of his business affairs, about which she knows nothing, might create problems for her. Perhaps he's run out on his debts, too, and she'll be left holding the baby.'

'Or holding nothing at all,' she said. 'For all the wife knows, Mr X is even now in the process of transferring his assets to wherever it is that he's gone. Or hiding them where Mrs X will never be able to find them, so that by the time she tracks him down the cupboard will be bare and she'll never see her share of the common property. She might even lose her home. Would that be fair, I ask you?'

'You really think Tony would do that to you?' I said.

'Not until he walked out on me,' she said. 'Now, frankly, I really don't know. Who knows what ideas that piece of trash has been putting into his head? It'd be different if I could talk to him about it. But nobody'll admit to knowing where he is. The staff at the restaurant say they haven't seen him. All I can be sure about is that I can't afford to take the risk he's doing the dirty on me.'

'So it's occurred to you that if some government agency had reason to suspect that Mr X was engaged in illegal activity,' I said, 'they might take steps to prevent him moving his assets out of the country?'

'Exactly,' she said. 'Freeze his bank accounts, something like that.'

Her brilliant idea lay there on the table between us, like a dead cat. I let it lie there for a while before speaking.

'I sympathise with your situation, Rita, I really do,' I said eventually. 'But you can't just go accusing Tony of criminal activity because you think he might be screwing you out of your potential divorce entitlements. You'll probably just make the situation worse with Tony when he eventually re-surfaces. Plus, you'll get yourself into trouble with the law. Making false allegations is a serious offence.'

'Even if they're true?' she said.

'So what's he done, Rita?' I said. 'Paid his casual staff cash-in-hand, watered the drinks, bribed the health inspector?'

'How about tax avoidance,' she said. 'Money laundering, stuff like that.'

'I thought you said you don't know anything about Tony's business activities.'

She ground her cigarette into the saucer, lit another and leaned forward conspiratorially. 'He's been going to Asia on business every few months for the last couple of years,' she said. 'Quick trips, just a day or so at a time. Hong Kong, Bangkok, Singapore. Meetings with his seafood export clients, he said. Last June, he took me along, made a bit of a holiday of it. Singapore. We went sightseeing, shopping, ate some fabulous food. But as far as I could see, the only business Tony did was visit the Oriental Bank to deposit some cash. A great big wad of it, $30,000 at least. Told me he was building up a nest egg for us.'

'It's a little unusual, I'll grant you that,' I said. 'But what makes you think there was something dodgy about the money?' I said.

She gave me a withering look. 'Get real, Murray,' she said. 'Even I know that there's a limit to the amount of currency you're allowed to export. And that banks in Australia have to report transactions that big. All I'm asking here is that you point me in the direction of the right government agency. Go into a cop shop with this sort of story, they'll put it down to a domestic, give me the bum's rush. A word to the wise, that's all I'm asking, Murray.'

'You're sure about this, Rita?' I said. 'You start the ball rolling, you won't be able to stop it.'

'It's Tony's ball,' she said. 'And right now, as far as I'm concerned, Tony's balls belong in a vice. As for me, I've done nothing wrong. I've signed nothing so I can't see how I can be implicated. I'm just an honest citizen doing her duty.'

She glowered across the table at me, as if any suggestion to the contrary would constitute a wilful obstruction of justice. 'You men,' she added gratuitously. 'I should have known whose side you'd be on.'

'That's unfair,' I said. 'And it's not a matter of taking sides. I'm just suggesting you give yourself a few days to think about this, not go off half-cocked.'

'And let Tony clean me out in the meantime?' she said. 'No way.'

I thought about Pontius Pilate. A much maligned figure, I reflected. I picked up the phone, dialled the state headquarters of the taxation department, identified myself and asked to speak with a senior officer.

I was put through to the state manager, a more senior seat-polisher that I'd expected, and explained that I was calling on behalf of a constituent with information relating to possible tax evasion and infringement of currency laws. Despite his understandable lack of enthusiasm for an unscheduled meeting on the afternoon of Christmas Eve, he agreed to spare said constituent fifteen minutes of his time, subject to her prompt arrival at the Moonee Ponds office.

'Can you be there in half an hour?' I asked, hand over the mouthpiece.

'Just try to stop me,' she said.

There was not the slightest chance of that happening.

As I escorted her to the door, Rita presented me with her Daimaru shopping bag.

'A little something for Christmas,' she said.

The bag held two brick-sized parcels wrapped in newspaper.

'A crayfish,' Rita explained, 'and a dozen abalone.'

'Thank you,' I said. 'That's very generous of you.' About a hundred dollars worth of generous by the heft of it.

'You've been a pillar, Murray,' she said. 'And Tony's got a freezer-load of this stuff in the garage.'

The instant she was out the door, I lowered the blind, shot the bolt and heaved a sigh of relief. Tony, I thought, you're a dead man. I was thinking metaphorically.

And then I wasn't thinking about it at all. As of that moment, my holidays had officially begun.

The house in Lorne was one of those sixties jobs, a cement-sheet box on stilts. Perched on a sloping block of land at the crest of the ridge overlooking the town, it had bare floors, throw-rugs, an antique television set with rabbit-ear antenna, ramshackle furniture and a timber deck from which the sea could be glimpsed through the raggedy tops of the surrounding bluegums. Sand had seeped into the nooks and crannies, pieces were missing from the board games and the bookshelf held only dog-eared fishing manuals, bird-spotting books and unfinished Peter Carey novels.

We arrived three days after Christmas, drove straight from the airport with a carload of holiday supplies and Tarquin Curnow. A three-man advance party, our mission was to establish base camp before the others arrived late on New Year's Day.

I had Christmas lunch with the Curnows, contributing

Rita's abalone to the spread, then trawled the Boxing Day sales for cut-price wardrobe essentials. My purchases included a selection of tropical shirts and a panama hat which, I felt, would serve me well in the resort-wear stakes.

I wore the panama hat to the airport. The day was hot, proper beach weather, with the promise of more to come. In deference to the season, Tark had shorn his Joey Ramone pageboy into a Travis Bickle mohawk and ripped the sleeves off his Nick Cave tee-shirt. The black jeans and mid-shin Doc Martens remained, however, welded to his lower body. For his part, Red was dressed for summer as God intended. Baggy shorts, a baggy shirt, blow-fly wraparounds, baseball cap and rubber thongs.

We drove across the Westgate Bridge, heat-haze rising from the oil depots, and fought our way down the Geelong Road with the rest of beach-bound Melbourne. Tarquin sprawled on the back seat, playing Tetris on his Gameboy, while Red gave me a run-down on his visit with mummy dearest, his twin half-sisters and Wendy's husband.

'Nicola and Alexandra are getting really fat,' he said, puffing out his cheeks. 'Biggest five-year-olds you've ever seen. I gave them swimming lessons in the pool and taught them to say fuck-bum. They're all going to Phuket for two weeks when Richard gets back from the Sydney to Hobart yacht race.'

'Phuket?' I snorted, flooring the pedal to pass a fish-tailing caravan. 'Fuck it! What's Phuket compared to this?'

I fed *Pet Sounds* into the cassette-deck and cranked up the volume. Tarquin groaned from the back seat but Red went with it, grooving on the antique vibrations. An hour later, it was Nirvana as we turned down the Anglesea hill and sighted the ocean. By then, we were following the Great Ocean Road, two lanes of blacktop threaded between the sea and the Otway Ranges.

We followed it past the Anglesea funfair and paddle-boat rentals, past the lighthouse at Aireys Inlet and along the straight stretch of surf beach at Moggs Creek. As we travelled further west, the hills became steeper, wilder, more thickly wooded.

The road began to climb, clinging to the forested slopes in a series of switchback curves, dropping away to wave-washed rocks, double lines all the way.

According to the annual report of the Australian Tourism Commission, the Great Ocean Road attracts more than four million visitors a year. Most of them, it was evident, should never have been allowed behind the wheel of a motor vehicle. For twenty minutes we were stuck behind a tortoise-shaming senior citizen in a spanking new all-terrain Nissan Patrol. When I pulled out to pass him, we were almost totalled by a dipstick in an Audi convertible.

At the Cinema Point lookout, I hit the left indicator and eased onto the gravel margin.

'Five minute break,' I said. 'Stretch legs, contemplate nature, allow blood to return to driver's knuckles.'

The sea extended to the horizon, vast and twinkling. Towering eucalypts and ragged scrub marched up the incline from the rocky shore, continuing past us, up into the grey-green vastness of the state forest. Looking back, we could see the surf at Eastern View, the breakers uncoiling in rows as regular as corduroy. Up ahead, beyond a series of blunt capes, we could just make out a broad arc of calico sand etched into the bush-covered ranges. And, packed tight around the sand, the township of Lorne.

'What's that pink blob?' asked Red.

'The Cumberland,' I said. 'A cutting-edge condominium-style time-share apartment complex.'

'Shipwrecks,' declared Tarquin, his hand sweeping the watery horizon. 'There's hundreds of them out there. Dozens, anyway. They sailed all the way from Europe, five months or more, then got smashed on these rocks.'

Red peered over the edge. 'Cool.'

'The dead bodies were washed ashore all along here. I did a project on it in Grade Six.'

An ancient kombi trembled to a halt beside us. Red nudged Tark and nodded towards a concert poster taped to its side door. Regurgitator. Hunters and Collectors. Spiderbait. Rock the Falls.

Two ferals got out of the van, little more than kids. He was covered in Celtic tattoos and she had feathers in her braids. A baby was slung across her chest in a raffia hammock. She sat on the lookout parapet, whipped out a tit and began to feed it. Magic Happens, read a sticker on the van window.

'So does shit,' muttered Tarquin, without apparent malice.

'Can I use the mobile?' said Red. He'd had his own, briefly, for emergency use and ease of essential son–father communications. Three hundred dollars worth of calls in a month, and I pulled the plug.

'Keep it short,' I said.

He strolled away as he dialled, reading the number off the back of his hand. 'Hey it's me. Wassup? We're almost there.'

Fifteen minutes later, the road dropped to sea level and

crossed the Erskine River where it tumbled out of the hills and turned into the lagoon beside the Lorne caravan park. We continued past the fruit shop called Lorne Greens, the joke lost on post-Ponderosa generations, and cruised along the main drag, an esplanade of shops that faced across the road to the foreshore carpark and the teeming beach. The old bait-and-tackle shops and milk bars were long gone, replaced by seaside-theme knick-knackeries and surfwear boutiques with swimsuit racks out the front. Holiday-makers ambled along the footpath, clinging to the shade, window-shopping. Some sat at tables outside coffee shops and juiceries, their hair still wet from swimming.

After a couple of passes, I found a parking spot between a Porsche and a Jeep Cherokee, then set off to pick up the house key while the boys found some lunch. As I headed along the footpath, I passed several nodding acquaintances. We smiled, delighted to see each other, even if we couldn't quite remember who we were.

I went into the real estate office and collected the key and directions to the house. As I came out, tucking the receipt into my wallet, a short man was rocking on his toes as he peered through the front window at the For Sale listings. He had less hair and more waist than the last time I'd seen him.

'G'day, Ken,' I said. 'Win the lottery, did you?'

Back when I was a ministerial adviser, Ken Sproule was factotum to a party heavyweight, the Minister for Police. Both Ken and his boss saw the chill weather ahead and jumped ship before the hull impacted the iceberg. Ken found himself a snug new berth as a consultant to the poker-machine business, a booming sector of the state's new growth industry.

'Hello, Murray,' he drawled. He did me the honour of tearing himself away from the array of ideal getaways with water views and in-ground pools. 'Checking the prices, mate. We've just built a place at Aireys Inlet, thought we might have over-capitalised. Look who's here, Sandra.'

Sandra was Ken's new cookie. Mid-thirties. Petite, well-toned, worked in PR. She was waiting her turn at the ice-cream counter next door. A small child was slung on her hip. Sandra was the chirpy type, foil to the blunt Ken.

'Hello, Murray,' she said, handing a cone to the kid. 'You in the market?'

'For an ice-cream?'

'A house, stupid.'

I showed her the key. 'We're renting for a few weeks,' I said. 'Sight unseen.'

'We?' She dropped her chin and looked over the top of her sunglasses. Wondering, I understood, if I had paired off since Lyndal.

'Me,' I said. 'My son. Some old friends.'

'Ah,' she said.

'Careful.' Ken lunged for the child's hand, narrowly averting a spilt vanilla crisis.

Sandra pulled a scrap of paper and a pen from the beach-bag slung over her shoulder. 'If you're free tomorrow evening,' she said, firming the paper against the estate agent's window as she scribbled. 'We're having a few friends around for drinks and a barbecue. A sort of housewarming for our new place.' She thrust the address at me. 'You will come, won't you?'

I made tentatively affirmative noises, then headed back to the car. The boys had connected. They were lounging in the shade of a big cypress, pizza slices in hand, communing with a mixed gaggle of teens. I recognised Max Kline from Red's rowing eight and some other kids from school. I waved the house key and Red and Tark came to the car, trailing a slim girl in a crocheted bikini-top and hipster board shorts with tousled, beach-wet hair.

'This is Jodie Prentice,' Red said. 'This is my father.'

The girl smiled shyly, displaying her retainer, and held out her hand, all very well-brought-up. Narrow hips, bare midriff, very little in the shirt-potato department. 'Pleased to meet you, Red's father.'

We shook, as though confirming a deal. She wore a butterfly ring, a puzzle ring and a black plastic spider ring. 'Charmed, I'm sure,' I said. 'Jodie Prentice.'

She was cute in a whippish, salt-flecked, young girl way. A bit cheeky. But no ditz, that much was evident. Heartbreak on the hoof.

Red shuffled in the gravel. 'I've got to go and, um…'

'He'll be back,' I told Jodie. 'After he's milked the cows, chopped the firewood and nailed Tark into his coffin.'

The gang began to gravitate beachward, trailing goodbyes. 'We'll be in front of Beach Bites,' Jodie told Red, hesitating for a second before dashing away.

'Ready to rock?' said Tark, drumming impatiently on the car roof.

I turned the Magna uphill and we climbed through the sunbaked town. Hemmed by inviolable forest, Lorne did not have room for lateral expansion. So, year by year, the old houses with their wide verandas, vegetable patches and couch-grass yards were giving way to low-rise cluster housing and sandstone mansions with garage access and touch-pad security.

But not our place, thank Christ. We found it at the end of the last street in town, nothing but bush beyond the back fence. We gave it a good going over, threw open the windows, checked the water pressure, tested the sofa, sniffed the empty fridge.

'Bit basic, isn't it?' concluded Red.

At six-fifty a week, it was no bargain. On the other hand, it was something of a classic, the last of its kind. Abalone-shell ashtrays, seventies stereo, flyscreen doors and a perforated surf-ski on the back porch.

'Nothing to maintain, nothing to keep clean,' I said. 'Perfect.'

Except for the noise. Every time Tarquin clumped across the bare floorboards in his Docs, it sounded like we were being raided by the Gestapo.

'No boots in the house,' I ordered. 'I'm here to relax, not have an Anne Frank experience.'

He clicked his heels. '*Jawohl, mein Fuhrer.*'

Opting for private quarters, the boys claimed a grove of tea-trees in the backyard and pitched an igloo tent. Until Faye and Leo arrived, the indoor accommodation was exclusively mine. I was stocking the refrigerator with Coopers Pale Ale and Pepsi Max when the boys ambled into the kitchen.

'New Year's Eve,' said Red, backside on the benchtop, bare feet dangling, Mr Casual. 'There's this music festival up in the hills.'

'Rock the Falls,' I said. 'I've seen the poster.' Not just on the ferals' kombi. They were taped to every light pole on the main drag. 'I'm getting a bit old for that sort of thing, but I'll keep it in mind.'

'Not you,' said Red. 'Us.'

'We were thinking we could maybe take the tent,' said Tark. 'Camp overnight.'

'Everybody's going,' said Red. 'We'll be social outcasts if we don't.'

'Pariahs,' said Tark.

I busied myself in the fridge, taking my time with the product placement. The boys were trustworthy, mature, capable. But they were only fifteen. And the music would not be the only experience they were seeking.

'Everybody?' I asked. 'That includes this Jodie Prentice?'

'Probably,' said Red. 'Her brother Matt is definitely going.' He rattled off some other names.

I shut the fridge and gave him the stop sign. 'I'll need to talk to Faye or Leo, see what Tark's parents think. And I'm not making any promises.'

The boys nodded, suppressing smirks of self-congratulation.

'In the meantime,' I said, hooking my thumb in the direction of the sea. 'Ready to rock?'

An hour later, I was sitting under a market umbrella at a table in front of Beach Bites, the snack bar on the foreshore. I was fresh from the water, togs still damp, legs bare. My Hawaiian shirt hung open, my panama hat was tilted low over my eyes and I was stirring the ice in my fresh-squeezed orange juice with a straw. A summery mix of ozone, hot chips, vinegar and sun-block hung in the shimmering air. Tarquin, dressed for a punk funeral, lounged beside me, sipping decaf macchiato and munching a vegan muffin. Spread before us was a tableau of the nation at play.

Innumerable near-naked bodies reclined on the baking sand, soaking up the full glare of the afternoon sun or sheltering beneath nylon hooches. Out from the shore, a row of surfers lay prostrate on the glistening water, staring seaward for the next break. Closer, where frilled curls dumped against the shore, swimmers bobbed in the water and little kids skittered though the shallows, dragging boogie boards behind them. Young men were playing cricket on the wet, hard-packed sand, defending plastic stumps against dog-gnawed tennis balls. A rainbow-tailed kite fluttered overhead. In front of the surf club, lifeguards with logo-emblazoned backsides stood sentinel in reflector sunglasses. Above the swish of the waves came the screeching of children and gulls.

'Uh-oh,' said Tark. 'Big brother.'

He nodded at a pile of bodies a few metres down the beach, the boys in peeled-down wetsuits, the girls in very little indeed. Young, free and girt by sea, they were chatting and joking and flicking each other with wet towels. Red lay sprawled in their midst, head turned towards Jodie Prentice. She was sitting, knees tucked up under her chin, squinting up at her brother Matt. He loomed above her, legs akimbo, proprietary.

'Protective type?' I said.

Tark shrugged and fluttered his hand. 'A bit,' he said. 'Not always friendly. Nothing weird or anything. They're pretty close, that's all. Real thick. Red's gunna hafta tread careful.'

Matt Prentice picked up his surfboard and padded towards the reef break at the far end of the beach. Jodie tapped Red on the shoulder, unscrewing the cap from a tube of zinc cream. He moved closer, offering his face and she began to paint his nose an iridescent pink.

Tark groaned in disgust. I, too, averted my gaze. It roamed along the shoreline, a frieze of nubile flesh. There were near-naked, magazine-strength babes everywhere. Face-down on towels, bikini straps undone. Jogging from the water, flanks glistening. Strolling in pairs, boobs straining at tiny scraps of lycra.

'Anybody looking,' said Tark. 'I'll be in the video arcade.'

My attention drifted to a woman dawdling barefoot along the edge of the water, sandals dangling from her hand, her straw hat pushed back on her short fair hair. She was long-legged, slender, a sarong knotted at her bosom, a billowy white shirt draped over her shoulders. Something about her bearing caught my eye, the poised way she held herself, her absorption in the play of the light on the water.

She drew nearer and I recognised her as the Prentice kids' mother, the woman who'd picked them up after the concert at Festival Hall. Jodie spotted her and waved. Their resemblance was obvious. The woman came up the beach, heading for the group of kids.

I should meet her, I decided. Make myself known, what with our children being friends. Say hello, in a purely social way. I stood, sucked in my stomach, ran my fingers through my hair, set my hat at a rakish angle and steered a converging course across the beach.

Rubber thongs sinking into the soft sand, I wove my way through the maze of prostrate bodies. Flip, flop, flip. Red spotted me coming, rose from his towel and shouted.

'Hey, Dad!'

He twisted, pirouetting on the ball of one foot, and whipped a Frisbee at me. It came low and fast. I took a couple of paces forward and firmed my stance to catch it. But the hurtling disc suddenly veered upwards. My arm shot into the air and I stepped backwards to intercept.

This was not a smart move. I immediately toppled over a pile of towels, ricocheted off a beach shelter and tripped over a child's bucket-and-spade set. My hat went west and my feet went east.

My fall was broken by a supine sunbather. A young woman. She was blonde, remarkably attractive, possibly Swedish, almost completely naked and glistening with oil. Her bikini top was unlaced. I registered these facts in the half second before my out-thrust hands closed around her busty substances. They were more than adequate to cushion my fall.

Blurting apologies, I leaped backwards, scrabbling in the scalding sand.

Bountiful Ingrid jack-knifed upright and lunged at me, emitting an outraged yelp. At that point, I realised I was clutching something. A wisp of floral fabric with a length of string attached. The string was taut. It was caught on something. A ring. A ring inserted through a nipple.

'Ikea,' yapped the Valkyrie, her face contorted with pain. Her right boob was coming at me like the nose-cone of an ICBM. 'Bang & Olufsen!'

She sounded like Marlene Dietrich gargling ball-bearings. Her companion, Sven Smorgasbord, loomed up and smacked the bikini top from my grasp.

'Häagen-Dazs,' he accused menacingly. 'Gustavus Adolphus? Björn Borg.'

No translation was required. His expression was sufficient. That, and the aggressive thrust of his posing pouch.

'Absolut!' I assured him, backing away. 'Hans Christian Andersen.' I realised my mistake immediately. Sven glowered.

'Ingmar Bergman,' I grovelled, displaying the Frisbee as

token of my innocence. 'Liv Ullmann.'

'Orrefors,' snorted the woman dismissively, and they sank back onto their towels.

Red was watching, writhing with embarrassment at his father's antics. I looked past him and saw that Jodie and her mother were occupied in conversation, apparently oblivious, beginning to walk away. Red glanced over his shoulder, following my gaze, then turned back, a relieved smirk on his face.

I unleashed the Frisbee, warp factor nine, and zapped the smarmy little smartarse.

The sign for Gusto stood at the corner of a narrow, bush-bordered road leading sharply uphill from the Great Ocean Road. The name was spelled in glazed turquoise tiles.

The moment I saw it, set in a curved adobe wall, I thought of Gusto's owner, Jake Martyn. And then of Tony Melina, in whose company I had met him.

I noticed the sign as I was driving out of town, taking Red to baptise his new surfboard. The surf scene at Lorne was tight and the local nazis took a dim view of blow-in grommets. I offered to drive Red to Fairhaven, just the two of us, so he could get some practice before strutting his stuff in full view of the gang. It was late morning, overcast and humid. The sky was the colour of dead grass, the swell even and glassy. According to the radio surf report the water temperature was eighteen degrees, the swell running at just over a metre.

It was two days after our arrival in Lorne and a week since Rita Melina had ambushed me at the electorate office, wanting my help to nail her husband's cheating arse to the wall. Since then, I hadn't given her or Tony a moment's thought.

In certain respects, a member of parliament is like a doctor, only less useful. An endless parade of people knocks on your door, each with their own problems. If you can, you help. If you can't, you refer them elsewhere. Either way, there's no mileage in busting your chops. And if the marital barricades are up, try not to get caught in the crossfire. Christ knows, you're never thanked, whatever the outcome. So when I shut the office door on Rita, I put the matter behind me.

But the Gusto sign set me thinking of Tony and, as I followed the twists and turns of the Great Ocean Road, I wondered if Rita had run him to ground yet. It revived my curiosity, too, about Tony's connection with Jake Martyn. According to Rita, Tony Melina was bent, at least a little. And the last time I'd seen him, he and Martyn appeared to be involved in some kind of deal. This offered scope for idle conjecture.

Idle being the key word. The restaurant game is a cash business. To those inclined, it provides ample opportunity to skim the till or dud the tax collector. If Tony was running some sort of scam, that didn't make Jake Martyn a crook just because I saw them together. After all, if it came to that, I myself had done business with Tony Melina over the years. Did that make the Melbourne Upper trivia nights a money-laundering operation?

'Forty dollars,' said Red. 'For that you get ten bands plus

a camp site. Pretty good deal, I reckon.'

'Hmm,' I said, hugging the cliff-face as we edged around a hairpin bend, a squadron of bikes roaring past, a sheer drop to the sea.

Value for money was Red's latest argument in support of the boys' plea to be allowed to stay overnight at The Falls festival on New Year's Eve. Tarquin had already phoned his parents and got the provisional nod, subject to my final endorsement, but the lads knew I wasn't going to announce my decision until I'd extracted maximum tease value from the situation. And that meant making them pitch their case.

'And this forty dollars?' I said. 'Where's it coming from?'

'Consolidated revenue,' said Red. 'I've got $63 in my bank account. And Tark's got even more, if he doesn't spend it all at the video arcade. He's met this girl there, Ronnie, one of the undead.'

'So you're both set for the night, then?' I said. 'Chicks-wise.'

'Guess so,' he said, not displeased with the idea.

'You'll be up there in the woods, no adult supervision, free to have your wicked ways.'

He gave a scornful snort, but he knew he'd fallen into a trap. 'Check it out,' he said suddenly, pointing to the view as we turned down the hill towards the long stretch of beach at Fairhaven. The waves were as advertised, a perfect beginner's break. Perfect, too, for an old guy who was long out of practice.

'Jodie's mother,' I said. 'What's she think about this overnight stay business?'

'Her name's Barbara,' he said. 'And I was wrong about her. She's not divorced.'

Fairhaven was a popular spot, a sandy bottom with even, regular sets. Vans and station wagons lined the tussocky dunes beside the road and it was hard to find a place to park.

'Let me know if you spot an opening,' I said.

'Actually, her husband's dead,' continued Red, eyeing me sideways. Checking my reaction, not getting one. 'Car crash. It happened when Matt and Jodie were little. They were trapped in the wreckage, all four of them. Jodie's still got this scar.'

He began to raise his right arm, his left hand reaching across his chest to show me where. The hand got half-way, then he changed his mind, wary, before I asked how he'd come to be so familiar with young Jodie's anatomy.

'Is that where her mother got that…?' I ran my finger from my earlobe to my collarbone.

'You've been checking her out, haven't you, Dad?'

'You should talk,' I said. 'You're the one planning to get her daughter into your tent.'

He shook his head, exasperated. 'Matt'll be there the whole time. They're hardly out of each other's sight.'

'That's reassuring.' I pulled into a spot at the Moggs Creek end of the beach, body-board territory.

'Yeah,' said Red, figuring maybe he'd found an angle he could use to his advantage. 'Anyway, in case you're wondering, Jodie says she's not involved with anyone at the moment. Her mother, that is. She lived with a guy called Dennis for a few years, but they broke up. He's married to someone else now, got his own kids. Matt was pretty cut up about it, apparently. So, like I said, she's up for grabs. I reckon you should go for it.'

'You're a sick puppy, you know,' I said. 'Trying to line me

up with your girlfriend's mother.'

'This thing with Jodie,' he said. 'I'm not a hundred per cent sure about it. She's nice, but she can get a bit clingy. Reckon I should play the field a bit before I commit. What do you think?'

'I think I should have you spayed while it's still legal.'

'No, really.' He went serious on me, man-to-man. 'If you're interested in her mother, don't let me stand in your way.'

'That's very considerate of you, son.' I mirrored his tone, meaning it.

'That's okay,' he said. 'You need it more than I do. Last chance before the retirement home.'

'Get fucked,' I said. 'Any other words of wisdom from the master of romance?'

'Just one,' he said. 'If you're fast enough, there's an empty parking spot next to that yellow station wagon up ahead.'

We hit the water and Red soon found his feet, the sharp-nosed thruster an easier plank to walk than my first board, a malibu. Or so it seemed, watching from the shore. When I finally managed to wangle a turn, it wasn't quite as manoeuvrable as it looked. We surfed up a hefty appetite, bought pies for lunch and drove back to Lorne through a squall that put coin spots on the Magna's dusty windscreen.

I spent the rest of the day lounging around the house. Intermittent showers, cricket on the radio, a book within reach, a nap. The lads were elsewhere, watching videos with better-resourced cronies, they claimed. Pressing their suits with the objects of their desire, I didn't wonder.

By seven-thirty, the cool front had passed, the streets were dry and the sky was clearing. Red and Tark were back, heads in the refrigerator, talking about having some friends over, kicking on. I dug out the address for Ken Sproule's place, changed into clean chinos and a polo shirt, forked over enough cash for a delivery of pizza, made a show of counting the beer, stuck a bottle of wine under my arm, then left the younger generation to its own devices and started for Aireys Inlet.

Sunset was still more than an hour away, but the ranges had already cast their long shadow across the Great Ocean Road. The beach at Fairhaven was murky and spray-shrouded, deserted by all but the most dedicated wax-heads. At the lifesaving club, I turned off the highway, climbed into the sunlight and followed the spine of the ridge that ran parallel to the coast.

Ten years back, a bushfire had descended from the hills and incinerated many of the houses along this section of road. New growth soon sprouted and new houses were built, but the inferno had left its mark. Charred trunks jutted from the greenery and many of the new dwellings had been constructed with an eye to the harsher realities.

Ken and Sandra's place was such a house. Low-slung and well clear of surrounding trees, it was recessed into a fold in the earth, the front cantilevered, the rear facing the road with a packed-gravel parking apron. Solar panels. External sprinklers. Slatted timber pergolas shading the north and west aspects. Slightly Spanish feel. Costa Monza.

The door was open. I gave it a passing rap and followed a short hallway into an open-plan space that was filled with convivial chatter and the smell of fresh paint. The furniture was sparse and modular. Ikea, I guessed. The feel was stylish but comfortable, tending to homey. Stray pieces of Lego littered the floor and cartoon noises leaked from behind a closed door. Pushing fifty, Ken was a come-again father.

About a dozen adults, none of whom I knew, were drinking wine and batting the breeze at a beechwood dining table. Past them, on a jutting deck, Ken was tending a Weber, aided by two blokes in fashionably lairish shirts, cans of beer in hand. He spotted me hovering uncertainly and beckoned with his barbecue tongs.

He introduced me to his friends, a Steve and a Boyd, ageing yuppies, then carved a wide circle in the air with his meat-grippers. 'Not bad, eh?'

It certainly wasn't. Undulating, scrub-covered hills extended from the deck, capped in the distance by the jade of the ocean. A froth of tangerine clouds rose from the horizon. Here and there, houses dotted the landscape and solitary trees emerged from the undergrowth, twisted into picturesque shapes by the sea winds. The building and the view were all of a piece, made for each other.

I whistled appreciatively, meaning it.

'We'll get built out eventually, of course,' said Ken. 'Lose the view. But not the capital gain.'

Sandra appeared, thrust a flute of bubbly into my hand, steered me inside and introduced me to her other guests. Couples, mainly. A few years younger, mostly. Media types and film people.

In keeping with the unspoken code of the beachside holiday, jobs were not mentioned nor shop talked. The topic was plans for New Year's Eve. Having none, I sipped and listened.

Ken, Sandra and some of the others had managed to get a table at Gusto, no mean achievement, apparently. 'We've got an in,' confided Sandra. 'The architect who designed this place also did Gusto. She had a word with Jake Martyn, fixed it up for us to join her party. We've become quite matey with her. Matter of fact, she said she might drop around tonight, see how the place works with people in it.'

What are the chances? I wondered.

My answer arrived twenty minutes later, a raw cotton skirt swishing at her ankles as she came down the hall. She hesitated for a moment before entering the room, examining the set-up. Unnoticed, possibly, except by me. She was buffed and moisturised, post-beach. Her ash-blonde hair was cut in an Annie Lennox crop and she wore a green coral necklace that might have matched her eyes. Hard to tell at the distance.

Sandra saw her and darted forward, smoocheroonie. The two women conferred, then waltzed around the room for a series of effusive introductions. In due course, it was my turn.

'Murray,' Sandra started. 'You really must meet…'

'Barbara Prentice,' I said. 'Jodie's mother.'

The architect raised a quizzical eyebrow.

'My son is a friend of your daughter,' I explained. 'Red Whelan. I'm Murray.'

'Ah,' she exhaled, putting it together. 'You're the polly, right?' Something in her tone conveyed the impression that my occupation wasn't the only thing she knew about me.

We held each other's gaze for slightly longer than was dictated by the requirements of common courtesy. Her eyes were grey.

'Quick,' called Ken from the deck, a rare enthusiasm in his voice. 'Showtime.'

A flock of sulphur-crested cockatoos had come flapping out of the hills, white plumage vivid against the darkening sky. There must have been a hundred of them, screeching and wheeling, then settling in the branches of a fire-blackened stringybark, the nearest tree to the house. We crowded the deck, all oohs and aahs, captivated by the wild splendour of the sight, children pressing to the front, television forgotten.

'Are they on the payroll?' somebody quipped. 'Ambience consultants?'

'All part of the design,' Barbara laughed.

The cockatoos worked on the tree for a while, their beaks shredding the foliage. Then they rose again, a restless whirlwind, and flapped away to feed elsewhere, screeching and carping. I thought of my ex-wife, Wendy.

Candles were lit and Ken's burnt sacrifice transferred to the dining table. As the other guests found their seats, I lingered on the deck, watching night settle over the lavender hills, and sea merge with sky. After a while, Barbara Prentice was standing there too.

'Nice house,' I said. 'It has such an open, welcoming feel. Wonderfully site-specific, too.'

'Sounds like you're out of practice,' she said.

'Badly,' I admitted.

'Your son, on the other hand, does not appear to be backward in coming forward.'

'I heard it was the other way around.'

She gave a derisive snort. 'Wishful thinking.'

'Well, that's no crime,' I said. 'Is it?'

Even in the waning light, the faint scar under her ear was clearly visible. A different haircut would have made it less evident, possibly hidden it completely. But she seemed to wear it almost as a badge of honour, the mark of a survivor.

There was something a bit dangerous about the woman. Smart dangerous, not whacko dangerous. Something challenging and, well, sexy.

'You comfortable about Jodie going to this Falls festival thing?' I said.

'Something I should be worried about?'

'Not Red,' I said. 'If that's what you mean. Born gentlemen, the Whelan boys.'

She gave me a sideways look that suggested both doubt and a degree of disappointment.

We're flirting, I thought. We're definitely flirting.

She waggled a hand, signifying ambivalence. 'The way I see it, Jodie will probably be a lot safer at the festival than hanging around in Lorne. It can get pretty ugly in town, all the boozing and brawling on the foreshore, yobbos coming from miles around. And her brother Matt will be there to keep an eye on her. He can be a bit of a tearaway at times, but he looks after his little sister.'

'So I understand,' I said. 'Not that…' I let the sentence fade away. Like she said, I was out of practice.

We leaned on the railing, saying nothing, watching the purple light seep away across the scrub.

'Murray,' she said.

'Yes,' I breathed.

'Did you bring your Frisbee?'

I didn't want to jump this woman, not straight off. I wanted to stand close behind her, put my arm around her waist, feel the fit. Just stand like that, looking out over the world.

'Get it while you can,' called Ken, summoning us to dinner.

Inside, Sandra was bustling with the seating arrangements, intent on placing us next to each other. But I wasn't about to have my match made. And neither, I could tell, was Barbara. We dithered, evading Sandra's attempts at shoe-horning, and finished up at opposite ends of the table. Soon after dinner, Barbara made her goodbyes and left.

Later, as I was helping Ken and his mate Boyd with the washing-up, Sandra floated into the kitchen, pleasantly pickled, and sidled up to the sink. 'Spoke to Barbara about New Year's Eve,' she slurred into my ear as I scrubbed a sauce-smeared plate. 'Asked her if maybe we couldn't squeeze you onto our table at Gusto. You know what she said? Said you could always turn up and'—she glanced around conspiratorially—'try your luck.'

'Luck?' I said.

There'd been bugger all of that lately.

'Mummy,' squeaked a voice near the floor. 'Damon stuck a piece of bread in the video player.'

As soon as Sandra turned her back, I handed the dishmop to Ken, thanked him for a splendid housewarming, and slipped away.

With five or six drinks under my belt, I was close to the limit. So I pushed Barbara Prentice and all she represented to the back of my mind and concentrated on the twists and turns of the road, my headlights sweeping empty air like the wandering beam of a lighthouse. Perhaps it was more than six.

Back in Lorne, I found a boat trailer blocking the driveway, a neighbour loading fishing equipment. He signalled his willingness to shift, but I wasn't fussed and parked a little further along the street.

Although the lights were lit, there was no sign of movement in the house. As I sauntered up the driveway, I was met by sounds from the backyard. The low strumming of a guitar and a girl's voice, singing off-key. Mopey, strangulated vocals of the Tracey Chapman variety, subset of the Joni Mitchell whine. Along with the music came the background burble of youthful conversation. And, as I drew closer, the unmistakable smell of something burning.

Ah shit, I thought.

Shit, pot, hemp, grass, weed, ganja, mull.

Marijuana.

In certain situations, discretion is the better part of parenting. I went back to the car, waited until the driveway was clear, then returned anew, advertising my arrival with engine noises, headlights and a banged door.

As I climbed the front steps, a camel-train of teenagers came loping down the side of the house, half-obscured in the shadows. Three boys and a girl.

The point man was Matt Prentice, sister Jodie in his wake. The other two boys were unfamiliar, generic tagalongs.

A year older than Red, Matt was taller and more confident. Nothing of his mother or sister in his features, not that I could immediately discern. He communicated an attitude, though. A cockiness that didn't necessarily have much to do with self-assurance. Something chippish in the shoulder region.

'I'm Jodie's brother,' he said with minimal courtesy. 'Picking her up.'

The two other boys nodded, confirming his claim. Jodie gave me a little hello-goodbye wave. And then they were gone, flowing down the hill.

I clattered through the front door and made a general presence of myself in the house. There was no smell of smoking but there were empty beer cans in the kitchen bin. Not a lot, not mine, not an issue. A half-dozen mid-teens were hunkered down in the backyard near the tent, propped on the rental's assortment of chairs, their outlines familiar to some degree or another. A boy I knew as Max, one of the many Maxes of his age, was noodling on the guitar, displaying an unsuspected talent.

Red wandered upstairs. 'Home already?' he said. 'No good?'

'It was okay,' I said. 'Jodie's mother was there.'

He tilted his head. 'And?'

'And various other people,' I said. 'So what's been happening here?'

'Nothing much,' he shrugged. If he was stoned he was hiding it well. 'Starting to drift away.'

'I passed Jodie on my way in. Big brother strikes again?'

'Matt's cool,' he allowed. 'Hung for a while, him and a couple of mates, Year Elevens. Came around to pick up Jodie, get her home before curfew.'

'Good idea,' I said, yawning and having a late-night scratch. 'Same goes for you and Tarquin. I'm going to hit the sack. Keep it down, will you, and don't leave the premises, okay?'

He shrugged, not fussed. 'Sure,' he said. 'Cool.'

I tossed and turned, just catching the low murmur of boytalk from the backyard and the faint sighing of the waves, somewhere out there at the furthest reaches of my hearing.

And as I awaited oblivion, I thought of Lyndal. And of a night like this, two summers back, when we lay entwined, the sea in our ears, moonlight seeping through a chink in the curtains, and conceived a child.

Then I tried to remember how many days had passed since Lyndal had last come unbidden into my mind. And what, if anything, the answer to that question might mean. It meant, I decided, that time is an active verb. And pondering in turn the meaning of that observation, I drifted into sleep, sure of only one thing. That I was sleeping alone and I wished I wasn't.

The morning dawned hot. By ten, it had muscled thirty aside. I nailed the boys at breakfast, got them with their snouts in the Nutrigrain. 'Order in the House,' I declared, gavelling the kitchen benchtop with the back of a spoon and firming the knot in my sarong. 'The Honourable Murray Whelan has the floor.'

The lads regarded me languidly, cereal-laden implements poised in mid-shovel.

'Regarding the smoking of dope,' I began. 'I'd like to take this opportunity to point out that the possession and use of cannabis is illegal in this state. A bust could get you kicked out of school. Furthermore, some authorities believe that marijuana can trigger adolescent-onset schizophrenia.'

Tark and Red gave each other the sideways eyeball, brows furrowing.

'Not if you don't inhale,' said Tarquin.

'According to the President of the United States,' added Red, helpfully.

'I'm not going to be hypocritical and pretend that I've never smoked the stuff myself,' I said. 'I know it's out there and you'll probably have a lash at some stage. Just let's not pretend it isn't happening.'

They twigged, realising why I had chosen that particular morning to raise the issue.

'Wasn't us,' said Red.

I raised my palms. 'No names, no pack drill. Just play safe, that's all I'm asking. And you might consider waiting until you're a bit older. That way, you can combine it with alcohol and cars, get more bang for your buck.'

'Chill, Dad,' said Red. 'We're cool.'

'I'm glad we had this little talk,' I said. 'Pass the sugar.'

'Now there's something can really kill you,' said Tarquin.

'Depends how hard you get hit with the bowl,' I said.

After breakfast, we went squinting into the heat and drove down the hill, looking to get wet. Mountjoy Parade was thick with traffic as party animals poured into town for the evening's revels on the foreshore, horns honking, car stereos cranked to maximum doof. On the sward of couch grass between the esplanade and the beach a concert stage was taking shape, roadies swarming over the rigging like a pirate crew.

We headed for Wye River, fifteen kilometres further west, a sandy beach at the mouth of a trickling creek. The water was wet but the tide was out, the surf was nowhere and the heat was so wilting that our swims wore off almost before we left the water. Within an hour, we'd had enough.

Back in Lorne, we found council workers erecting crowd-control barriers along the main drag, heat haze rising from the asphalt. Police buses were disgorging coppers from Melbourne, all aviator sunglasses and peaked caps, and a mobile command centre was parked at the kerb outside the Chinese take-away. An FM radio station was broadcasting from the foreshore, its studio in the shape of a giant boom box.

I spent the rest of the day in a wilting torpor, the boys drifting in and out of frame. In due course, late afternoon, we set out for the Falls festival. The lads were tarted up for the festivities. Tark had gone for the romantic-consumptive look in a pleat-fronted dress shirt with a wing collar and no sleeves. Red's hair was sculpted into the vertical with enough gel to grease a Clydeside slipway. Taking the Erskine Falls turn, we followed the shuttle-bus up a meandering road that climbed past the town tip and fern-shaded picnic grounds towards the divide at the top of the ranges. Somewhere to our right, invisible in the dense bush, was the Erskine River and its eponymous falls.

For the last couple of kilometres, the traffic crawled, bumper to bumper. There was shade between the trees, but not a hint of breeze. The leaves hung motionless, limp, the light filtering through their drab greenery from a baked enamel sky. Then, at the top of a crest, they parted to reveal the festival site, a neat patch of grazing land that sat in the midst of the forest like a crop circle in a wheat field. A squarish circle, cyclone-fenced and sloping to an array of big-tops, canopied stages and food stalls, a bass thump washing up the hill to the main gate. A mini-Woodstock.

Eight thousand were expected. Most were there already, the rest arriving by the minute, the tribes gathering. I parked in the designated drop-off zone and told the boys that I'd pick them up in exactly the same spot at exactly noon the next day. After extracting sworn assurances that they would enjoy themselves without doing anything health-threatening or egregiously illegal, I issued a small cash bounty and left them to find their friends in the milling mass at the main gate.

On the way back down to Lorne, I passed a dark grey Landcruiser coming up the hill, Barbara Prentice at the wheel, a full load of teens. I gave her a beep and a wave but I couldn't tell if she recognised me.

By seven-thirty, I was back in town, replenishing my stock of grog at the pub drive-through. The show on the foreshore was firing up. Elements of the crowd were already well lubricated, and mounted police were patrolling the fringes on horses with clear plastic visors. I'd been giving some thought to my options for the evening and hanging with the headache crowd wasn't one of them. I took my beer back to the house, stripped to my jocks, put Ry Cooder on the CD player, ripped the scab from a Coopers Pale Ale, sat in the shade on the deck and watched the sinking sun reach over the ranges and caress the molten sea. Fuck it was hot.

One beer down, I was talking to myself out loud. 'Nothing ventured,' I said, far from convincingly.

Two beers down, I was staring into the rickety wardrobe beside my rented bed, looking for the right kind of statement. The pre-faded Hawaiian, I decided, with the dark hibiscus motif. Khaki shorts and loafers. Laid-back but snazzy.

I finished the third bottle under the shower, out-and-out Dutch courage, then dressed and drove to Gusto. It was nine, the sun was gone and a syrupy twilight was taking its place, the sea flat, the air motionless. Inbound traffic on the Great Ocean Road was backed up to the town limits, cops at a row of witches hats running random breath tests. I was safe, headed the other way, but I popped a mint anyway and summoned my sobriety. Chill, I ordered. Be cool.

If I was serious about this, I'd have done some spadework. I'd have called Sandra, made exploratory noises, got the low-down. Instead, I was playing an outside break sucking a peppermint, for Christ's sake. All dicked up in my new-bought leisure-wear, hot to trot with a mother of two who probably wasn't even in the market.

By the time I took the turn at the adobe signpost, I was moving beyond second thoughts, entering cut-and-run terri-tory. But there was nowhere to run. The sharply ascending strip of asphalt was squeezed by tea-trees and there was a car behind me, pushing me forward. At the first opening, three hundred metres up the slope, I was extruded into the restau-rant carpark.

I fed the Magna into the first available slot and sat there, engine idling, aircon blasting, fingers drumming on the steering wheel, sucking my mint.

The carpark was a quadrangle of crushed gravel toppings, fifty or so spaces, filling fast. The car that had followed me up the road, a big old banger of a Merc, decanted a party of four. Thirtysomething couples, the men in high spirits, the women in high heels. Passing a dark grey Landcruiser with roof-racks and Ripcurl stickers, they bantered and crunched their way down steps flanked with enormous terracotta pots sprouting an exuberant arch of raspberry bougainvillea.

Another carload arrived, then another, then another. This was getting ridiculous. Time to screw my courage to the designated place. But which one?

It wasn't rocket science. I had two choices. I could return to the house and get comfortably numb on self-pity, Coopers Pale Ale and *B. B. King's Greatest Hits*.

Or I could slip into the restaurant, ease my way into the evening's *joie de vivre*, suss my prospects with Barbara Prentice and play it as it came.

Go wild, I told myself, live dangerously. You're on holidays after all.

I turned off the motor, checked my charm in the rear-view mirror and stepped out into the sticky night air. The twilight was thickening, thrumming with laughter and music, the sound of salsa. Gusto's facade was an eclectic amalgam of peeling weatherboards, fibro sheeting and rust-hued corrugated iron. The effect was of a beachcomber's shack slapped together by a castaway with an artist's eye. Gilligan meets Georgia O'Keeffe. Or Barbara Prentice.

A strip-door curtain of rope and crimped bottle caps marked the entrance. I parted the strips and found myself in a narrow, badly lit corridor. The sound and light and laughter lay ahead, drawing me forward. All part of the design, I realised. The customer as privileged insider, a mate of the owner. The cook's cousin, granted back-door access.

A gaggle of diners milled at the edge of the light, pressing their credentials on the head waiter. One wall of the corridor became a plate-glass window, a view into the kitchen. Another design flourish. No miserly dribbles of truffle oil here, no pernickety plating of filleted fava beans. This was

Gusto's fiery forge, a seething engine-room of white-clad minions, flaming sauté pans and flashing knives. I watched a cook emerge from a back door, a heavy bucket in each hand, and pour a stream of glistening black mussels into a huge pot on the cooktop.

Past the waiting customers, the lucky guests were roaring at each other across long tables covered with butcher's paper, carafes of wine and Duralex tumblers. Some of the tables were outside, running around the edge of a broad patio. Party lights hung in droopy loops, illuminating the scene.

At one end of the terrace a four-piece combo was doing a playful *mucho maracas* Carmen Miranda routine. Snack jockeys were circulating, aproned tweenies with nibbles on trays. Couples sat on the low adobe wall that surrounded the terrace, soaking up the view. All two-seventy degrees of it. A wedge of moon glowing through a thin gauze of clouds crept across the sky. The sea extended forever, eerily phosphorescent. And immediately below, the snaking lights of the cars on the Great Ocean Road.

Hooley-dooley, I thought. Whacko the did. All the senses, all at once. Count me in.

I scanned the moving bodies, peering into the muted, multicoloured light, searching for a slender woman with a talent for the casual chic, a mannish haircut and an elusively attractive way of carrying herself. The knot of supplicant customers dissolved, approved *en masse* by the head waiter. As I shuffled forward to plead for admission, Barbara emerged from a clump of conversation on the far side of the room.

She was wearing a sheathy jade-green thing with shoestring straps. One of them slipped off her shoulder and

114

as she turned her head to fix it, our eyes met. Hers were still grey.

'Ay-ay-ay-ay-ay I like you verrry much!' warbled Carmen on the veranda.

Barbara gave a little self-satisfied smile. I knew you'd come, it said. Let the games begin.

I gave her a smile back, the hapless here-I-am one. I poked at my chest, then at the head waiter, shrugging. She nodded and began to make her way across the crowded room. Some enchanted evening, I murmured.

The kitchen door flapped on its hinges and a big man came sailing out into the restaurant. He wore a loose cotton shirt, cuffs rolled to the forearm, and an air of proprietary bonhomie. It was Signor Gusto himself, Jake Martyn. He paused for a moment, cast an appraising eye over the proceedings, then advanced into the throng, arm raised in hearty salutation.

A burst of flame drew my eye to the window into the kitchen. A flambé of prawns in Pernod, perhaps. Beyond the cooktops and the steaming molluscs, a man in a khaki work shirt and matching stubbies had also turned towards the sudden flash. He was glancing back over his shoulder from the semi-darkness of a doorway to the delivery bay. Stocky. Bushy beard. Ravaged baseball cap, the bill pulled down. A working man. Delivery driver, rubbish removal, hump and grunt.

Head tilted sideways, eyes peering out, his expression exactly mirrored an image which I had seen many times before. A still photograph printed from a few seconds of video footage, then enlarged. A three-quarter profile of a handcuffed prisoner being bustled into a remand hearing, tossing a sideways glance in the direction of the television camera. A picture at which I had stared long and hard, simmering with impotent rage.

A picture of Rodney Syce.

And then he was gone.

My stomach dropped away beneath me like an elevator in freefall.

I stood rooted to the spot, mind spinning, staring into the empty space where the man had been. Was it really possible that I had just looked through a plate-glass window at Lyndal's killer?

Only one thing was certain. I could not ignore what I had seen. Try, and the doubt would drive me nuts, poison the promise of the evening. And beyond.

I had to get another look at the man. Satisfy myself, one way or the other.

Dashing back along the corridor, I squeezed past a phalanx of incoming guests and burst through the rope-and-bottle-cap curtain. An irregular hedge of tea-tree separated Gusto's public entrance from its service area. I shouldered my way through the thicket and glimpsed a curved driveway leading from a loading bay at the back of the restaurant to the road above the guest carpark.

A runabout tray-truck was parked half-way up the driveway, a well-used Hilux utility. Its driver's-side door was open and the figure in khaki was hoisting himself aboard. He glanced back, not noticing me as I parted the shrubbery.

I was thinking very fast. His general description fitted Syce. Height, shape, approximate age. The beard didn't appear in the picture, but that proved nothing. Stood to reason that he'd attempt to disguise himself. More to the point, there was a nagging similarity between my snapshot and what I could see of the man's face. The oval shape, the full lips, the sloping cheekbones.

But still I couldn't be sure. The light was murky and he was a good ten metres away.

The door of the Hilux slammed shut and it started up. I began to run towards it, but its wheels were spinning, tyres spitting gravel, tail-lights glowing.

I pulled up short. But only for a heartbeat. And then I was running again, sprinting back to the Magna, slamming the key into the ignition, backing out of the parking slot. Acting, not thinking, except to think that I couldn't let him vanish into the night. That there was no way in the world the cops were going to believe me a fourth time.

The Hilux had turned right, heading uphill. Fifty metres past the restaurant driveway, the road became graded gravel. It climbed through low scrub for a couple of minutes, crossed the hump of the hill and emerged into a residential area, cars at the kerbsides, lights in the houses, party time.

But the utility was nowhere in sight. I arrived at a T-junction. Two lanes of asphalt, double yellow lines, cats-eye reflectors on white roadside markers. Deans Marsh Road, the back-door route across the ranges. Cars whizzed past, barrelling downhill, revellers heading into town. Which way had he gone? Downhill or up? Towards the activity or away from it?

Go back to the restaurant, I told myself. Make enquiries. Find out if anybody knew him. By the look of it, he'd been making a delivery of some kind. So even if nobody knew him, they'd at least be able to tell me who sent him. What could be gained by chasing him?

A better look at him, for a start. The chance to cross him off the list, mark him down as a false alarm. And without going through the rigmarole of interrogating the Gusto staff, parading my obsession. Without the risk of making a fool of myself in front of Barbara Prentice.

Uphill, I decided, away from town. I swung the wheel and floored the pedal, spraying gravel as my front tyres gripped the bitumen. The road climbed steadily, joined at irregular intervals by smaller side roads and tracks. Had he taken one of those? I stuck with the main road, a theory taking shape in my mind, consistent with what I knew about Rodney Syce. As scenarios went, it made as much sense as anything the coppers had told me.

On the lam, solo, Syce had gone to ground, grown some fungus. Stayed in Victoria, where he had no criminal connections, less chance of being fingered. Picked up jobs on the margins, cash-in-hand stuff, melded into the here-today-gone-tomorrow casual workforce. Maybe even built a new identity.

The road twisted and turned, climbing continuously, its course hemmed by thickening bush. The traffic was all downhill, oncoming headlights at the frequent corners. It was almost nine-thirty, night coming down. If I didn't spot the Hilux in the next few minutes, I told myself, I'd pack it in, turn around, contact the cops. Persuade them to make enquiries at Gusto. Let the appropriate authorities deal with it, like I'd been told.

I checked my watch, stepped on the gas. Two minutes, that's how much longer I'd give it. *Dangerous Turn*, read a yellow advisory sign.

Then it was there, right in front of me as I rounded a bend, nothing between us. I dropped back, not showing my hand, waiting for an opportunity to overtake, study the driver as I passed. I tried to read the number plate, but it wasn't lit.

It was double lines all the way, not a chance to swing around him. We continued uphill, north-west into the ranges. At some point, twenty or thirty kilometres further along, the road would pop out of the hills and run through farmland to the Princes Highway. If he went that far, he could be headed anywhere in Australia. Literally. The Princes Highway circled the entire fucking continent.

The road straightened and I moved closer, preparing to pass. But the Hilux slowed, indicated left and turned down a side road. I continued past for a hundred metres, then doubled back. The road was a single lane of asphalt, gravel-edged, tree-lined, a trench cut into the forest, well signposted. Mount Sabine Road. Never heard of it, or its mount. The ute's tail-lights bobbed in the distance, beckoning.

This is crazy, said the voice of reason. But since when has reason been reason for anything? I dipped my lights to low beam and kept going, deeper into the night.

Rodney Syce was an experienced bushman. And what were

the Otways if not the bush? Dense, virtually impenetrable bush, all just a few hours from Melbourne. A tall timber bolt-hole, exactly the sort of place where a wanted man could lie doggo, grow a beard, pass unremarked among the locals. Scruffy transients, back-to-nature hermits, hippy farmers, breast-feeding ferals, bush mechanics, timber cutters, sleep-rough surfers, mind-your-own-business truckies, law-leery bikers. The full panoply of tree-dwelling, kit-home, cud-chewing yokeldom. The only thing missing was a banjo-plunking soundtrack.

I twiddled the dial of the radio, caught wavering snatches of pop music and the hiss of static, the signals baffled by the timbered folds of the hills. The road rose and fell with the signal, snaking around tight-coiled corners. The trees got bigger, closer together, the understorey more dense. My headlights swept the fronds of giant ferns, bare rock walls, mossy clefts.

Occasional chinks opened in the curtain of bush. The brutal gash of a firebreak. Obscure clearings stacked with saw-logs. Unmarked forestry tracks. Machinery sheds, hunched in the middle of nowhere. All the while, up ahead, the pickup's tail-lights winked and blinked, luring me on.

The road meandered, lost its paved surface, became a rutted blanket of beige dirt, forever changing direction. As it followed the twists and turns, the pickup vanished for minutes on end. Then, just when I thought I'd lost it, I caught the flicker of headlights amid the trees ahead, slatted radiance. Or the abrupt flare of brake lights at some sharp bend.

Where was he going? A farm? That would explain the delivery to the restaurant. Strawberries? There were signs along the Great Ocean Road for pick-your-own berry farms. Kiwi fruit, maybe. Some sort of bush tucker, myrtle berries, gummy bears. Not very Jake Martyn, that sort of stuff.

And why the late-night delivery? An unexpected shortage of canapé garnishes? If this guy was indeed Rodney Syce, he should be hunkered down in the native shrubbery, not gadding about the place, running taste treats into a town crawling with coppers.

The road forked, then forked again, the Hilux nowhere in sight. I guessed, guessed again. Kept left, tightened my grip on the steering wheel, imagined it was Rodney Syce's neck.

The track kept getting narrower. Its surface was potholed and corrugated. It hammered my suspension, peppered my undercarriage with gravel, sent my tail slewing at the turns. A tight bend loomed and suddenly the track disappeared, replaced by a sheer drop into a scrub-choked gully. I stomped on the anchors, the steering juddered and the Magna went into a skid, wheels locked.

I wrestled for control, steering wildly for the inside edge of the road. The Magna slid to a halt, then stalled, side-on to the direction of the road. My fingers were rigid around the wheel, my ears roaring with adrenalin.

I killed the lights, got out and took stock. The car's rear wheels were sunk to the rims in a pothole, its tail dangling over the edge. Another half a metre and I'd have joined the choir eternal. Or worse, been trapped in the wreckage, ruptured and bleeding, lingering in agony for days, waiting for help that never came. Situation like that, a body could remain undiscovered for decades, like some shot-down Mustang pilot in a New Guinea jungle, a bleached skeleton buckled into a rusting machine.

I reached into the glovebox for another cigarette. My second in an hour. I was practically chain-smoking. Then, squatting at the side of the road, I tried to gather my wits. The bush was motionless, monochromatic, an ancient daguerreotype. Pools of black gathered at the feet of massive trees, grey slabs of bark peeling from their trunks. The milky wash of an overcast sky seeped through their dappled foliage. The humidity was oppressive and beads of sweat trickled from my armpits.

What the hell did I think I was doing? Right at the very moment that my life was regaining balance, when romance seemed not likely—okay—but possible, I'd headed for the hills in hot pursuit of a half-seen face. What was more important, settling the scores of the past or making something of the future?

It was nearly ten. Down on the Lorne foreshore, beer and sunburn were brewing a heady mix, testing the tolerance of the coppers. At the Falls, Red was moshing it up with Jodie Prentice. Back at Gusto, the Domaine Chandon was flowing and an intriguing, accomplished woman in a jade-green dress was wondering, I hoped, where that Murray Whelan fellow had disappeared to.

The bush, stilled by my noisy arrival, was coming back to life. Mopoke calls, cicada thrums, possumy ruttings in the canopy. I ground my cigarette under foot, making sure it was completely extinguished. It was time to stop chasing geese around the ranges.

As I rose from my haunches, I heard the clunk of gears being engaged, then the muted wheeze of an engine. I dropped back into a crouch and leaned forward, every fibre straining into the variegated night. Across the gully and slightly below me, a vehicle was labouring through the bush. I squinted in the direction of the noise, attempting to pinpoint its source. I caught the whine of a gearbox, the slow crunch of tyres. But no lights. The driver, it seemed reasonable to assume, didn't want to be noticed.

The sound receded. I got into the Magna, manoeuvred it back onto the track and crawled forward, aircon off, window down, ears cocked, headlights off. Whoever he was, the fact that he didn't want to be followed was reason enough to follow him.

The track hugged the rim of the gully, switched back, then turned again, heading away from the source of the noise. The ground became flatter, the vegetation less dense, stringybarks with an understorey of scrubby vines. I cut the motor, got out, and listened. Nothing.

I walked back along the track, eyes fixed on the ground.

Enough light from the overcast sky made it through the canopy to throw a faint shadow in the wheel ruts. Fifty metres from the car, tyre treads had squashed the edge of the track. The treads ran into the bush. I followed them. The ground was hard-packed and thick with tufts of native grass. The tyre marks petered out.

Maybe they'd been made by the Hilux. Maybe not. What did I know? I was no black tracker. But I'd come this far, so I figured I might as well exhaust the possibilities before turning around and going back to Gusto.

I slipped the Magna into neutral and rolled it off the track. I left the key in the ignition ready for a fast getaway and put my wallet under the seat. I took a torch from the glovebox, pocketed my mobile phone and set off.

Swinging the torch back and forth across the leaf litter, I

advanced into the undergrowth. After a few minutes, the beam found a patch of exposed earth, the clay ploughed by wheel ruts. Somebody had come this way in a wetter season, broken the surface. But the ground had turned back to iron and the trail faded away, lost in a thicket of bracken between towering gums.

The torch beam flickered, then faded completely. I pressed on, picking my way through a stand of flattened bracken. The terrain dropped away to a fern-filled gully, the ground spongy with rotted logs and leaf mulch. I climbed back up the slope and started again, casting about for spoor like an illustration in *Scouting for Boys*. Absurd figure in Bombay bloomers demonstrates correct technique for detection of rogue wildebeest. I might as well have been wearing a blindfold. It was so dark in places that a man would have been hard put to find his local member.

My shirt was sticky with sweat, my knees caked with dirt, the bare skin of my legs and arms livid with nicks and scrapes. Fuck this shit, I thought. Time to pack it in, come at the matter from a different angle.

For some reason, the track wasn't where I left it. I retraced my steps, scanning the forest for previously noted landmarks. A dappled gum with a skirt of shredded bark, a cleft boulder with a sapling sprouting from it, a quartz-strewn slope. But they, too, seemed to have wandered away. I began to suspect that I might not be headed in the right direction.

No immediate cause for alarm, I told myself. The track must be somewhere nearby, it's just a matter of taking a methodical approach, applying your mind to the problem. You are not lost. You have merely paused to orient yourself.

Five minutes later, I conceded that I was utterly bushed.

According to received wisdom, the correct procedure when lost in the bush is to remain where you are. Do not risk exacerbating the situation by wandering around. If you have a pack of cards, deal yourself a hand of patience. Before long someone will lean over your shoulder and point out that the red queen goes on the black king. Failing that, simply wait for your absence to be noted and a search initiated.

On the other hand, I could ring for help. I pulled out my mobile phone, switched it on and looked down at the keypad.

Ring who, I wondered? Roadside assistance. The Hansel and Gretel helpline. The House Ways and Means Committee? I dialled 000 and pushed the send button. 'Out of Range' glowed the LCD. I tried again, my number in Melbourne, testing. Same result. Zip.

I scrabbled uphill, hoping for a better outcome on higher ground. Still no luck. The ground kept dropping away, always some gully yawning before me. The understorey was so thick that I almost needed a machete to get through it. And still no signal. If I kept punching at the phone, it would go the way of the torch, battery flat. Panic began to take hold. I was trapped in a labyrinth, hoist on my own petard, an idiot.

I changed strategy. Rather than heading uphill in search of a signal, I hunted the lower ground, plunging down gullies, hoping to reach a creek bed. If I was not entirely mistaken, always a possibility, I was somewhere on the seaward side of the divide. If I followed a creek downstream, it would lead me in the right direction.

Down, down, I went, momentum building. Then my left foot hooked a root and I fell, crying out as a bolt of pain shot through my ankle. Flat on my arse, I skidded and skittered down a sharp incline, snatching at branches to slow my descent.

I landed hard, ankle throbbing, chest heaving. Keep thrashing through the mulga like this, I decided, and I'd do myself a serious damage. No point in continuing to buggerise around in the dark, risking a fatal accident. Follow the manual, stay put, wait until morning. I pressed my back against a tree fern and tried to get comfortable.

As the thump of my heartbeat slowed and the rasp of my breathing settled, I became acutely aware that night was filled with sound, alive with movement. Faint rustlings in the leaf litter, reptilian slitherings, bandicoot scuttlings, the snick and hum of insects, the omnipresent chorus of cicadas. Soon, my every sinew was tuned to the concert of the forest. I was in the dress circle.

Gradually, I became aware of an intermittent murmur at the far periphery of my hearing. Two distinct components, two alternating tones, snatches. It was coming from further along the debris-choked gully in which I was sitting.

I stood up and began limping towards it, picking my way over rotting logs and lichen-covered boulders. The sound grew clearer. Somebody was talking.

I heard the words quite clearly.

'A pizza.'

There was a contemptuous hoot, then silence.

I kept going, all my senses alert, creeping through the undergrowth. Maybe the owner of the voice was benevolent, a potential rescuer. Or maybe it was Syce.

A hundred metres along, the gully became a dry creek bed, a floor of sand and pebbles between sharply rising banks. High above, the canopy parted a little and a milky wash leaked down from the night sky, creating a chiaroscuro world of deep shadows and luminous space. I felt my way forward, ankle throbbing but not unbearable.

'Bag of ice. Any warmer, you could poach an egg in this beer.'

'I'm not your fucken errand boy, you know?'

The voices had started again, just above me now, at the top of a steep rock wall. Snatches. Two men, it sounded like. Bickering about who was responsible for the poor quality of the catering.

'Anything'd be better than this canned crap you've been feeding me.'

'Yap, yap, yap…nothing but bitch the whole time.'

The exchange was intermittent, lethargic, rehearsed, like the conversation of a long-married couple. But it offered no clue as to the identity of the speakers, apart from the fact that there were two of them and they were men. Neither was a member of the Royal Shakespeare Company. Both spoke a flat, workaday Australian, one with a tinge of second-generation wog.

Hunched, darting, all very commando, I worked my way along the narrow watercourse to where the bank became less steep and overhanging. Looking back, I caught a flicker of movement, elongated shadows reaching up into the branches, thrown by the white glow of a camping lantern.

I caught the glint of water, a necklace of shallow pools, hovering mosquitoes, the ribbit of a frog. A low wall of sand-filled plastic bags had been laid across the creek bed. Water was banked up behind it, its surface flecked with dead leaves, busy with bugs. A heavy-duty hose emerged from the pond and disappeared into the darkness. I raised a cupped palm of the tepid, musty-tasting water to my lips, then skirted the pool and continued, my ear tuned to the murmur of voices at the top of the bank.

A few metres past the dam, the creek bed widened into a flat wash of gritty sand and loose pebbles, maybe ten metres wide. Tyre tracks led downstream and a vehicle had been driven up onto a flat area on the bank. It was the Hilux. I put my hand on the hood to be sure, felt the lingering heat of the engine.

The bank was low, easy to scale, but the ground was

uneven and densely thicketed. I tiptoed up the bank, my left ankle still not pulling its weight, trying to get some sense of the set-up without betraying my presence. The dam and the creek bed roadway pointed to an established campsite. Illegal, in that the state forest was off-limits to campers, but playing fast and loose with forestry by-laws was hardly a federal case, not in itself. Point was, whose camp was it?

Wired, every nerve at battle stations, I circled around, looking for the best approach to the light. At least now I had a potential exit route, the creek bed. If the driver of the Hilux turned out to be Rodney Syce, or if things just got too hairy for me, I could follow the tyre ruts to the nearest police station.

In the meantime, I was edging through a clump of saw-toothed shrubs, the ground between them cut with shallow trenches. I plucked a leaf, crushed it between my fingers and sniffed. Cannabis. A small crop of it, irregularly spaced, twenty or thirty plants, head-high.

Okay. So we had a dope-growing operation of some sort. That accounted for the dam, the hose, the concealed location. And weren't petty crims sometimes employed to baby-sit dope plantations? The Syce scenario was firming.

And my nostrils were twitching, picking up a pungent smell. Not the dope but something fishy, its source closer to the light. I edged forward, the hiss of the gas lantern now audible. A square-edged structure loomed in faint silhouette.

I waited, letting my eyes adjust to the complexities of the near-total darkness, until the outline became an aluminium shed, garage-sized, its metal surface camouflaged with rough dabs of paint. The pong was coming from inside. A dark-on-dark rectangle suggested an open door. From the other side of the shed's thin walls came the voice I had come to think of as The Grumbler. It was grumbling.

'Jesus, what a way to spend New Year's Eve, hanging around this god-forsaken dump with a half-wit possum fucker. What's keeping him, for Chrissake? You said he'd be here in half an hour, it's been twice that.'

'Sooner he turns up the better,' said the other voice. 'Ten days of listening to your fucken belly-aching, I'm fed up.'

Easing the torch from my pocket, I stepped to the opening in the shed. The flashlight summoned its reserves, glowed wanly for a few seconds, then expired once again. Before it did, I glimpsed an earthen floor, a pump, a generator, gas bottles, a bench with a four-ring burner and grimy sink, a cooking pot. By the look of it, and the smell, the cultivation of marijuana was not the only illicit activity taking place here. If I wasn't mistaken, this was some sort of abalone-processing set-up. It seemed reasonable to assume that it was not a government-licensed, industry-standard, health-inspected facility. The fishy smell was vile, overwhelming.

A weathered aluminium dinghy on a boat-trailer was parked beside the shed, brick wheel chocks. Above it, a tarpaulin was slung between the shed and the branches of a tree. Even from a helicopter, the place would be almost impossible to spot. Peering between the shed and the boat, I saw a clearing lit by the spill from a Primus lantern, a gas bottle with a glowing white mantle above it. The lantern sat on a folding table in a tent walled with insect-screen, the side flaps rolled up. Tiny moths swarmed over the screen.

A man was sitting at the table, his back to me. Shorts, work shirt, the outline of a beard. My suspect. I could see that he was playing solitaire, hear the faint slap of the cards.

A man well equipped for the bush. But I couldn't see his face.

'Christ,' he said. 'How many fucken times I gotta tell ya? You want a slash, go into the bush. Stop fucken stinking up the place.'

The other bloke was standing a few metres away, at the far edge of the circle of light. He, too, had his back to me. He was stocky, roughly the same shape as the card player. He was naked except for a pair of mustard-coloured jockettes and rubber flip-flops. His hairy shoulders drooped above the sagging flesh of his torso. He was pissing loudly against the trunk of the tree.

'Yeah, like it doesn't stink already, those abs you been cooking up.' He shook himself and turned. Sweat glistened on his high, domed forehead and stubble crawled down his face, thickening into a goatee.

I saw but I didn't believe. It was Tony Melina, proprietor of La Luna restaurant, steaks and seafood a speciality. Tony Melina, runaway spouse.

Dumbfounded, I squeezed my eyes shut, shook my head and looked again. Yup, it was Tony all right. But what was he doing here? It didn't make sense. According to his wife, Tony Melina was disporting himself with some floozie in the flesh-pots of Asia. That, at least, was plausible. This was utterly baffling, as incomprehensible as Section 27(a) of the Health Insurance Act. More mystifying even than a Liberal's ethical framework. Tony Melina? Here? With Rodney Syce? I sniffed my fingertips. That dope, maybe it was some hybrid superstrain. Perhaps I was hallucinating.

Tony stepped forward into the light. He looked like a washed-up gorilla, the missing link between man and doormat. He raised his foot and shook it.

'You want a hygienic camp?' he said. 'Try showing a little trust.'

A chain rattled. It was connected to his ankle, running across the ground to the screened tent. The card player gave a derisory snort and shuffled the cards.

'And have you take off again? Not on your nellie.'

'Why would I take off now?' Tony whined. 'Soon as he arrives, we do the business, I'm out of here.'

'Just doing my job, pal. You'll get unlocked when he gets here, not before. You know the drill.'

Tony grunted, then shuffled into the tent, dragging the chain after him. 'Far as I'm concerned, it won't be a minute too soon,' he said, plonking himself down and curling his fist around a can.

Things were getting weirder by the second.

Tony was obviously a prisoner, yet his demeanour suggested that to some degree he accepted the situation. Did Rita have a hand in this? Was some sort of rough justice being dispensed here? It was one thing to dob her philandering husband in to the authorities, quite another to chain him up in the Otway Forest wearing only last week's underpants. Who was the card player? Was he Rodney Syce or not? And what was that fucking terrible smell?

Every fibre of my being was telling me to get the hell out of there, follow the creek bed downhill, find a road, summon the cavalry. Let the coppers sort it out.

But I couldn't leave yet, not without getting a clearer view of the card player's face, enough to satisfy me on the Syce front. Heart pounding, I inched into the gap between the boat-trailer and the shed. The inky shadow of the tarpaulin canopy ran right to the edge of the clearing, as close as I could creep without giving myself away. But to get a well-lit view of the man's face, I needed a bit of altitude and a better angle. Slowly, heartbeat by heartbeat, I put my right foot, the good one, on the mudguard of the boat-trailer. Easing down on the springs, I hoisted myself upright. Left leg jutting sideways for balance, I leaned over the boat, craning for a clearer view.

That's when I saw the mutt. It was lying on an old sack beside the screened tent, licking its balls. A short-haired mongrel of a thing, a stump with legs, some sort of kelpie-pitbull cross.

The trailer's springs squeaked beneath me. The sound couldn't have been softer. The dog pricked up its ears and raised its muzzle, did a radar sweep. I froze. The bloke at the table turned over a card, oblivious. The dog stood up. I stared at it, not daring to breathe, my mouth dry, my ears filled with the *boomf, boomf, boomf*ing of my heart.

The dog's ears quivered. It took a step forward, sniffed the air, tensed. Somewhere in its canine recesses, input was being assessed, conclusions drawn, sinews mobilised. It swung its snout in my direction and emitted a low, carnivorous growl.

'Wassat, boy? That feral again?'

The card player swivelled in his seat, following the direction of the dog's stare. But I didn't notice his face. I wasn't looking that way. My eyes were glued to the dog. It was hurtling towards me, a fanged missile, barking savagely.

My fight-or-flight instinct took the floor. Flight had the numbers. Run, Murray, run. Now. Fast.

But I wouldn't get far, not with a dodgy ankle and set of canine canines embedded in my fleshy extremities. Nor, prudence dictated, would simply revealing my presence be a good idea. 'Evening gents, Murray Whelan here, Member for Melbourne Upper.' For a start, I still wasn't absolutely sure if the solitaire-shuffler was Rodney Syce. I was pretty sure, however, that he was engaged in some sort of criminal activity and he was unlikely to be well disposed to a stranger blundering into his operation. A lost and vulnerable stranger.

And as for Tony Melina, although he wasn't hostile, not as far as I knew, he was in the unreliable category until proven otherwise. Besides which, he was chained to a frigging tree.

Instinctively, even as these thoughts were racing through my mind, I stepped into the dinghy and dropped to a crouch.

My hands swept the floor, searching for something with which to defend myself, should the situation so require. Furious barking rent the air. Creatures scarpered in the canopy. But the dog came no closer. It snapped to a halt at the end of a rope tether, capering and baying, filling the night with its clamour.

'Shuddup, you,' snapped the card player. 'Quiet.'

The dog reluctantly obeyed, firing off a final volley of yaps. But it continued to bristle, snout pointed my way, trembling eagerly. I sank lower on my haunches, eyes level with the edge of the boat, hand closing around a light metal object. The shaft of an oar, I guessed. A serviceable implement, if paddle came to whack.

The card player emerged from the screen shelter and stood beside the dog, staring out of his pool of light directly into the darkness in which I was immersed. The lantern behind him formed a nimbus around his head and threw his features into shadow. He was holding a shotgun.

That did it for me. I no longer needed a full-face close-up. Forget the Cecil Beaton portrait, the whole murky ball of wax spoke for itself. If the man with the gun wasn't Rodney Syce, I'd go down on the Premier in front of the entire parliamentary press gallery.

He stared long and hard, head tilted to one side, listening. My heart was pounding louder than the Burundi National Drum Ensemble. My mouth was so dry that the skin was making crackling noises. I had ceased entirely to breathe.

From somewhere behind me came the faint drone of an approaching motor.

Syce relaxed, reached down and ruffled the nape of the dog's neck. 'Good boy,' he said. Then, over his shoulder to

Tony, who was hobbling from the annexe, dragging his chain behind him. 'Here he comes now.'

The dog yapped, its muzzle still pointed directly at me. 'Settle,' Syce ordered. The mutt gave a disappointed growl, padded back to its bed and lay down.

Syce moved out of my frame of vision for a couple of seconds, then reappeared minus the shotgun. He busied himself with undoing the shackle at Tony Melina's ankle. 'Behave yourself and you'll be out of here tonight,' he said.

'Yeah, yeah,' said Tony impatiently. 'I know the score.'

I allowed myself to inhale. I needed to get out of there, fast and quiet. I let go of the oar, took hold of the rim of the dinghy and tensed, ready to vault to the ground beside the ab-processing shed. But the advancing vehicle was already labouring up the slope from the creek bed, headlights angled high into the treetops. Up the bank it came, *vroom, vroom*, a blaze of light preceding it. Light that began to sweep across the tarpaulin above my head.

I dropped flat, cheek pressed to the dinghy's aluminium hull. Fetid bilgewater rose in my nostrils. The vehicle came around the boat, very close, and pulled up. The engine cut out, but the lights stayed on, spilling their glow to the very edge of my hiding place. A door creaked open, then snicked shut. Footsteps crunched.

'Tony,' hailed a man's voice. 'Mate.'

'Nice to see you, Jake,' replied Tony, his tone heavy with sarcasm. 'Good of you to pay us a visit. Busy night at Gusto, I imagine.'

Jake Martyn. It couldn't be anyone else.

This did not compute. Nothing computed. My mental mainframe could not do the arithmetic.

'Busy enough,' came the reply. Relaxed. Hail-fellow. 'So what's the problem? Something in the paperwork you didn't understand?'

I managed to roll onto my back. Shadows flickered across the tarpaulin suspended above the boat. An unobserved exit was now out of the question. The voices were no more than ten paces away.

A million questions swarmed through my mind, not many of them finding answers. Jake Martyn and Tony Melina belonged in the same frame, that much I could grasp. Two men in the restaurant business. Men in the process of conducting a business deal of some sort. A dirty money deal, poached abalone in the picture. Some degree of duress involved, hence Tony's captivity. This had nothing to do with Rita. And the whole tall-timbers hideout set-up made sense in terms of Rodney Syce, wanted fugitive and experienced bushman. But what was the connection between Jake Martyn and Rodney Syce?

'What's the problem?' echoed Tony Melina, his tone incredulous, angry. 'I've been chained to a fucken tree, you ask me what's the problem?'

'Chained to a tree?' Martyn mirrored Tony's incredulity, but with a larding of mock outrage. 'I had no idea. Is this true, Mick?'

Mick clearly meant Syce. An alias was only to be expected. Tony, evidently, didn't know the true identity of his jailer. Or he was in on the act.

'Not to mention the bloody awful stink,' Tony went on. 'It seeps into your pores.'

Martyn laughed. 'That's the sweet smell of money, mate. Mick's little abalone kitchen might not be Health

Department approved, but we'd both be poorer without it.'

'You said I'd only be stuck here for a couple of days,' whined Tony. 'It's been ten, for Chrissake. What the fuck am I going to tell the missus, the staff.'

'It's been far too long, mate, I agree,' soothed Martyn. 'And you've been very patient. I appreciate it, I really do. And so would Phil, I'm sure, if he knew how uncomfortable you've been. But delays are inevitable at this time of the year, any kind of international transaction. Banks closed for the holidays, different time-zones, it's been frustrating for all of us. But I sent up the papers the minute they arrived, just like I promised. All you had to do was sign them, have Mick bring them back. If you'd done that, you'd be on your way right now. Instead, you send him to fetch me, busiest night of the year, insist on seeing me in person before you sign. And here I am. So, can we get on with it?'

I tensed my stomach muscles and raised my torso until I could just see over the bows of the boat. Jake Martyn—it was definitely him—had a briefcase in one hand. His other hand was on Tony Melina's hairy shoulder, leading him towards the screened tent with its table and hissing Primus lantern.

That wasn't the only thing I saw. Rodney Syce was walking directly towards me. I dropped back and felt the bows of the boat dip as he lowered his backside onto the trailer hitch. He grunted as he dropped into place and the springs of the trailer squeaked beneath his weight. My bowels turned to liquid. I clenched my buttocks, scarcely daring to breathe.

'I don't fucken believe this,' Tony Melina was saying. 'You act like it's perfectly normal to do business like this. Grab me, get me pissed. Keep me that way for days on end, pouring grog down my throat every time I wake up. Drag me up here, wherever the fuck this is, tie me to a tree like a dog, then expect me to sign on the dotted line, go home like nothing unusual's happened. This is the deal from hell, Jakey boy. I might as well kiss my money goodbye, right?'

Syce made a low, irritated noise, then stood up, restless. His footsteps moved away, into the bush.

'Not at all, Tony,' Martyn soothed. 'It's going to be exactly like we agreed in the beginning. We'll be partners in the restaurant, you and me. Fifty-fifty. Straight down the middle. I'll run things, you'll be the silent partner. Very silent. As long as you keep your mouth shut, things will be sweet. You'll get your fair whack of the profits. Believe me.'

'Sure,' said Tony bitterly. 'If there's any profits to share. Which there won't be, of course. Why don't you admit this whole thing's been a scam from the word go.'

'Listen, mate. Things got off to a bit of a rocky start, I'll admit. But there'll be plenty for everybody. You keep your side of the deal, I'll keep mine. It's a matter of trust. And, frankly, you've been the weak link in that department, you've got to admit. You were eager enough to come into the business when I first proposed it, you'll recall. Keen to play with the big boys. It was even you who first suggested we go the offshore loan route, remember?'

I could hear twigs snapping and the clump of Syce's footfalls as he stalked the perimeter of the camp. The hull was hard against my back, my mobile phone jammed against my kidneys. I hoped to Christ it was still out of range. The last thing I needed right then was an unexpected call, some cold-canvasser ringing to discuss my insurance needs at ten past eleven on New Year's Eve. Shifting position, I propped on my elbow, casting about with my free hand, taking blind inventory. Two lightweight metal oars, a tangle of fishing line, a life-jacket. Nothing remotely useful.

'And if you hadn't tried to back out at the last minute, upset the applecart, it wouldn't have been necessary to remind you of your obligations,' Martyn was saying. 'So stop being such a cry-baby, Tony. Sign the fucking papers, join the firm. Then Mick can see you out of here and I can get back to my guests.'

I hazarded a peep. Tony and Jake Martyn were facing each other across the table in the screened tent, the briefcase open between them. Martyn was reaching in, removing a sheaf of documents. The dog was reclining on its sacking bed, back to doing what dogs do because they can.

As far as I was concerned, Tony Melina and Jake Martyn could do the same. And the sooner the better. My interest was Rodney Syce. And if I'd understood what I'd just heard, as soon as Martyn and Melina finished transacting their business, Syce was going to escort Tony elsewhere. If I was patient and kept my head down, all three of them would soon be gone. This offered a much more satisfactory prospect than attempting to sneak past Syce, who was still lurking out there somewhere in the mulga.

I sank back down, immersing myself in the pool of darkness on the floor of the dinghy. My shirt and shorts were soaked with bilgewater and sweat, and a plague of mosquitoes was gorging on my skin. I didn't dare swat them but I managed to get the life-jacket under my head, ease the crick in my neck. Ears cocked for Syce, I could hear nothing but the drone of the predatory mozzies and the back-and-forth of Jake Martyn and Tony Melina as they talked about their deal.

As far as I could make out, a company owned by Tony, incorporated in the Cook Islands, was buying a half share in Gusto. This was somehow concealed as a loan to a company registered in Panama, a Chesworth Investments. The entire exercise was doubtless a means of concealing the transaction from the scrutiny of corporate regulators and the tax man. Was the Senate estimates committee aware of this, I wondered?

'Sign here, here and here,' said Martyn. 'X marks the spot. This authorises the transfer of funds from your account with the Farmers Bank of Thailand to Phil Ferrier's account with the National Bank of Cartagena.'

I cupped a hand around one ear, fingers splayed, fending off an insistent anopheles, straining to hear what they were saying. Who was this Phil Ferrier that Martyn kept mentioning? A faint bell rang in the west wing of my mind. It rang, but nobody came.

'Take no notice of the repayment schedule,' Martyn was explaining. 'As per our understanding, the debt is purely nominal. On receipt of your $750,000, Phil's company transfers its ownership of a fifty per cent share of the restaurant to you. As you see, he's already signed the relevant documents. Trust, Tony. Like I said, this is all about trust.'

'Yeah, yeah,' said Tony. 'No need to labour the point. Just show me where to make my mark.'

'Here and here.'

'And that's it?'

'Signed, sealed and delivered. Here are your copies. And here's your passport, your credit cards and the other ID that Phil needed to set up the relevant accounts. Congratulations, mate. You now own a half share in Gusto and the land on which it stands. And you're getting a bargain, if you don't mind me saying so. And all that dough you made selling my abalone is now nicely laundered.'

'Yeah,' said Tony drily. 'It's a real steal.'

'Don't be like that,' said Martyn. 'You'll be well looked after, I promise you. Now, if you don't mind, perhaps I can get back to our restaurant, schmooze our guests. I'd invite you to join me, toast our partnership, but you're not really dressed for the occasion, are you?'

I heard the snap of a briefcase closing, then the zip of the door flap on the screen tent.

'You there, Mick?' called Martyn. 'A quick word before I go.'

'Here.'

The response startled me with its proximity. It came from right beside the dinghy. Without my noticing, Syce had stepped into the gap between the boat and the shed. The slightest move and he would have heard me.

Martyn's footsteps approached and two men conferred in hurried whispers.

'You still up for this?' said Martyn.

'Leave it to me.'

'The places for him to sign are marked in pencil. Make sure he signs them all.'

'I'm not fucken stupid, you know,' hissed Syce. 'You sure his wife still hasn't reported him missing?'

'She's telling anyone who'll listen that he's fucked off overseas. It's perfect.'

'What about the plane ticket and the fifty grand?'

'I'll be back with them mid-afternoon. I can pick up the signed documents, shave back your hairline, trim your beard into a dapper little goatee, dab on a bit of grey.'

'You sure this'll work?'

'I guarantee it. You'll be a dead spit for his passport photo. Seven tomorrow night you'll be on a plane to Bali, just another tourist, fifty grand in your pocket. They won't look twice at you, I promise. And Tony Melina will have left the country.'

'Okay, leave it to me. See you back here tomorrow arvo.'

'Just one more thing. Make sure you don't get any blood on the documents, okay?'

Blood? What the hell did that mean?

The rest was clear enough. Aided by Jake Martyn, Rodney Syce was planning to leave the country the next day, using Tony Melina's passport.

It was a risky proposition, but not without a fair chance of success. Tony was ten years older but the two men shared certain general characteristics. Both had egg-shaped heads, for a start. Thick necks. Facial hair. Beyond that, the differences could be fudged with judicious tinkering. Australian passports do not specify the height or eye colour of the bearer. And a Bali-bound tourist was unlikely to get the fine-tooth-comb treatment from the overworked guy behind the outbound desk at the airport, not at the height of the holiday-season crush.

Spotting Syce was a lucky break. Spotting him in the process of leaving the country was even luckier. But my luck wouldn't be worth a pinch of shit unless I could raise the alarm. I shrank down into the hull of the dinghy, silently urging them to hurry up and go.

'Mick'll see you out of here,' Martyn was saying, his voice receding towards his vehicle. 'Pleasure doing business, Tony.'

The vehicle started up, backed away, beeping as it reversed. I risked a quick look and glimpsed a dark 4x4, a Range Rover or Landcruiser, tail-lights flaring as it angled down the slope to the creek bed. One down, two to go.

Syce was standing at the screen tent, watching Tony Melina pulling clothes from a plastic garbage bag, replacing them with documents scooped from the table. 'Let's get out of here,' said Tony. 'Sooner the better.'

Amen to that, I thought. Tony tugged a tee-shirt over his head and emerged from the tent, garbage bag in hand, clambering into a pair of pants.

'One more thing.' Syce brandished a document. A4, longwise fold. 'Jake needs a couple more signatures.'

'On what?' said Tony, irritably. 'Jesus, what a fucken shambles.' He snatched the papers from Syce's hand and turned them to the light. 'Why didn't he say so while he was here?'

The dog got up, yawned and trotted to Syce's side. Syce bent and scratched its ears, his eyes never leaving Tony Melina.

Tony moved closer to the light, lips moving as he read, brow furrowing as he flipped the pages. 'This authorises the transfer of my half of the business to some offshore company I've never heard of.'

'So?' said Syce.

'So it was never part of the deal,' he said. 'I've just forked over three quarters of a mill for a half share in Martyn's restaurant with fuck-all prospect of a return on my investment. Sign this, I'm out of the picture entirely.' He ran a cupped hand over his glistening scalp, then tugged at this goatee. His eyes darted nervously towards Syce. 'Must be some sort of mistake,' he said. 'Tell you what. Get me to a phone, I'll give him a call, clear it up.'

Syce took a step forward. 'He was pretty clear just then,' he said. 'Told me to make sure you signed before we left. Very specific, he was.' He took another step.

The tip of Tony's tongue flitted across his lips. Then he bolted for the trees. He hadn't gone three steps before Syce slammed into him, knocked him to the ground and snatched the papers from his hand.

The dog started yapping again, but Syce was too busy to notice. He had Tony in a head-lock, hauling him across the clearing. Tony flailed, bare heels scuffling as he tried to writhe free. With a sickening thud, Syce rammed his bare head into the trunk of a tree, the one Tony had been pissing against.

Tony slumped, stunned, the wind knocked out of him. You could almost see the little birdies twittering around his cranium. Syce propped him against the tree, legs splayed, and stuffed a rag into his mouth. Scooping up the chain, he passed it under Tony's arms and ran it around the tree. In a matter of seconds, Tony was trussed like a turkey.

'Go,' screamed every sentient atom in my body. 'Run, now, while Syce is looking the other way. Fuck caution, just run.'

Hands pressed against the sloping sides of the boat, I bore down, knees bending as I came into a coiled crouch.

Knees not bending. Legs not responding.

I'd been lying there for so long, body contorted, hugging the bottom of the dinghy, that my ambulatory extremities had gone to sleep. Dozed off, like the Minister for the Arts at the opening night of *Götterdämmerung*. I pounded my thighs with a balled fist, felt pins and needles. I sent jiggle messages to my toes and instructed my knees to bend, frantic to get going, desperate not to reveal my presence prematurely.

At the far edge of the pool of light, muffled protests were leaking through the gag in Tony's mouth. He writhed and thrashed, eyes rolling in his head. Syce kicked him in the ribs. He made a noise like a chihuahua being dropped down a lift-shaft, then went quiet.

Sensation was returning to my legs. I eased myself into a low crouch, levered myself up and down on the balls of my feet. Up, down. Up, down. Toe aerobics.

Syce planted a booted foot on Tony's knees and dropped the lid from a cooler into his thighs. He twisted his captive's right arm free of the encircling chain and shoved a pen into his hand. 'Do what you're told, stupid cunt.'

Tony tossed the pen away, flung it right across the clearing. It bounced off the side of the aluminium dinghy. Ping. As Syce turned to find it, I dropped back onto the stinking floor of the miserable, shitty little boat.

Light bobbed as Syce picked up the Primus and came towards the dinghy. Tony spluttered and coughed, spitting out his gag. 'I'll double it,' he gasped. 'Whatever he's paying you, I'll double it.'

He should have screamed at the top of his lungs, not wasted his breath trying to negotiate. Syce didn't bother to reply.

Tony started babbling, pleading, saying he wasn't going to sign anything. The light went back towards him and he made a gurgling noise as the gag was shoved back into his mouth.

'You'll sign, nice and proper,' said Syce. 'Even if it takes all night.'

I peeked over the gunwale, preparing again to make my escape. What I saw was a tableau from Hieronymus Bosch. A hallucination straight from hell.

The lantern sat on the ground beside the tree, hissing, pounded by kamikaze moths. Syce had one foot planted on Tony's chained legs, the other braced against the ground. There was a blade in his hand. Short and blunt. An oyster knife. He was sawing at the side of Tony's head with it.

A keening was rising from Tony's throat, a guttural groan of despair and pain. A combination of muffled scream, prayer, wail and whimper.

The dog growled, straining at the end of its leash. Moths battered the light. Shadows jumped in the leaf canopy.

Syce's arm sawed back and forth. Tony moaned.

Then Syce stepped back. The side of Tony's head was red raw, a blood-gushing wound. Syce held the knife in one hand, Tony's severed ear in the other. He held it up, dripping, then tossed it to the dog. Fido rose and its jaws clamped around the tasty titbit before it could hit the ground. A chomp, a snuffle and the gory morsel was gone.

The mutt licked its chops and stared expectantly at Syce.

But Syce was bending again to Tony. 'What next, you reckon? Other ear? Nose? Fingers? What about your dick? How about I cut off your wedding tackle?'

I shuddered and felt myself sink backwards onto the floor of the dinghy. My legs had again turned to jelly. But it wasn't poor circulation that was stopping me from moving. It was fear. Sheer, nameless, gut-wrenching dread. A kind of shame, too, as if my failure to intervene in what I was witnessing somehow made me complicit in it.

For more than a year and a half, I had fantasised about coming to grips with the man who killed my Lyndal. This scum-sucking piece of shit, Rodney Syce. This despicable, gutless loser. And now he was within reach, not more than ten metres away.

And me? What was I doing? I was cowering in the dark, watching him torture a man, feed the poor bastard's ear to his dog, for fuck's sake. If only I could get my hands on the shotgun. But I had no idea what he'd done with it. If only I could be sure that my legs would do what I told them, when I told them. If, if, if.

The dick threat had done the trick. Tony's hand was fluttering, signalling surrender. Syce pulled the plug from his mouth long enough for him to gulp down a lungful of air, then jammed it back. Tony was limp, a rag doll, the fight gone out of him, blood squirting from the side of his head. Syce ripped a strip from the towel, pressed the balled wad against the gash where Tony's ear had been, tied it in place. He tore Tony's tee-shirt from his torso, drenched it with water from plastic jerrycan and wiped Tony clean of blood. I caught the glint of a small gold crucifix in the dark mat of Tony's chest-hair.

Syce acted quickly, a man who knew what he was doing. He tilted the jerrycan, cleaning himself, then dried his hands and arms. Then he replaced the lid of the cooler on Tony's thighs, fitted the pen into his fingers and guided it towards the paper. 'Do it properly,' he commanded, holding Tony's head back. No blood on the documents, as per Martyn's instructions.

Tony's hand moved. Syce turned the page. Tony's hand moved again. Then Syce was stepping away, bending to the light, checking that all was correct. Satisfied, he folded the pages and slid them into his back pocket. Tony was slumped, forehead on the lid of the cooler, motionless, sobbing.

He knew what was coming next. So did I. Transfixed, incapable of action, I watched it happen.

Syce stepped out of the light and vanished behind the tree. Seconds later, he reappeared with a long-handled shovel. A latrine digger. A grave digger. Gripping the handle like a bat, he swung downwards, putting his full power behind the blow. The flat of the blade hit the back of Tony's head with a dull thud. For a brief moment, a metallic reverberation quavered in the air. When it stopped, Tony Melina was no longer sobbing.

Lizards and scorpions crawled up my spine. A python writhed in my stomach. 'Holy fuck shit Jesus Christ,' I thought.

Syce propped the shovel against the tree and began to unchain Tony's limp body. The logic of the situation unfolded before me. Syce did not intend to merely borrow Tony Melina's identity. He was going to steal it. A plan which wouldn't work if Tony's body was found. At the very minimum, a shallow grave would be required. Hope flared. While Syce was burying Tony, I could make myself scarce.

But instead of dragging Tony out of the circle of light, he was dragging something into it. Something heavy. A roll of chain-mesh fencing. He unrolled it and stomped it flat. Hauling Tony by the armpits, he manoeuvred his limp form onto the wire mesh and straightened his limbs. Grunting and pushing with his boots, he rolled up the mesh with Tony bundled inside.

He disappeared again, moving out of my line of sight. I heard an engine start, the Hilux. He was driving away, leaving the body behind. I scrambled to my feet, legs buckling beneath me. This was it. The moment had come.

But he wasn't driving away. He was driving up the slope from the creek bed, coming the way that Jake Martyn had come, headlights catching me as I stood in the dinghy, poised to spring over the side.

I froze as the beam passed over me, a prison spotlight. The light kept going, sweeping into the campsite. I dropped back to the floor of the dinghy. If this kept up, I might as well send for my furniture, have my mail re-directed. The Hon. Murray Whelan, The Old Runabout, Club Torture, Hidden Location, Otway State Forest.

The Hilux continued. Syce hadn't seen me. Fresh hope welled. He wasn't going to bury Tony near the camp. He was going to haul him somewhere in the back of the utility. Again, it was just a matter of keeping my head down and waiting until he'd gone.

I kept it right down, pressed myself to the floor of the boat. No peeking. Too risky.

The Hilux was reversing, beep-beep-beep. Then the door was opening, engine still running. Feet shuffled. Shuffle, shuffle. Syce grunted and wheezed, exerting himself.

There was more foot shuffling, then a flicker of movement at the periphery of my vision, a writhing in mid-air. It was coil of rope, first ascending, then slithering downwards. Then again. Syce was attempting to toss a line over the branch of a tree.

He succeeded on the fifth attempt. Then the Hilux was creeping forward. The rope went taut and the roll of chain mesh rose into sight. When it got to about three metres off the ground, the Hilux stopped. The mesh cylinder swung on the end of the rope, rotating like the needle of a compass.

Syce's intentions eluded me. Did he plan to conceal Tony Melina's body in the branches of a tree, I wondered, cocooned in fencing mesh? Was this a practice he'd encountered in remote backblocks of the country? Had he got the idea from some sort of aboriginal burial rite? It was certainly not a custom usually associated with the interment of second-generation migrants from Melbourne's inner-northern suburbs.

I heard the ratchet of the Hilux's handbrake above the idling of its engine, then footfalls headed for my hiding place. The bow of the dinghy dipped. It began to move. Syce had the boat trailer by the hitch. He was pulling it forward, steering it towards the dangling bundle. I began to get the idea. The mesh was weight. Tony's body wasn't going up into a tree. It was going down into the sea.

I pressed myself as flat as possible against the floor of the shallow dinghy. One glance and Syce would see me. But he was already back in the pickup, reversing. Beep, beep, beep. Down came the awful package. Thump. It landed right on top of me, pinning me to the floor of the boat.

Syce's footsteps crunched. The dinghy went horizontal and rolled forward a little. With a judder and a clunk, Syce hitched it to the tow-bar of the pickup. An arm reached out and jerked the rope holding the mesh. Its coils slithered into the boat. The mesh bore down on me. I writhed beneath it, discovery imminent.

Then, utter darkness. A covering had been flung over the load.

The door of the Hilux slammed shut and the trailer began to move forward, rocking and bumping. I put my palms against the mesh and pushed upwards, gasping for air. The dog started barking, wondering where the rest of its supper was going. Syce yelled for it to shut up. It did. A tepid, viscous liquid was seeping through the mesh. It dribbled onto my face, pooled in my palms and trickled down my wrist.

The boat tilted as if plunging over a waterfall. The load shifted, slipping towards the bow. As I tried to squirm free, something brushed against my cheek, swaying back and forth. It was, I realised, Tony's crucifix, dangling from the gold chain around his neck.

Fat lot of good it had done Tony. But the way things were going, I'd need all the help I could get.

I closed a sticky fist around it and squeezed tight.

Hell is other people, said Jean-Paul Sartre. Take it from me, he didn't have a clue.

Hell is being pinned on your back to the bottom of a cheap aluminium dinghy by a crushingly heavy roll of fencing mesh containing the mutilated corpse of a murdered trattoria proprietor from Ascot Vale, while being hauled cross-country through a trackless forest in the middle of the night by a criminal maniac with a propensity for gratuitous violence who's already slaughtered your pregnant lover, trapped in absolute darkness beneath a black plastic tarpaulin, drenched in sweat and struggling blindly to get out from under a shifting cargo of metal links and oozing body fluids.

As distinct from having to share your breakfast croissant with Simone de Beauvoir, for example.

Twigs and branches scraped the hull of the dinghy as it

bounced along the dry creek bed, plunging down invisible gradients and lurching over hidden obstacles. Desperately, I wriggled free of the pitching, bucking, bitching bale of wire and got my head clear of the suffocating plastic tarpaulin.

For all the bump and grind, our progress was slow. I rapidly assessed the situation. Syce's attention was focused on the way ahead. He was unlikely to notice if I rolled over the side and slipped into the surrounding scrub. With luck, I might even be able to find a phone signal, get a description of the Hilux and boat trailer to the cops, have them nail Syce with the corpse in tow.

I gave my pocket a reassuring pat. The phone was gone. Ducking back under the plastic tarpaulin, I put my shoulder to the mesh cylinder and groped the hull beneath it. As my fingertips found the phone, the load shifted, grinding my digits between steel mesh and aluminium hull. The mobile slithered beyond my grasp. By the time I succeeded in getting a firm grip on the elusive little fucker, the Hilux had found level ground. Shifting up a gear, it accelerated forward.

Hidden by the tarpaulin, I prodded at the touchpad of the phone. No light, no dial tone, no nothing. A shake and a rattle did nothing to improve the situation. The useless piece of plastic was kaput. And my chance of an easy exit had gone west. Or possibly south or even east. The pickup was moving along a proper track now. It was narrow and bumpy but our speed was increasing. A brisk leap overboard was off the agenda.

I was wedged into the gap between the side of the dinghy and the roll of wire mesh, swathed like a papoose in black plastic, the blade of an oar jammed up my kazoo. Branches flashed overhead. My chest rose and fell. The roar of adrenalin filled my ears, overlayed with the hum of the wheels, the squeak of the suspension and an intermittent, almost inaudible groaning.

At first I thought it was me. Gradually, I realised that the groan was emerging from the folds of wire. Sweet Jesus, was it possible that Tony Melina was still alive? I pressed my head against the mesh, all ears. Which was more than could be said for Tony.

Tony was a tosser and a letch, and his garlic bread was mediocre, but those aren't capital offences. So what if he'd fiddled his taxes and done business with crooks? Start killing people for that sort of thing and you'd have to execute the entire Australian corporate community. Apart from the Murdoch family, of course. And the Packers.

The moan became a gurgle. Melina must have been tougher than an overdone veal scaloppine. 'Hang on, mate,' I urged. 'Just hang on. We'll get you out of here.'

We? Me and my regiment of crack commandos.

The headlights of the Hilux lit up, sweeping the bush ahead of us. Syce's silhouette was visible in the rear window of the cabin. We moved onto a road, an even surface. No longer pitching wildly, the dinghy was hurtling through the night, speed increasing. The surface firmed, turned to bitumen. We were racing downhill, the cat's-eye reflectors on the roadside posts winking as we flew past. Down, down.

The roadside verge widened. Gaps opened between the trees, then closed again. For a fleeting moment, the sea glinted in the cleft between two humped-back crests, a distant mirror. The pickup's tail-lights flared. On-off-on. On-off-on. SOS.

A radiance lit the horizon, a spreading sheet of lightning.

A rocket rose, trailing incandescent showers, then burst into a glittering ball of emerald sparks. Even as it faded, a scintillating yellow cascade took its place, followed by an explosion of vermilion.

The midnight fireworks show in Lorne, I realised, squinting into the dial of my watch.

Happy New Year, Murray. My first resolution was to get out of that fucking dinghy toot sweet. My second was never again to act on impulse.

I thought about Red, imagined him in a sea of youthful faces. Goofing it up to a wah-wah Auld Lang Syne, flanked by a supercilious goth and a clinging pixie. Thought, too, about the festivities at Gusto. Jake Martyn presiding. Barbara Prentice in attendance. Me not.

We were flying now, the boat-trailer bucking and fish-tailing. Fingers sunk to knuckle in the steel mesh, I clung for dear life. The tarpaulin flapped and rustled around my ears. If Tony was still breathing, I could no longer hear it.

The Hilux slowed, then jerked to a halt. The load slid forward, carrying me with it. Then we were moving again, turning right, the trailer swinging wide, the load sliding back. I heard the crashing of surf, saw the flash of oncoming headlights, felt the buffeting rush of passing vehicles.

I figured the geography, conjured the map. Sea to our left, hills to our right. We were west of Lorne, heading along the Great Ocean Road. Ahead lay a long stretch of sparsely inhabited coastline.

A car was approaching from the rear. I crawled to the very back of the boat and extended an arm, waving in a way that I hoped would be understood to be a sign of distress. The headlights moved closer and closer, blinding me. I continued to wave, hunched across the stern of the boat. The car veered to the other side of the road and accelerated, beginning to pass. A figure leaned from the passenger window.

'Whackaaaaa,' he yelled, raising a can of beer in salutation. The shitfaced peabrain in charge of the wheel hit the horn, a doppler wail of appreciation at my daredevilry.

The car picked up speed, overtook the Hilux and disappeared. On we drove, our speed unchanged. Hoping that Syce had not twigged to my presence, I ducked back beneath the tarpaulin.

We were moving fast, 90 k at least. Soon there would be fewer and fewer cars on the road. I needed a more compelling attention-grabber than a wave and a grimace.

The dinghy's outboard motor was held in place by a pair of salt-encrusted wing-nuts. Sprawled flat on my stomach, head down, I went to work on one of them. It was corroded tight. If I got it undone, I could drop the motor into the path of an approaching vehicle. That should do the trick. Or send some poor innocent hurtling off the road into the ocean hundreds of metres below us.

The nut refused to budge. I tried the other one. Ditto. I persisted, wincing with the pain of it. Same result. I pounded the inert metal with my mobile phone. Even as a blunt instrument it was useless.

From far behind us, headlights began to approach. But just then we began to slow down. The Hilux swung off the highway, cut its lights and bounced towards the sea. Dry sand spattered against the trailer mudguards.

I slid back into the gap between the hull and the freight and got my hands around the shaft of an oar. I lay there, staring up at the blackness of the covering tarpaulin. Oar clutched to my chest like a quarterstaff, I awaited developments.

We rocked across broken ground, then stopped. The cabin door opened. It snicked shut. The hitch fastenings of the trailer squeaked and clattered. The trailer moved backwards, bumpity-bump.

Now, I told myself. Go for broke. Toss the tarp aside, jump out of the boat, run, head for the highway. If tackled, clobber Syce with the oar, keep running, find somewhere to hide.

As I began to rise, the front of the boat jerked upwards. The top of my head slammed against the stern of the dinghy. The boat slid off the trailer, scraped across a hard, uneven surface and splashed into the water. It bobbed, righting itself, then rocked again as Syce jumped aboard.

I lurched upright, oar at the ready. But the tarpaulin didn't rise with me. Syce was standing on it, yanking the rope toggle to start the outboard. I pushed upwards against the unyielding sheeting, and flung myself recklessly in the direction of the stern. Flailing with the oar, I tried to bat the slippery plastic aside.

The motor fired. The boat rocked in the swell as it chugged forward. I bore upwards, jerking like a frog in a sock and tried to hoppo-bumpo the helmsman into the water.

Syce must have thought I was Tony, rising from the dead. Or some avenging spectre in black plastic.

'The fuck?' he said.

Spooked or not, he had a firm grip on the tiller handle. I bounced off him and sprawled backwards onto the roll of mesh, scrabbling free of the tarpaulin.

Syce was an ominous presence in a wrestler's stance, arms

spread, legs akimbo. I teetered on the mesh roll, the tarp wrapped round my shins, firming my grip on the oar. Lit by the phosphorescence of the sea, we confronted each other down the short length of the bobbing boat.

'The fuck are you?' demanded the dark shape.

That was for me to know and him to find out. Kicking free of the tarp, I lunged forward and took a swing. Syce dipped and the oar whistled over his head. He snatched it and tried to wrench it from my grip.

We see-sawed back and forth, fighting for ownership of the oar, the boat pitching beneath us. We were about fifty metres from the shore, moving parallel to it. Then Syce pushed instead of pulling and I felt myself toppling backwards. It was the Frisbee incident revisited.

'Mamma mia,' I thought. 'Here I go again.' I let go of the oar and dived overboard.

The sea was bracing cold, pitch black. I kicked hard and made as much distance as possible before broaching the surface. When I bobbed up, whooping for air, the boat was already turning. The vibrations of the propeller hummed in my ears as Syce gunned the throttle. The swell rose beneath me and the low outline of the shore reared at the periphery of my vision. I struck for the land, clawing at the water with a frenetic overarm.

The tempo of the outboard increased, closing fast. The sea was dark, the land darker. The boat sliced through the water, bearing straight at me. I filled my lungs and dived. The hull brushed my shoe and I kicked harder, deeper, lungs at full stretch, ears popping.

I broke the surface in the wake of the boat and immediately resumed my wild stroke for the shore. The boat came around, Syce trying for another pass. But before he could reach me, I was taken in the grip of a wave, hoisted aloft and pitched towards the shore.

The swell dropped, then rose again, clutching me to its heaving bosom. Directly ahead, just metres away, white water slopped over a shelf of jagged rocks. The rocks were mottled with seed mussels, thousands of tiny shells, sharp as razors.

For the moment, I was flotsam. Soon I would be jetsam. The difference being a fractured skull, a broken spine, a ruptured spleen and multiple lacerations.

The fatal shore rushed towards me. I hit it chest-first and rocketed forward, careering across slimy straps of wet leather. A bed of uprooted kelp. Limbs flailing, I skittered like a buttered duck. The wave subsided and my fingers closed around a projecting knob of rock. I dragged myself upright. White water streamed around my shins, trying to drag me back. I tottered forward, escaping its pull.

Somehow, miraculously, I was alive and ashore. I bent, hands on knees, shivering and retching. Then, I looked back to sea. Thirty metres away, the dinghy sat low in the water, a grey smudge. A dark shape crouched at the stern, arm on the outboard rudder, watching me.

I turned and headed inland, wading and hobbling across the pitted table of exposed rock. My shoes squelched and my ankle throbbed but I was well on my way to the highway, to a passing car, to the police.

I would have been, at least, if a cliff wasn't blocking my way. A sharp incline of crumbling sandstone, it rose almost vertically from the rock shelf. I groped along its base, sloshing through ankle-deep water, looking for a way up. It crumbled at my touch, showering me with sand and pebbles.

The boat was still there, outboard idling, Syce watching. My landing place was a shallow bite mark in the encompassing cliff, a dead-end street.

I started to scramble up the cliff, clefts and crannies crumbling under my weight. The putt-putt of the outboard came across the water and I glanced over my shoulder. The dinghy was moving, heading back the way it had come. I kept climbing.

The cliff face had all the substance of a coffee-dunked donut. I slipped back, advanced, slipped back again. Gradually, I gained height. Nearer the top, stunted vegetation sprouted from the loose rock. Seizing roots and stems, I worked my way upwards, clinging like Spiderman to the friable rock.

Eventually I reached the top. Greyish waist-high bushes extended for as far as I could see, melding into wind-bent trees at the top of a far incline. A figure was wading through the scrub. He was holding a long thin object.

Syce. He must have put the boat ashore.

Bent almost double, I fled along the clifftop and picked my way through the maze of bushes. But the soft ground gave way beneath my feet. Slithering downwards, riding my backside, grabbing anything within reach to slow my descent, I found myself back at the bottom of the cliff. A cascade of pebbles and sand rained down on my head. Syce was close, moving fast. A wave broke across the rock platform and lapped at my feet. The sea was my only way out.

Desperate for deeper water, I hobbled and limped, winced and pirouetted through the rock-strewn shallows. I stubbed toes, lost my balance, tripped and stumbled. The grunts and curses from above told me Syce was coming fast down the incline. A few more seconds and he would be at the bottom, raising the shotgun, getting a bead on me.

Water flooded my nose and mouth. I sank into deep water, a hidden rockpool. A wave washed over me and I grabbed the jutting rim of the pool, looking back in terror.

Syce had stopped, pulled up short by my sudden disappearance. He cast around, trying to spot me in the churning water. I held tight and ducked as the next wave passed over me. Syce advanced, scanning the roiling shallows. A bigger wave broke, sending water surging to his thighs. He swayed and teetered but held his ground. I gulped down a lungful of air and another wave washed over me.

The rock pool was maybe a metre and a half deep, jacuzzi-sized. I clung to the overhang, willing myself invisible, daring to raise my head only in the brief intervals between waves. Gasp, duck, cower. Gasp, duck, cower.

An eternity came and went. My teeth began to chatter. The tide was going out. If I stayed where I was, I would soon be exposed. Syce, if he was still there, would walk across the rocks and shoot me dead. I risked raising my head a little. Syce was not visible. But that didn't mean he'd gone.

Taking a punt, I edged my way to the seaward extremity of the rock pool. Then, flat on my belly in the surging foam, I slithered out towards the ocean.

A wave broke over the rocks and the ebbing tide sucked me off.

Nostrils at the waterline, I breaststroked along the edge of the deep water, rising and falling with the chop. The water was deep and dark, cool and creepy, but it was infinitely better than being shot.

The land lay to my left, about fifty metres away, so the current was running east in the general direction of Lorne. This was good. Once I'd put a bit of distance between myself and Syce, I could swim ashore. After that, all I had to do was make my way uphill to the Great Ocean Road, follow it to human habitation, sound the alarm and collapse in a convulsing heap.

The land loomed, a sheer wall, the sea foaming at its base. With no immediate opportunity for landfall, I rolled onto my back and sculled, letting the current carry me, conserving my strength for the push to shore. My shorts clung to my thighs, chafing the skin, and my ankle throbbed faintly. The leather of my watchband had shrunk, tightening around my wrist. My mobile phone and flashlight were long gone, dropped in the dinghy during my tussle with Syce. But I still had Tony Melina's cross tucked in my change pocket.

I heard a faint putt-putt, the signature of Syce's outboard. Treading water, I strained to get a fix on its position. Cool currents swirled around my legs. Gradually, the sound grew fainter, then faded away entirely.

The land, too, was fading. With a sudden sense of urgency, I struck for the shore, freestyle now. The continent appeared to be receding. I slogged on, pounding at the water.

Face down, arm over, turn and breathe. Face down, arm over, turn and breathe.

Urgency became panic. Despite my efforts, I was making no progress. I was panting, unable to suck down enough oxygen. My pulse was racing and so was my imagination. I was electric with fear. Freaking out, big time. Gripped by the gut-wrenching terror of a man adrift at night in the bottomless abyss, a puny speck in the immensity of the inky ocean. Shark bait.

Even now, a great white or a blue pointer was rising from the deep, circling for the kill. It would strike without warning, hit me like a freight train, clamp its monstrous jaws around me, shred my flesh with merciless, serrated teeth. Then others would join the attack, a pack of them, whipped to a frenzy by the blood in the water. My blood. Even now, myriad minor abrasions were spreading my scent, sounding the dinner gong.

A shark, or something worse. Some nameless horror from the primordial depths. A creature of suckered tentacles or poisonous spines. Anyone familiar with the leading personalities in the NSW branch of the Labor Party would know exactly how I felt.

Onwards I thrashed, adrenalin, sea water and my own asthmatic gasps roaring in my ears. Whatever they are, I told myself, you can't outswim them. Don't exhaust yourself trying. I slowed down, shifted to sidestroke, focused on the blurred smudge of the land. Specks of light showed along the coast, some of them moving. Houses and cars, all just beyond my reach. I let panic settle into mere hysteria, then struck again for the shore, aiming for a ragged line of white, the slosh of waves on rocks.

Churning through the black water, I collided with a pedestal of nubbled stone. It was slightly below water level, table-sized and flattish. I scrambled onto it. For several minutes, I knelt there, clinging to its uneven surface. My chest was heaving and relief surged through me.

When the gasping subsided, I climbed to my feet and took my bearings. Ankle-deep in the encompassing briny, I must have looked like a try-hard Jesus pausing for a leisurely look-see on my way across the Sea of Galilee.

The shoreline proper was about two hundred metres away. Here and there in the intervening water, dark patches could be faintly discerned, fragments of submerged reef. If the tide continued to fall, it might eventually be possible to get ashore by jumping from rock to rock. I decided to wait and see.

No man is an island, according to the constitution of the Australian Labor Party, but I certainly felt like one. At the very minimum, I was a shag on a rock. A shivering shag in sodden shoes squatting on an almost invisible rock, water swirling around me, waiting for the tide to ebb away.

'Aarrkk,' I cried, just to hear my own voice, reassure myself that I was still alive. 'Aarrkk.'

I raised my watch to my face. Waterproof to 30 m, it said. 1:33 a.m. Four hours since I'd got myself lost in the bush. For most of that time I'd been in imminent danger of being discovered, mutilated, shot, drowned or eaten by killer whales. By comparison, being perched on a semi-submerged rock waiting for the tide to ebb was a moment of quality solitude, an opportunity to reflect on what I'd seen. My chance for an end-of-year stocktake.

I reviewed the contents of my mental in-tray.

Rodney Syce was hiding in the Otway Ranges. He was calling himself Mick, growing marijuana and processing poached abalone for Jake Martyn, celebrity eatery proprietor. The two of them had abducted Tony Melina, a less celebrated but evidently cashed-up restaurateur. Someone called Phillip Ferrier was involved too.

On the promise of a cash pay-off and Martyn's help getting out of the country, Syce had tortured Melina, forced him to sign certain documents, then murdered him. He was currently in the process of dumping Melina's body in the sea.

Had Syce been hiding in the Otways ever since the Remand Centre break-out? Was the restaurant owner involved in the escape? If so, how? And why?

It was a bizarre scenario. Too bizarre.

A new fear suddenly took hold of me.

This was a story that strained credulity to the limit, even mine. How could I expect anyone else to believe it?

My credibility with the Victoria Police was not exactly money in the bank. Surely they would conclude that I was having one of my periodic visions. Maybe even that I'd mislaid my last marble.

How could I convince them that I was telling the truth? What evidence could I produce?

Syce had doubtless rolled Tony Melina overboard by now, so there was no body. I had no idea how to find the camp again. And judging by what I had seen of him, Jake Martyn wasn't likely to fess up the moment the coppers put the question to him.

No evidence, no admission, a lunatic witness.

I rummaged in my pockets as if they might possibly contain some means of proving my story. Or some means of getting off that damned rock. An inflatable life-raft, a signed confession, a map of the Otways with X marking the spot.

I found $125 in notes. Waterproof polymer banknotes, thanks to the cutting-edge washing-machine-proof technology of the Australian Mint. A half-full pack of Tic-Tacs. And Tony Melina's little gold crucifix.

It was circumstantial at best, but it was the only hook on which I could hang my credibility. Rita would be able to identify it. She could also attest that he was missing, whereabouts unknown. And the fact that I possessed an item of Tony's personal jewellery might persuade the police at least to investigate.

Poor Tony. He slept with the fishes tonight. At least he was getting some rest, which was more than could be said for me. I slipped his little Jesus back into my change pocket and gave it a reassuring pat. Then I ate the Tic-Tacs.

An hour passed, making no effort to hurry. My shirt began to dry out, the accumulated heat of the day radiating from the nearby landmass. The air was balmy, the ambient temperature still in the high teens. Little by little, the water level receded. My plinth became a pyramid. Add a deckchair and a daiquiri, I could have sold tickets.

Time crawled. I flexed my knees and windmilled my arms, shag-aerobics to keep myself from cramping up.

An archipelago slowly emerged from the sea, a path of stepping stones leading to the tide-exposed shore. Problem was, it fell far short of my perch. Walking ashore dry-shod was off the agenda. Apart from the fact that my shoes were soaked, the nearest visible outcrop was a good hundred metres away.

At 3:40 a.m., I climbed down from my shag-roost and lowered myself into the water. A hundred metres was nothing, after all. Four lengths of the pool at the City Baths. A mere bagatelle.

Small beer but big trouble. A powerful current was surging through the channel. For every metre I advanced towards the shore, I was swept five sideways, a cork in a stormwater drain. I tried to fight my way back to Whelan Island but soon lost the battle. Again, I was being swept out to sea.

I pounded for the land, relentless, determined. Kick, stroke, breathe. Kick, stroke, breathe. Thirty strokes, fifty, a hundred. My arms turned to lead and still I kept clawing at the water. My thighs were red-raw but still I waggled them. I shucked off my shoes, hoping it would help.

It didn't. I was going nowhere fast. Nowhere I wanted to go, at least. The current was running parallel to the shore, dragging me with it. The land remained in view, contours rising and falling as it rushed past, but I couldn't reach it, try as I might.

You're finished, Murray Whelan, I told myself. This is it.

You are going to die. And for nothing. By the time your body washes ashore, if there's anything left to be washed up, Syce will be long gone.

The sea wanted me bad and I no longer had the strength to resist. Water filled my mouth and visions flooded my mind. Deeds regretted, hopes unfulfilled, a terrible sense of waste. All the usual shit. And worst of all, the gut-wrenching, aching realisation that I would never see my little boy again.

I shuddered, gasped and groaned. Then, marshalling my strength, I made one last effort to reach the land. If I was going down, I'd go down fighting.

I went down.

Jesus, it was dark down there. My lungs were burning. My arms were flailing. My hand struck something slimy and ropy. A slimy rope. I grabbed it and hauled with the last of my strength.

Blood raged in my ears and a glowing ball of white rushed towards me out of the darkness. It grew larger and larger until it filled my entire field of vision. The mystery of life and death was revealing itself to me.

It struck my head with a hollow *bonk*. I broke the surface gulping for air and discovered that the secret of the universe was a basketball-sized polystyrene sphere. I grabbed it and clutched it to my chest.

Christ alone knew how long I hung there, and He wasn't telling. A bamboo cane extended from the centre of the bobbing white ball. A limp scrap of orange plastic hung at its far extremity. I was clinging to the marker buoy for a crayfish trap.

I grabbed the cane mast, wrapped my legs around the buoy and mounted it. It sank beneath my buttocks. Instead of being chin-deep in the water, I was now midriff-deep.

From my marginally improved position, however, I could see the shore. A faint light flickered on the beach, a fire perhaps. A sound came across the water. It was almost human.

'Tonight's the night,' wailed the voice. 'Gonna be all right.'

I didn't believe a word of it. Party noises joined the music, well-oiled revelry.

'Help,' I bleated. Help me if you can. I'm feeling drowned. But help was beyond earshot. My strangulated plea was a reedy vibration.

After Rod Stewart came Dire Straits. As if things weren't bad enough already.

My body heat was being leached away. My skin had turned to gooseflesh and my teeth were castanets striking up the overture to hypothermia. I had, at most, another two hours. By the time the music faded, half an hour later, my respiration rate was so high that I couldn't get enough air in my lungs to raise a decent shout.

I hugged the thin sliver of bamboo, jiggled up and down, braced for imminent shark attack and tried to distract myself with hot thoughts. The blazing sands of the Sahara. A steaming mug of cocoa. Nicole Kidman and Tom Cruise in bed. When that didn't work I pissed my pants, luxuriating in the brief suffusion of warmth.

But the cold was unendurable. I slid off the polystyrene ball and examined the orange nylon rope that moored it to the pot on the floor of the sea. Somewhere far below me, a trapped lobster was facing an identical problem, racking its crustacean brain for a means of escape.

The rope was spliced, tighter than a preference swap in a leadership spill. Impossible to untie. I bit a chunk from the polystyrene, then another. Gnawing with my teeth and tearing with my nails, I worked at the ball.

Water flooded my mouth. My fingers were numb. My jaw jack-hammered. After an eternity, I managed to break the buoy in half. The bamboo mast toppled into the water. The rope sank without trace. I'd done what I could for my incarcerated crustacean companion. He was on his own now.

All that remained of the buoy was two irregular hemispheres of polystyrene and a scattering of little white pellets. I stuffed the two lumps of foam up the front of my shirt and began to breaststroke, high in the water.

This time, I didn't fight the current. I let it carry me along, steering across it at an oblique angle, working my way gradually shoreward, alternating between backstroke and breaststroke. Gradually, the land moved closer. But Christ on a bike, I was fucking freezing.

It was nearly five o'clock. I was hyperventilating, numb and shivering. Rolling onto my back, I twitched and gave up the ghost.

High above me, the firmament faded to a blur. One by one, the stars went out. Through the water came the grind of icebergs. The sands of time turned to crystals of ice. A pale radiance was all that I could see. Faces looked down at me. Curious, not unkind.

It came to me that I was passing between rows of columns like those of a temple. And that the faces staring down at me were those of ancient Greeks.

My shoulder struck something hard. Thought flickered in my sluggish brain. The current had carried me all the way to

Lorne. I was passing beneath the pier. The faces belonged to old Greek men, jigging for squid. Was there some law, I wondered, some clause in the Fisheries Act which required that at least one male of Hellenic origin with a squid rig be permanently present on every pier or jetty in Australian territorial waters?

I rolled over and the swell surged beneath me. It hefted me forward as the current pivoted like a hinge around the point at the end of the bay. Beyond it, rimming the curve of Loutitt Bay, the town glowed. The shore was just a few metres away. I clawed at the water and felt the grainy drag of the bottom against my toes. Another surge of the swell and I was flopping through the shallows, Robinson Crusoe crawling up the beach.

You're alive, I told myself. Hallelujah. Praise be to Whatsisname. That little guy in your pocket. The one on the thingamabob.

My brain was frozen. My thoughts moved at the speed of glaciers. Fingers trembling, I fished the cross from my pocket. It was important, that much I remembered. But why?

A gaggle of youths materialised, staring down at a barefoot man with bloodshot eyes, his clothes sodden, two foam hemispheres bulging in his shirt like skewiff falsies. Unable to speak, I held up the cross.

'You're too late, mate,' slurred one of the juveniles, a pimply half-wit with his hat on backwards, his shirt tied around his waist and a can of rum and lolly water in his hand. 'We've already sold our souls to Satan.'

He snatched the cross from my hand and flung it into the sea.

Misery on a stick, I discarded my primitive flotation device and lumbered along the beach. Blue with cold, teeth hammering out the Rach 9. Heat, I needed heat.

A downy light suffused the scene with the pearl grey of pre-dawn. Empty cans and crumpled food wrappers littered the trampled sand, the detritus of a massive communal booze-up. A faint whiff of cordite hung in the air, a reminder of the fireworks five hours earlier. Figures shifted obscurely at the periphery of my vision, hunkered down in the boulders and vegetation at the edge of the beach.

'Not here,' whispered a female voice. 'I'll get sand in it.'

Lights were still blazing at the surf lifesaving club. I lurched towards it, shorts clinging, bow-legged as a crotch-kicked cowpoke. Two and a half hours deep-sea marination had done wonders for my twisted ankle. My hobble was now merely a limp. My jaw, however, was snapping so violently that I feared for my tongue. Goosebumps covered my flesh like a relief map of the Hindu Kush. Get to the lifesaving club, I urged myself, to people who know the art of defrosting. That's why it's called the lifesaving club.

I reached a door, yanked it open, found a concrete-floored corridor. I wobbled inside, tottered, careened off a wall, felt a door handle, smelled disinfectant. A light switch found my hand. The changing rooms. Metal lockers, slatted benches, a row of showers.

The water ran tepid. Tepid was encouraging. I cranked up the volume and stood beneath the stream, clothes and all. Miracle of miracles, it grew warmer and warmer, until it was so hot that I was reaching for the cold tap.

I don't know how long I stood there, turning from pale blue to pale pink, stripping off my clothes to find a penis so puckered and brine-bleached that it looked like an albino axolotl. I slumped to the floor and let hot water cascade over me, sobbing and retching and pissing down the plughole. Me, not the hot water.

Just as my inner permafrost was beginning to melt, a man appeared in the doorway. He was about seventy years old. Leather face, leather arms, leather legs, immaculate white tee-shirt, shorts, socks and trainers. He blazed with irritation and rapped at the sign on the door with his knuckles.

'Can't you read, bloody idiot?' barked the surfside ancient. 'This is the Ladies. Gawn, out you get.'

His steely gaze brooked no contradiction. I climbed back into my sodden clothes and beat a retreat, finger-combing my hair as I went.

The foreshore was deserted, its swathe of couch-grass mashed and litter-strewn. At its centre sat the skeleton of a cuboid whale, the scaffolding of the deserted concert stage. I thought again about Red, wondered what kind of a night he'd had up at the Falls.

Lorne was a hangover waiting to happen. Streetlights shone down on empty asphalt, their sodium glow bleeding into the grey wash of the imminent day. A girl in a bikini-top and denim mini tottered down the middle of Mountjoy Parade in absurdly-high platform sandals, her mascara smeared, a bottle of Malibu in one hand. Drunken shouts reverberated in the far distance, punctuated by the honking of plastic party horns. The mating call of the shitfaced dickhead. In the foreshore carpark, the flashing light of a stationary ambulance showed the limbs of crashed-out party animals protruding from car windows and the tail-gates of station wagons.

The police temporary command centre was gone, along with the reinforcements bussed from Melbourne for the revels. The only sign of the law enforcement community was a scattering of horse-shit and a few piles of orange plastic crowd barrier in the gutter.

It was almost six o'clock. Magpies were carolling and kookaburras cackling. Where the sky met the sea, the nicotine-stained fingers of dawn were already at work, levering open the first day of the new year. Even in my half-thawed state, I could tell that it was going to be a hot one, a real stinker.

The police station was up the hill behind the pub, a weatherboard building in a residential street, a small cellblock out the back. I took a deep breath, wiped my nose on my shoulder and pushed open the front door.

The counter was unattended. A ragged chorus of 'Born in

the USA' was coming from the direction of the lock-up. I pushed the buzzer. After a couple of minutes, the racket out the back subsided and a beefy young rozzer appeared. He had damp patches at the armpits and the demeanour of a man at the fag-end of a long shift. The tag on his shirt pocket identified him as Constable Leeuwyn. He gave me the once-over, unimpressed, and suppressed a yawn.

'Can I help you?' His tone implied that he hoped not.

'I'd like to speak to the senior officer on duty,' I said.

'I'm the watchhouse keeper, if that's senior enough for you. Or you can wait for the sergeant. He'll be here at seven.'

'Is there a CIB attached to this station?'

'Nearest CIB's Torquay,' he said. Torquay was nearly an hour's drive away. 'What's it concerning?'

'A murder,' I said. 'And the whereabouts of Rodney Syce. The Remand Centre escapee. He's got a bush camp somewhere up there.' I jerked my thumb over my shoulder at the hills behind the town. 'There's a fair chance of collaring him if you're quick enough.'

The cop narrowed his eyes, letting me know that he'd spent a long night listening to bullshit and his tolerance was pretty well exhausted. 'Is that right, sir?'

'I can assure you this is not a joke. I'm not crazy. I'm a member of parliament.'

Constable Leeuwyn's expression suggested he did not consider these categories to be mutually exclusive.

'And I'm not drunk, either,' I went on. 'If I look like crap, it's because I've spent half the night in the sea in fear for my life. I am not playing funny buggers here, officer. I'm here because I've just witnessed a number of very serious crimes involving a wanted fugitive.'

My high-horse tone did the trick. The copper, alert now, laid a clip-board on the counter between us. 'Do you have any identification, sir?'

'Not on me,' I said. 'But I'm sure you can check. My name is Murray Whelan. I'm the member for Melbourne Upper in the Legislative Council.'

The constable took down my name, address and DOB, then disappeared through a door into a muster room with computers on the desks. I paced the worn linoleum of the vestibule in bare feet, keeping the blood flowing to my still-chilled extremities. The walls were hung with framed certificates of appreciation and commemorative photographs of civic events. In one picture, a representative of the Rotary Club was shown presenting the results of a fund-raising fun-run to an officer of the Country Fire Authority. Jake Martyn was holding one end of the cheque.

After ten minutes, the constable reappeared. Word had evidently come down the line that I was to be treated with kid gloves. 'Sorry to keep you waiting, Mr Whelan,' he said. 'The sergeant will be here shortly to take charge of matters. In the meantime, you'd better tell me all about it.' He raised the flap on the counter, inviting me to step through. 'Can I get you a cup of something?'

'Tea with milk and sugar,' I said, my gratitude unfeigned. 'Please.'

We went through to the muster-room where I dictated my statement between sips of hot tea. Three cups, it took, and twenty minutes. Leeuwyn two-finger typed my account of the night's doings straight into a computer, interrupted only by periodic visits to the cells to quell outbreaks of communal singing. I stuck to the bare bones and he tapped at the keys without comment or question, even when I mentioned Jake Martyn, whose name was almost certainly known to him.

When I got to the part where Syce fed Tony Melina's ear to the dog, the young copper looked up from the keyboard and opened his mouth as if about to warn me that telling outrageous fibs to the wallopers is a chargeable offence. I held his gaze until he turned back to the computer.

He printed out the finished statement and, as I was signing it, the sergeant arrived.

He was a solid man in his iron-grey fifties, with a military moustache and the bearing to match. His cheeks and chin were still raw from the razor and, judging by the bags under his eyes, the shave had come on the heels of a minimum of sleep. The buttons of his powder-blue shirt were taut over a midriff like a sack of concrete.

He introduced himself as Sergeant Terry Pendergast, took the statement from my hand and led me into his office, his demeanour correct and businesslike.

The sergeant's office was a cubby hole off the muster room. There was a large map of the district on the wall and a stand of fishing rods in the corner. He wedged himself behind an almost-bare desk and invited me to sit on the other side of it. He put on a pair of reading glasses and studied my statement. He took his time. Occasionally his gaze shifted from the page to my face, then back again. He stroked his moustache once or twice. There was coming and going in the outer office. I may have tapped my feet and chewed on a knuckle or two.

'Hmmm,' said the sergeant at last. 'Quite a story.' He laid

down the statement, folded his reading glasses and slipped them into his shirt pocket. He pushed his seat back and crossed his hands on his stomach. The ball, I understood, was in my court.

'If you've spoken to Melbourne,' I said, 'you'll be aware that I have a history in regard to Syce. You might even have been told that I've got a tendency to imagine I've seen him.'

Pendergast gave a slight nod, confiming that he'd been backgrounded. 'And do you?'

'Syce killed the woman I loved,' I said, 'and our unborn child. So, yes, I'll admit to a degree of obsession. But this isn't like those other times. I realise it all sounds pretty far fetched, Jake Martyn's involvement and so on. And I don't have anything to substantiate my claims. But I'd have to be certifiably mad to make up something as unlikely as this.'

Pendergast gave me the copper's eyeball, as though considering the possibility. The salt encrusted on my printed hibiscus didn't help. Then, abruptly, he swivelled in his seat and directed his freshly shaven chin at the map on the wall. 'So where do you reckon this bush camp is, Mr Whelan?'

The map was large-scale, the contours of the hills so dense they showed as crumples in the paper. Filaments of blue ran between the wrinkles, dozens of creeks and rivers. I got up, put my finger on Lorne, ran it up to Mount Sabine Road and traced the route along the ridge of the ranges to an unnamed road that led back down to the coast.

'Somewhere here,' I said, placing my palm on an area of perhaps a hundred square kilometres. 'It's hard to be more precise. You'll need to get in a helicopter.'

'Let's start by trying to find your car,' said Pendergast.

A Constable Heinze was summoned. He didn't look more

than twenty, a sinewy lad with a flat-top and a lazy drawl.

'Any sign of this Syce,' the sergeant instructed, 'let me know immediately. Do not approach.'

'Understood,' said Heinze. 'No worries. This way, sir.'

He rustled me up a pair of thongs, fed me into a police 4x4, dropped a pair of mirror shades over his eyes and hauled me back up into the hills. It was a tad more civilised than the trip down.

The sun was climbing, turning the sea to tinfoil and flooding the town with a harsh light. Work crews were clearing the foreshore of rubbish and stay-over party beasts were emerging from parked cars, blinking and wincing.

I tried to make myself comfortable, damp knickers wedged up my bum crack, eyes puffy with salt and glare. I wished I had a pair of sunglasses and some lounging pyjamas. I wished I were waking up in Barbara Prentice's bed, but the last time I thought about her was a lifetime ago.

'Busy night for you blokes,' I said, making conversation.

'Not as bad as usual,' said the young constable. 'So they tell me. Only twelve arrests.'

'How about the Falls?' I said. 'How'd that go?'

'No problems, if that's what you mean,' he said. 'Hunters and Collectors stole the show, I heard.'

'Were they charged?' I said.

'Very amusing, sir,' said Heinze. 'Where to from here?'

At first, I had no great difficulty in retracing the route I'd taken the previous evening. Landmarks and side-roads appeared in the right places. The twists and turns of the track resonated in my memory. But as we advanced deeper into the bush, my self-assurance began to wane. The whole aspect of the terrain was transformed by the daylight, even if that daylight was strained through a rainforest canopy. The tracks and trails, no longer revealed by headlights, twisted and forked in ways I didn't anticipate. The sheer vastness of the bush threatened to overwhelm me.

I hunched forward in my seat, staring through the windscreen, scanning the sides of the track, directing Heinze down dead-end tracks that were little more than faint ruts in the hillsides. We backed up and tried again. And again.

'It's around here somewhere,' I kept repeating. 'It has to be.'

But the damned thing had vanished, swallowed up by the landscape like some dingo-snaffled Adventist infant.

After an hour of buggerising around, Heinze got a call on the radio, a string of letters and numbers, unintelligible code.

'A4, copy that, 7–11,' he replied, or words to that effect.

We'd been summoned back to Lorne. Developments had occurred.

'What developments?'

'Sarge'll fill you in,' said young Heinze.

Hitting the nearest sealed road, we dropped down to the sea. I scanned the outline of the hills, concluding that this was probably the road I'd ridden in the boat with Tony Melina. Syce had turned south-west at the Great Ocean Road. We turned north-east. The tide was coming back in. Tony's body was out there somewhere, catering to the bottom feeders.

Sergeant Pendergast was waiting outside the cop shop, lips compressed, thumbs hooked in his belt. There'd been developments all right. 'Your car's been located,' he announced. 'It's parked near the Cumberland River caravan park, twenty kilometres back along the Great Ocean Road. It's been there for several hours, apparently.'

My shrivelled dick shrivelled further. I stared at the copper, struggling to understand. I was back to square one.

'Somebody must have moved it…' I said.

The sergeant raised his hands, cutting me short. 'This obviously raises a number of questions, Mr Whelan. But I'm sure we'll soon get some answers. A member of the Syce Task Force is on his way from Melbourne to take charge.'

Was he bringing a straitjacket, I wondered? A ticket to the funny farm? Or just the Victim Liaison shrink, ready with some on-the-spot counselling for the bitter and twisted Murray Whelan, headbanging fantasist.

I nodded bleakly. 'The car?'

'For the moment, we'd prefer to leave it where it is,' said the sergeant. 'If you don't mind.'

As if I had any choice. I felt hollow inside. I must have looked it. Pendergast took pity on me.

'This time of year,' he said, 'Christmas and whatnot, it can be very emotionally difficult for some people.' The sergeant twitched his moustache in the direction of the cop shop. 'You can wait inside. We'll get you something to eat if you like.'

At the mention of food, I felt a sudden ravenous hunger.

'Okay,' I said. 'I'll have an orange juice, two fried eggs, bacon, mushrooms, grilled tomato, wholegrain toast, a selection of jams and a black coffee with sugar. And a cigarette, thanks.'

'Best we can do is a cup of instant and a slice of cold pizza I'm afraid, Mr Whelan. This isn't the parliamentary dining room.'

Delving into my cling-shrunk shorts, I confirmed that my

cash was still there. 'Maybe I'll just pop down the street,' I said.

The sergeant dispensed an indifferent shrug. 'Better make it quick,' he said. 'The officer from Melbourne will be here soon.'

'I'll try not to keep him waiting.' I hoisted my shorts, turned and hobbled away in my borrowed flip-flops.

It was getting towards nine and the early risers were up and about. The pock of ball on catgut came from the tennis courts on the foreshore. A man with a bowling-ball beergut was hosing the footpath outside the pub. Couples pushed toddlers in strollers. Kerbside parking places were filling fast. The air of normal life seemed discordant, bizarre.

As I trudged back down the hill towards Mountjoy Parade, I contemplated my situation, seething with frustration. The business with the car had trashed my fragile credibility with the coppers. This dick from Melbourne had been dispatched to hose me down. At best, I might be able to persuade him to contact Immigration and have Tony Melina's name put on a passport watch list. An immediate full-scale manhunt for Syce was clearly out of the question.

There were other law-enforcement buttons I could push, of course. Corporate Affairs. The tax department. But that was a long-term approach. In the meantime, Syce would slip through the net again.

I found breakfast being served at tables on the terracotta-tiled terrace outside the Cumberland Resort. Some of the other customers looked a little the worse for wear, although none of them came near my level of unkempt. The waitress asked for cash upfront when she took my order.

As I peeled off the notes, I recalled that I'd left my wallet under the seat of the Magna. Where it had probably been found by whoever moved the car. An image came to me of Rodney Syce in Bali, spending up big on my Visa card. But there was more than plastic in my billfold. As well as a creased ultrasound Polaroid, it also held my driver's licence and the rent receipt for the holiday house.

So, chances were, the person who moved my car also knew my name, my face and where I could be found. Was I being watched, even now? By Jake Martyn, perhaps? The mystery ingredient.

My eggs arrived. I wolfed them, warily scanning the dog-walkers and newspaper-buyers as they strolled past. Cars cruised the strip, the sunlight from the ocean searing their windows.

Lucky the boys weren't at the house, I thought. I'd have to get out of Lorne, of course. A draft agenda began to take shape. Deal with the cops, try to persuade them at least to organise a helicopter sweep of the camp area and have the airport watched. Get my car back. Pick up the boys as arranged at midday. Should I phone Faye and Leo, I wondered, who were due to arrive later in the day?

A man appeared on the other side of my toast. Wiry and fiftyish, he wore shorts and a threadbare tee-shirt. A towel hung over his shoulder as if he'd just come from an early-morning swim. Without asking, he pulled out a chair and sat down.

'Murray Whelan?' He squinted at me with a kind of cock-eyed leer.

Straggly greyish hair hung to the nape of his neck. His face was tanned and weather-lined. It was a face I had seen before, I realised, nearly gagging on my multigrain. Just once and very briefly. But I remembered. It had been a memorable occasion. The owner of the face had been tossing the finger over his shoulder from the helm of an escaping shark-cat.

There were maybe thirty or forty people in the immediate vicinity, sipping coffee, browsing newspapers, nursing hangovers.

'There's witnesses,' I said, loud enough to turn heads. 'Try anything, these people are witnesses.'

The abalone poacher looked at me like he'd been warned that I was somewhat eccentric. He chuckled, letting the onlookers know that he was in on the joke. At the same time, he made a small placatory gesture with his hands, stroking the air between us.

'My associates are hoping for a word.' He spoke softly, reasoning with me.

'I'll bet they are,' I said. 'But if you think I'm going anywhere without a fight, pal, you'd better think again.'

He furrowed his brow, disappointed and perplexed at the vehemence of my response.

'Before you make a scene,' he said, 'I suggest you take a look at this.'

He took something from his pocket and placed it on the table between us.

It was a business card.

The logo of the Department of Natural Resources was embossed at the top. Printed beneath it: Bob Sutherland—Director, Fisheries Compliance.

'Bob said to remind you, if need be, that you met him a couple of months ago in San Remo. He'd like a few minutes of your time, if possible. He's a couple of minutes' walk away.'

I picked up the card and studied it. It looked real enough.

'So you've got Sutherland's card,' I said. 'Doesn't prove he sent you.'

The man shrugged, stood up and handed me a mobile phone. 'Ask him yourself.'

He strolled away and stood on the footpath, a hand shading his eyes as he stared across the road towards the sea.

Two phone numbers were printed on the card, office and mobile. I punched in the office number. Sutherland's voice said he wasn't at his desk, that I could leave a voice-mail message or call him on his mobile. The number was the one on the card. I dialled it.

It was answered immediately. 'Sutherland.'

'Murray Whelan,' I said.

'Thanks for calling, Mr Whelan. Excuse the cloak and dagger. Appreciate a few minutes, face-to-face.'

'What's this about?' I said.

'Nutshell, hope you can clarify some matters.'

Typical skewiff priorities, I thought. Sceptical about my tale of a wanted fugitive, murder and mayhem, the cops report the shellfish-rustling aspect to the fish dogs.

'The police have been in touch, have they?'

'Not as such,' said Sutherland after a brief pause. 'Far as we know, they're not aware of our presence in the area.'

'I'm not sure I understand.'

'Coastal communities, all kinds of connections, family and whatnot. Word gets around pretty quick, fish dogs in the neighbourhood.'

That wasn't what I didn't understand. 'So how did you know where to find me?' I said.

The lank-haired man was watching me keenly, not pretending otherwise.

'Strayed onto our radar,' said Sutherland. 'And like I said, we think you might have information of interest.'

Damn fucking right I did. This was manna from heaven. If the cops didn't believe me, perhaps the fish dogs would. I'd thrown up on his boat and been seen with Dudley Wilson, but at least Sutherland didn't think I was a fruitcake.

'I'm just up the road,' continued Sutherland. 'My man will show you where.'

'With the department, is he?' I said.

'Not as such,' said Sutherland. 'Technically.'

'Seems familiar,' I said.

Again, a pause. Then, 'Employed by the Abalone Industry Association, the licensed divers. Liaises with us, enforcement-wise. See you soon.'

He hung up. The man in the falling-apart tee-shirt tilted his head sideways, a question. I nodded. He began to walk away.

I downed the last of my coffee and followed, weaving through the foot traffic. Twenty paces up the street, outside Tourist Information, I fell into step and gave him back his phone. 'You work for the licensed ab divers?'

He nodded, not stopping.

'Liaison with the fish dogs?'

He nodded again.

'Doing a little liaising down Cape Patterson way a few months ago, were you?'

He looked at me sideways.

'You must be mistaking me for someone else.'

I heaved a heartfelt sigh of exhaustion. 'I've been a member of the Labor Party for more than twenty-five years,' I said, 'so I've been bullshitted by grand masters. And I've had a long night. I'm not in the mood to be treated like a moron.'

We were passing a surfwear shop with racks of swimsuits on the footpath. New Year Special, announced a sign on a bin of footwear just inside the front door.

'Give my regards to Bob Sutherland,' I said. 'Tell him maybe some other time.' I turned into the shop, rummaged in the bin and selected a pair of rubber-soled strap-overs. I paid a not very special price and tossed my perished police-issue thongs into the wastepaper basket under the counter.

My escort was waiting on the footpath. 'Was it that obvious?'

'Fooled me,' I said. 'At the time.'

'What about Dudley Wilson?'

'He was the target, was he?' I said.

'He's the influential one. Ear of the Premier and all that. We thought it'd be a good way to dramatise the poaching problem.'

'It was dramatic, all right.'

'The guy overboard? Yeah, that was a real bonus. We only planned on a chase sequence and a bit of show and tell. But Wilson ended up believing he'd compromised a real operation.'

'How did you know he'd insist on gate-crashing the expedition?'

'Calculated gamble. And if he hadn't risen to the bait, it would've been no problem to cancel. We were only fifteen minutes ahead of you. Bob would've got on the blower, pulled the plug. Nothing ventured, nothing gained.'

'I can see Sutherland's motives,' I said. 'Fending off staff cuts. How about your lot? What was in it for the Abalone Industry Association?'

'The same thing,' he said. 'Our members pay up to a million dollars for a licence, then find themselves competing with poachers. Complain that the resource is under pressure, we run the risk the government will respond by lowering the quota rather than beefing up the enforcement.'

I was impressed. Behind his sturdy bosun exterior, Bob Sutherland was a crafty bugger.

'So what's all this about a hush-hush operation?' I said. 'Not another pantomime, I hope.'

The pretend poacher shook his head. He'd said too much already. 'Talk to Bob.'

He moved ahead and I followed in silence, dodging pedestrians. At the corner of Erskine Falls Road, the shuttle bus arrived from the concert. A horde of tired-but-happy campers tumbled out, chattering in a range of foreign languages, several of which might have been English.

We turned up the hill, tramping along the nature strip past a shop window where a woman in a sailor's hat was arranging a display of distressed sheet-metal pelicans. After that, it was mostly houses. There were few other pedestrians and most of the road traffic was flowing the other way, down from the festival. It was a little after nine-fifteen, still almost three hours before I was due to pick up Red and Tarquin. A police divisional van came down the street. The driver was Constable Heinze from the wild goose chase for the Magna. I raised my forearm in a gesture of recognition as he cruised past.

Just before the water supply reservoir, we entered a side road and went through a gate into a compound of utilitarian, shed-type buildings surrounded by tall trees. My guide indicated a door marked 'Forestry Survey', then turned and walked away.

My skin was sticky with sweat and I was puffing from the hike up the hill. I was just a tiny bit short of sleep, standing alone on an apron of sun-baked concrete, not sure why I was there.

I'd jumped at the chance to talk to Sutherland, who represented another way of getting at Syce. But now I was beginning to think I had been a bit rash. What if this was a set-up?

'Appreciate your assistance, sir.'

Bob Sutherland stepped from the doorway, hand extended. He was dressed for a round of golf. Pastel yellow polo shirt, beige slacks and a wide-brimmed white hat, shark logo on the band.

He gave me the once-over, but said nothing.

'I hope this isn't another of your theatrical productions,' I said. 'No use lobbying me, you know.'

Sutherland grinned. 'Told you, did he?'

'Sang like Pavarotti,' I said. 'Couldn't shut him up.'

Sutherland guided me to the open door. 'Low on resources, high on resourcefulness, that's us,' he said. 'And I'm not wasting your time today, sir.'

The door opened into a room with frosted windows and a row of tables running down the middle. Grey steel map cases lined two of the walls. An all-in-one television–video sat on a desk, together with some kind of radio communications equipment. Looked like the fish dogs had borrowed the place from their tree-counting colleagues. A boyish bloke was sitting on the desk, legs dangling, murmuring into a mobile phone. About thirty, he wore hiking boots with khaki socks, shorts and shirt.

Sutherland took off his Greg Norman hat and wiped his brow with the back of his wrist. 'This is Geoff Crowden,' he said. 'Runs things for us in this part of the world.'

Crowden snapped the phone shut and clipped it to his belt. He pumped my hand, a real eager beaver. Cheerful as Chuckie the Woodchuck. 'You look like you could do with a cold drink.'

Not to mention a shave, a comb, a change of clothes and twelve hours' shut-eye.

He reached into a bar fridge and tossed me a tetra pack of apple juice. I half-expected him to break out the trail mix and rub two sticks together.

'So what's this all about?' I said, lowering myself into a chair at the table.

Sutherland was propped on the edge of one of the map cases, hat in hand.

Crowden climbed back onto the desk and picked up a clipboard. He leaned forward, bare elbows on his bony knees. When he spoke, his tone was formal, interrogatory. 'You drive a dark green Mitsubishi Magna sedan?' He checked the clipboard and recited the registration number.

'That's correct.'

'Your vehicle was observed in a remote location in the state forest last night.'

I felt a surge of elation. 'By who?'

'Officers of this department.' He turned the clipboard towards me, displaying a list of rego numbers, makes, models and times. 'We have the area under surveillance.'

'Excellent,' I said. 'That's great news.'

Crowden and Sutherland exchanged perplexed glances.

'We'd like to know why you were there,' said Crowden. 'And if you encountered any other vehicles or individuals.'

I wanted to leap to my feet and cheer.

'Before I answer,' I said, 'can you tell me the target of your surveillance?'

Crowden looked at Sutherland.

Sutherland looked at his hat.

'These enquiries relate to an ongoing investigation into a

poaching and distribution ring,' said Crowden. 'You'll appreciate we can't say more than that.'

'This ring,' I said. 'Does it include Tony Melina and Jake Martyn?'

Sutherland's hat was suddenly less interesting. His head came up sharply. 'You know these individuals? You saw them last night?'

I made the stop sign. 'Another question before we go any further. The man with the beard, drives the Hilux utility. Is he still at his camp?'

Crowden looked to Sutherland, got the nod. 'That's our understanding,' he said.

'You know who he is?'

'First name Mick,' said Sutherland. 'Surname currently unknown. Plates on the utility were stolen. Wrecker's yard in Colac. This matter—you know something we don't?'

'I know that I'm very grateful for your diligence,' I said. 'And I'll tell you why.'

I laid it out for them, pre-dinner drinks at Gusto to breakfast on Mountjoy Parade. The whole blood-drenched kit and caboodle.

This time, there was no question of diminished credibility. The fish dogs listened without interruption, galvanised. When I'd finished, Crowden gave a low whistle.

'Incredible,' he said.

'That's what the police think, unfortunately.'

Sutherland picked up the clipboard. 'This should sort them out. Log of all traffic in that part of the state forest between 6 p.m. and 3 a.m.,' he said. 'The Hilux was also observed at the Gusto restaurant.'

'And you had no idea that you were watching Syce?'

Sutherland shook his head. 'Came to our attention a year or so back, courtesy of our friend from the divers' organisation. Seen to be a regular buyer of abalone and crayfish from small-time poachers along the west coast. Not a priority target at the time. Had our hands full with a major Asian gang. Then, lo and behold, up he pops on a video surveillance tape. Routine monitoring, carpark at the Cape Otway lighthouse. Same frame, Jake Martyn.'

'We already had our eye on Martyn,' explained patrol leader Crowden.

'Tip from the federal money monitors,' said Sutherland. 'Questionable transfers. Period of time, we pegged him as a mover of illegal abalone and crayfish. Selling it to other restaurants and certain seafood exporters.'

'Such as Tony Melina,' I said.

Sutherland nodded. 'Been looking for a chance to bust him. Big time possession. But he's cagey. Doesn't shop around for product. Supplier unknown. Then he's spotted with this Mick character.'

Crowden dropped off the edge of the desk and turned to a map pinned to the wall. 'We finally managed to tail him to a sector of the state forest designated as a reference area.' He pointed to the spot, like a student teacher launching into a geography lesson. 'Pristine bushland. Kept that way for long-term study purposes. No forestry. No tourism.'

Bottom line, as Sutherland put it, several months of intermittent surveillance and a quick look-see of the man's camp confirmed that he was operating a makeshift abalone processing plant.

'He was cooking them up, vacuum-sealing them,' said Sutherland. 'Large quantities, buyer unknown. Martyn suspected. But no firm evidence. We were getting ready to bust him, see if we couldn't get him to roll over on his buyer. Then, week before Christmas, bingo.'

Crowden explained. 'Our phone scanner started to pick up calls to Jake Martyn's mobile. Our man Mick, calling from a payphone up the coast. Coded references, something about a guest. We cranked the surveillance back up. Martyn made two visits to the camp.'

'Late at night,' said Sutherland. 'Thing is, no warning. No chance for us to act. Then, last night, a flurry of activity.'

Crowden put his clipboard on the table in front of me and ran his finger down the log entries.

Hilux to Gusto. Hilux to camp. Magna enters area. Jake Martyn's Range Rover enters area. Range Rover returns to Gusto. Hilux emerges, towing a boat. Hilux returns, no boat. Hilux leaves area, towing Magna. Hilux returns. Surveillance ends, 3 a.m.

Surveillance recommences, 6 a.m. Police vehicle from the local station enters area. Appears to be searching for something. Police officer and civilian.

'We'd checked the registration of the Magna, identified you as the owner,' said Crowden. 'Thought that you must've strayed into the area, got bogged or had a breakdown, walked out and left your car behind. Figured our man had found it, decided to move it further from the camp. That was our thinking when we approached you after you left the police station.'

Which brought us back to square one.

'Better escort you back there pronto,' said Sutherland. 'Get the ball rolling.'

As we got to our feet, the door swung open. A figure

stepped into the frame, side on, backlit by the glare of the sun. Coiled tight, he scrutinised us through rimless sunglasses. The jacket of his lightweight suit was drawn back at the hip and his right hand rested on the butt of a holstered pistol.

'Who the hell are you?' demanded Sutherland.

'Allow me,' I said, 'to introduce Detective Sergeant Meakes of the Victoria Police.'

Within an hour, I was surplus to requirements.

I'd been conveyed back to the station house, pumped dry, offered tea and trauma counselling, then left to cool my heels in an interview room while assorted components of the law-enforcement community got their ducks in a row.

Everybody was lining up for a suck of the Syce sausage. Two other members of the task force had arrived with Meakes. Homicide turned up soon after. The Special Operations Group was on its way with kevlar vests, shin-high combat boots and surface-to-surface missiles. The fish dogs were having a field day, the drug squad was sniffing around, the local cops had been conscripted and, for all I knew, the Man from Snowy River was galloping Lorneward with a detachment of alpine cavalry.

'You should've informed the sergeant of your intentions,' Meakes reprimanded me as we drove back to the police station. 'Naturally we were concerned about your safety when we arrived to find that you were missing. Particularly when one of the local officers reported seeing you with a unidentified person.'

'I appreciate the way you came to my rescue,' I said. 'But until that point I was under the impression you lot didn't believe me.'

'Why would you think that?' he asked.

Back at the police station, Meakes loosened up. I had, after all, delivered Syce to him. Done his job for him. Once Syce was back in custody, DS Meakes would be the man of the moment, his mug on the box, his pic in the paper, his tailoring the envy of the aspirational classes. So he rapidly recast himself as my confidant and collaborator.

As we worked our way through the details, he brought me up to speed on the background investigation.

For starters, I was wrong to assume that the moving of the Magna had scuppered my story. It was irrelevant. Meakes and his crew were half-way to Lorne by the time the car was found. Their scramble button had been pushed by two names that appeared in my statement to the Lorne coppers. Persons already of considerable interest to them.

One was Jake Martyn. The other was Phillip Ferrier, who was a Melbourne solicitor, Meakes informed me. And one of Ferrier's clients was Adrian Parish, the hold-up man who masterminded the motorbike escape. It was Ferrier who briefed Parish's barristers. He also assisted Parish with financial matters. Investments and the like.

After Parish's untimely death, his estate went to probate. It came to light that his goods and chattels included a shelf company whose sole asset was a half share in Gusto. It further emerged that Parish had assigned his share in Gusto to his lawyer as security against any outstanding fees, should he find himself unable to pay.

'Because he was doing fifteen years in prison, for example,' explained Meakes.

Adrian Parish died owing his lawyer money and so, in due course, Phillip Ferrier became half-owner of Gusto.

In the meantime, Meakes and his merry men were putting Jake Martyn under the microscope.

When interviewed, the restaurateur denied all knowledge of Parish. As far as he knew, the equity in his restaurant was owned by a trust fund operated by a reputable solicitor named Phillip Ferrier, a man he had met several years earlier when seeking investors for Gusto. Solicitors' trust funds are not an unusual source of capital for enterprises such as restaurants, he pointed out, and his dealings had been exclusively with Ferrier, an arm's-length investor who took his share of the profits but played no role in the business. Martyn was shocked to discover that the actual investor had been a notorious criminal. So he claimed.

Ferrier backed Martyn's account. Parish had wished to remain anonymous, he explained. Client confidentiality, blah, blah.

As to Rodney Syce, Martyn claimed to know only what he'd read in the newspapers.

Lacking hard evidence to link either Martyn or Ferrier directly to Syce, the police had no option but to bide their time. And when I was washed ashore with their names on my lips, lights flashed and buzzers buzzed.

'You hit the trifecta,' said Meakes.

My eye-witness account of the previous night's events,

combined with the investigative work done by the cops and the fish dogs' surveillance, produced a working hypothesis to explain the connection between Jake Martyn and Rodney Syce.

It ran like this. When Parish escaped from the Remand Centre, he planned to rendezvous with Jake Martyn, his bent business associate. After Parish was shot, Syce connected with Martyn, who hid him, then put him to work. First in the illegal seafood racket, then as an extortionist and killer.

Had I not spotted Syce, the two of them would probably have got away with it. As Meakes generously conceded, I'd been a very real help to the investigation.

Once the big picture came into focus, police attention moved to operational issues, the tactical implementation of Operation Snaffle Syce.

Surveillance was upped on the bush camp and Jake Martyn was kept under observation at Gusto, where he was choreographing preparations for New Year's Day brunch. And, presumably, preparing for his assignation with Syce at the bush camp.

No contact had been detected between the two men since Martyn's trip into the hills the previous night. This indicated that Syce was now playing a lone hand, the cops concluded. That he was keeping quiet about the complications that had arisen during the disposal of Tony Melina's body. That he was waiting for Martyn to arrive with the blood money, Tony's passport and the airline ticket out of the country.

Martyn had told Syce he'd bring the dough and the getaway kit to the camp during the afternoon. The moment he got there, the police trap would spring shut.

By eleven-thirty, I was out of the loop and growing bored

with sitting around waiting for my underpants to dry. Besides, if I didn't do something I would fall into a coma. My request for a lift to the holiday house for a change of clothes was denied—it would be better to wait until the dust settled. Just in case. Likewise, pending forensics, the Magna was to remain at the Cumberland River caravan park.

Meakes had taken over the sergeant's office as a field headquarters. Busy, busy. I waited until he finished a phone call, something about a helicopter landing area.

'I have to pick up my son and his friend from the Falls music festival,' I reminded the detective.

He beckoned over my shoulder to the muster room, a minor hive. 'One of the boys will drive you.'

But I didn't want a free trip in a police car. What I wanted was an hour's respite from the thump and grind of the previous twelve. A chance to feel normal again. Not a victim, not a witness, not a man possessed. Just a father doing his fatherly thing. Meeting his boy, asking him about his big night out. Not a man with a police escort and awful things to explain. In time I'd have to explain them, of course. But not yet.

'Thanks,' I said, 'but I'll take the shuttle-bus.'

'It's no problem,' insisted Meakes.

'It is for me,' I said. 'I need a bit of breathing space.'

'Not a good idea. We don't want a repetition of that earlier business, do we?'

'You think I'm in danger? Think you might have to rescue me again?'

'No, it's just better this way.'

Better for him, he meant. Better to keep me filed away until after his moment of triumph. We batted it back and forth for a couple of minutes, but short of arresting me, he couldn't detain me against my will.

'I'll keep my head low,' I said. 'And I'll be back in an hour with two teenage boys.'

'Suit yourself,' he said. 'But you're acting contrary to my advice.'

Outside the copshop, I found the weather turning, the heat dissipating before it reached its threatened peak. Concrete-coloured clouds scuttled across the sky. A gusty onshore breeze was raising whitecaps and rattling the treetops. Frankly, I was more than a little rattled myself. Rats-arsed, anyway. It had been a big night, what with one thing and another, and I was fuzzy-headed and heavy-limbed.

I was also not in a fit state to been seen on the main drag of a fashionable resort in the middle of a public holiday. The Labor Party's reputation was already at an all-time low. Sticking to residential side-streets, I steered an inconspicuous course to Erskine Falls Road and hailed the mini-bus as it returned up the hill.

I was the only passenger. Picking my way towards the back, I found a yellow terry-towelling hat on the floor. I sprawled across the back seat and laid it over my face, resting my weary bones and red-rimmed eyes.

Fifteen minutes later, the bus jerked to a halt at the festival gate. Yesterday's pasture was now a mosh-trampled cow-paddock littered with abandoned tents, wayward groundsheets and half-dismantled vegan-burger stalls. A bunk-chukka-bunk beat was washing up the slope from the direction of the circus bigtop that housed the main stage. Youthful punters were straggling from the scene of the all-night beano, their duds crumpled and flecked with grass.

Here, at least, I was dressed for the occasion.

I found Tarquin on the grassy verge beside the pick-up area. He was dozing, mouth open, his back against a big grey-gum. His dress shirt was scrunched and sweat-stained, the wing collar gone entirely. He was buttressed on one side by two backpacks, his and Red's, and on the other by a girl in a black knee-length slip. She had black, magenta-streaked hair, purple lipstick, flour-white make-up and Cleopatra eye-liner. Around her neck was a black velvet ribbon. She was about fourteen years old. She, too, was slumbering, slack-jawed.

I looked around, but saw no sign of Red.

'Wakey, wakey,' I croaked, nudging Tark's prostrate form with a rubber sandal.

He came upright. He looked at me, looked around, looked at his watch and looked around again. His little friend from the Addams family came awake and stretched fetchingly.

'This is Ronnie,' explained Tark.

Veronica gave me a watery smile. Then she stood, flapped her wrist in Tark's general direction, mumbled something about seeing him later, and wandered away.

'No need to ask if you had a good time, then,' I said.

'Likewise,' said Tark. 'Love the hat. It's very you.'

'Get fucked,' I said. 'Where's Red?'

Tark clambered to his feet, smacking the dust off his backside. Shading his eyes, he took a long look around. No result. He scratched his scalp-tuft and shrugged. His put-upon air suggested that he'd been left to guard the baggage while Red amused himself elsewhere. 'Not back yet,' he said.

'Back from where?'

'Nature ramble.' He said it with disdain. 'Red, Jodie, Matt

Prentice, bunch of them. Been gone a while. Supposed to be back by now.'

I sighed and slumped down onto the backpacks. They were very comfortable, stuffed with tent and sleeping bags. So Red was a bit late. No big deal. Busy enjoying himself, he'd probably lost track of time. He'd turn up. I settled back to wait, shoulders against the grey-gum, my new head-wear pulled down against the glare.

'Good, was it?' I yawned in Tark's general direction. 'I hear Hunters and Collectors stole the show.'

'If you like that sort of thing,' he allowed. 'Think I'll get a drink. Want one?'

'Uh-huh.'

I dozed, lulled by the swish of the leaves above my head. Images from the previous night flashed past. Barbara Prentice at Gusto. The pursuit into the ranges, tail-lights dancing ahead. Bafflement at the discovery of Tony Melina. Dark and horrible things. White knuckles, severed ears. The immensity of the ocean.

'Mineral water.'

'Huh.'

'Mineral water,' repeated Tarquin. 'It's all they had left.'

He lifted the towelling hat and dangled the bottle in front of my face. Deep Spring.

Deep mouthfuls, then a glance at my watch. A half hour had slipped past. I eased myself upright and scanned the scene. Vehicles were coming and going in the pick-up area, parents collecting offspring. Red was still nowhere to be seen. Nor Jodie or her big brother.

'Still not back?' I said.

Tarquin prodded the ground with a steel-capped toe, a

man on the horns of a dilemma.

'Better tell me what's going on,' I said.

Tark heaved a sigh. He'd talk, but only because I'd beaten it out of him. 'They went to get some plants.'

'Plants?' I said, 'What do you mean plants?'

Tark shrugged. Not tomato plants. Not hardy perennials. Not specimens of endangered native vegetation.

'Little bastard,' I said. 'I'll wring his fucking neck.'

Tarquin shook his head furiously. 'It wasn't Red's idea. He doesn't even smoke, honest. Okay, maybe a puff now and then. But he doesn't inhale. Only reason he went was because Jodie went. And she only went because Matt was going and she wanted to make sure he didn't get into any trouble. The whole thing's down to this dickhead eco-warrior called Mongoose. He's the one found the plants, talked Matt and the others into going with him. Reckoned they were just sitting there for the taking.'

Great timing, I thought. Today of all days, rope-a-dope Red decides to join a band of bhang-burglars.

Then came an even more disturbing thought. I stared past the fences to the featureless bush. There's bound to be more than one clump of hemp out there, I reassured myself. And the one I happened to know about was at least two hours solid hiking to the west.

'And where exactly are these plants?' I said.

Tark shrugged. 'Mongoose was pretty vague. They left about eight. Mongoose said they'd be back by midday.'

'Which way did they go?'

He looked around, settled on a direction and tossed his mohawk west-ish.

'On foot?' I said.

Tark nodded. 'You think they might have got lost or something?'

I wasn't sure what I thought. I was fully occupied trying to calculate the chances that the target of the half-baked dope raid was Rodney Syce's camp.

'Who is this Mongoose guy anyway?' I said. 'Friend of Matt Prentice, is he?'

Tarquin shrugged again. 'Friend of a friend of a friend sort of thing,' he said. 'He's a feral. Walked here cross-country from a logging protest camp with a bunch of tree-huggers.'

'I want to know exactly where they went,' I said.

Tark caught my antsy tone. 'I dunno,' he pleaded. 'Honest. But that lot over there might.'

A pod of ferals was moving towards the exit, a half-dozen soap-shy, low-tech, bush-dwelling hippies. Crusty chicks in shaman chic, fabric-swathed and spider-legged. Bedraggled boys in scrofulous face-hair and army-surplus pants, matted dreadlocks stuffed into tea-cosy tam-o'-shanters.

'They're the ones Mongoose came with,' explained Tark. 'Want me to ask if they know anything?'

'Go,' I commanded. 'Ask.'

Tark jogged after the ferals and hailed them. They encircled him, bobbing in time with the faint pulse of the music, beaming at him like he was a strange and fascinating artifact. A conference commenced. Everybody had something to contribute. I hung back, impatiently awaiting the outcome.

The talk continued, back and forth, heap big pow-wow. The People's Consultative Congress. Then, abruptly, the ferals resumed their march for the exit. Tark returned.

'Off their faces,' he reported. 'But they know where Mongoose took Red and the others. They camped near the place on their way here, night before last. They heard this dog barking somewhere in the bush, nobody around, houses or anything. Mongoose went for a look, came back with fresh leaf. Said he'd found a dope patch. He wanted to go back in the morning, check it out, maybe rip it off. They said no, so he convinced Matt and his mates to help them instead.'

I didn't like the sound of that dog.

'They're headed that way now,' said Tark. 'They reckon they'll probably meet Red and the others on their way back.'

The ferals were trucking out the gate, disappearing down the road. Should I wait here? Should I follow the furry freaks, hope to connect with Red and the Prentice kids?

Should I contact the cops and share my concerns?

I decided on all three.

'You wait here,' I ordered Tark. 'If I'm not back in half an hour, or if Red hasn't shown up, contact the Lorne police. Mention my name. Tell them what you told me and what the ferals told you. Tell them I think these dope plants might be the ones at Rodney Syce's camp. Tell them I've gone to find Red and the others. Okay?'

Tark was a fast study. 'Rodney Syce?' he said, 'Wasn't that the guy…'

'Later,' I said, stuffing the bottle of mineral water into my back pocket and starting after the vanishing ferals.

They were setting a cracking pace, moving faster than a runaway budget deficit. I hurried to keep them in sight as they powered along the roadside.

A dark-grey surfwear-stickered Range Rover came up the hill and whizzed past, Barbara Prentice behind the wheel.

Come to collect Jodie and Matt, no doubt. Chances were, Tark would spot her, fill her in. Good.

Or was it? Barbara had connections with Jake Martyn. Could word leak back to him somehow?

The ferals had walked into a picnic area. Tree ferns, log tables, families. They entered a slot between the trees, the beginning of a hiking track. I pursued them along the narrow defile. The bush rustled around us. The path rose and fell.

I put on a spurt of speed and caught up with the rearguard feral. She was a thin girl, her collarbones jutting above a flat chest bandoleered with ragged scarves. A wide headband and a ring though her septum, she looked like the door knocker from a Mayan temple. She was sucking a Chupa-Chup and making a vibrating noise in her throat as she marched.

'Excuse me,' I panted, falling into step beside her.

She shook her head briskly and continued to hum, lips tight around her lollipop stick. Headphone plugs stoppered her ears, leading from a Discman in an embroidered sack on a cord around her neck.

'I'm trying to find out...'

She shook her head again, making it clear she wasn't going to speak.

Suppressing the urge to rip the wires from her lugholes, I hurried up the line to the next crusty. He was bare-footed with vulcanised soles, Celtic tattoos, a braided beard, a moonstone pendant and a walking staff incised with a rainbow serpent. All of twenty years old.

'Excuse me,' I gasped. 'I'm looking for my son. He's with a guy called Mongoose. I'm worried...'

Gandalf did not break stride. He beamed benignly and stroked his beard. 'You've got to learn to let go, man. You can't, like, stifle the people you love.'

'I'm not trying to stifle him,' I said. 'I'm trying to find him.' And then, it was true, I'd throttle him.

'Find yourself first, man,' opined the wizard. 'The answer lies within.'

More likely it lay ahead. Stacking on the pace, I reached a brace of feralesses. One was tall and ethereal, all bracelets and bells. The other was stocky and wore a shearer's blue singlet. ''Scuse me,' I wheezed. 'I'm looking for my son.'

Tinkerbell slowed a little and smiled beatifically. 'What's his name?'

'Red,' I said.

'Cool,' she said. 'It's, like, very vibrant.'

The little shearer sheila clocked me for a suit in mufti. She eyed me suspiciously. 'We don't know anyone called Red.'

'But you know a guy called Mongoose, right?'

Grasping my line of enquiry, she shook her head. 'It's nothing to do with us.'

The wind was getting stronger, snatching at our words. I had a stitch in my side and a raging thirst. My ankle was throbbing and my new sandals were rubbing at my heels. I downed the last of my water.

'I just want to know where they've gone,' I pleaded.

Tinkerbell extended a long delicate finger threaded with silver rings. The trees on the side of the trail were thinning. Through them I could see a vast open space. A firebreak. The lead ferals, a cluster of young bucks, had left the path and started across it.

I checked the time. It was past one-thirty. The half hour

had come and gone. Either Red and the others were safely back at the concert pick-up area or Tark had contacted the coppers. Should I go forward or back? I decided to press on, give it another few minutes.

The firebreak was a desolate gash in the grey-green fabric of the forest. Two hundred metres of torn earth, flattened vegetation and chain-sawed tree stumps. By the time I was half-way across, the pathfinder ferals had vanished into the bush on the far side.

Pixie and Poxie and Whacko the Wizard were nowhere in sight. The sky roiled with clouds. My brain was turning to mush. What was I doing?

A rutted track intersected the firebreak, two shallow undulations in the hard-packed dirt. I followed it into the trees for a couple of minutes, then sank onto a fallen branch.

Time to pack it in, go back the way I'd come.

The wind roared in the canopy and stirred up willy-willies of leaves and dust. Shards of bark and dry twigs flew through the air. The temperature dropped. Rain coming.

I pulled the empty water bottle from my pocket and cursed my stupidity. So much for my New Year resolution about going off half-cocked. I unpeeled the velcro tabs on my sandals and massaged my raw heels.

The Australian bush. I hated it. The sooner it was turned into woodchips, toilet paper and florists' accessories, the better.

As I climbed to my feet, a spanking new Nissan Patrol came lumbering along the track from the direction of the firebreak. Bullbar on the front grille. It juddered to a halt beside me and a flush-faced, silver-haired man in a crisply ironed check shirt leaned out the window.

'G'day,' he said, in an unconvincing attempt to sound as if he hadn't spent his entire adult life in a corporate board-room.

'G'day,' I responded, spotting an opportunity. 'Got myself a bit bushed here, mate. Any chance of a lift back to civilisation?'

A brittle-coiffed matron scrutinised me from the passenger seat, not entirely thrilled by the idea. Her R. M. Williams collar was rakishly turned up. Protection against the harsh outback sun for both a well-preserved neck and a string of rather good pearls.

'Hop in,' said the silverback.

I climbed into the back seat, inhaling the ambience of the leafy suburbs. The vehicle had a dashboard like a B-52. Traction control, six-speaker CD, floating compass, artificial horizon, dual airbags. 'Murray's the name,' I said.

'Douglas,' said the man. 'And my wife Pamela.'

The massive machine crawled forward. Douglas craned over the steering wheel, concentrating on the narrow, rutted track.

'Bit new to this,' he explained. 'We're planning a big trip to the Top End later in the year. I thought I'd get some off-road experience first.'

We bumped and rocked to the top of an incline, then ploughed downwards. Douglas hadn't counted on an audience. He kept wiping his hands on his thighs. Wet patches darkened the armpits of his shirt.

'Sure this is the way?' I said. 'You got a map?'

The wife had one on her knee. 'This track leads to the Mount Sabine Road,' she said primly.

You're the one who got lost, her tone implied.

I lapsed into grateful silence.

Pamela stared fixedly ahead. I couldn't tell if her tension was caused by her husband's driving or a suspicion that the rough-looking stranger in the back seat was about to cut their throats and steal their expensive new car.

The track was little more than a fissure between close-packed trees. Branches scraped the doors and the vehicle yawed from side to side.

'Honestly, Douglas,' said his wife, clinging to the handrail. The minutes ticked past. I grew prickly with impatience.

'I really appreciate this,' I said.

Suddenly, Douglas hit the brakes hard and the Patrol lurched to a halt.

A wild-eyed figure was blocking our path.

He was compact and sinewy, his scalp razored back to a braided topknot. Sweat and grime covered his nut-brown skin and his bare chest heaved beneath a shark-tooth necklace. His army surplus pants had been sheared off mid-calf and cinched at the waist with a tattered saffron scarf.

He was semaphoring desperately for us to stop.

I hit the ground running and reached him in ten seconds flat. He had a sharp, tapered face, small ears and darting eyes. A mongoose if ever I saw one.

He teetered on the spot, sucked down air and steadied himself. He was much older than I'd assumed. Twenty-five at least.

You prick, I thought, bracing for the worst.

'Need help, man,' he panted. 'I was, like, taking these young dudes to check out this place where I'd, like, seen this amazing platypus and next thing there's this loony pointing like a shotgun at us and sort of herding us into this kind of shed but I'm like basically behind a tree and he doesn't see me so I, like, see my chance to go get help so I make a break and…'

The torrent dried up and he paused to catch his breath. I clamped a hand around one of his Polynesian wrist tattoos.

'Cut the outdoor-education crap, Mongoose. I know all about you ripping off the dope.'

The twerp stared at me, eyes wide with astonishment. His mouth did a passable impression of a dying carp.

'Are those kids okay?' I demanded. 'Tell me exactly what happened.'

Mongoose licked his lips, cowering slightly. Probably because I was twisting his arm behind his back.

'There's five of them,' he said. 'Four guys and a chick. We were doing a run-through of this guy's crop. He springs us, and suddenly he's waving this gun around, yelling out stuff like, "Hands in the air, shuddup, get in the shed." The others, they're like totally freaked but, "Sure, man, whatever you say" and I'm out of there, so I don't see what happens next. But there's no shots, nothing like that. He's, like, taken them prisoner or something. I think.'

Douglas was hovering apprehensively. All this, and he wasn't even in the Northern Territory yet. He glanced back at the Patrol. Pamela stood a few paces behind him, fingering her pearls. In her other hand she held a bottle of water.

'Where's this happening?' I said.

Mongoose flapped his free arm. 'Back that way. Along a creek, bottom of a ridge.'

'Take me there.'

He wrenched free. 'What for, man? Take me to the cops, I'll show them the way.'

'The cops already know where it is.'

'Bullshit. How could they?'

'You don't know the half of it, you dopey deadshit,' I said, with more assurance than I felt. 'Take me there and I'll put in a good word for you at the trial.'

He accepted a swig of water from Pamela and gulped, his adam's apple pulsing. As he drank, he eyed me warily as though I might snatch the bottle from his grasp and deck him with it.

'You're out of your fucken tree, man. No *way* am I going back there. Not without an army of cops.'

I turned to Pamela and Douglas and adopted my doorknocking-in-a-marginal-seat tone. 'This sorry specimen has put a group of teenagers in serious danger. They're in the hands of an escaped convict, a murderer. One of them is a young girl. We need to get to the police, ASAP.'

'That's what I'm telling you, man,' bleated Mongoose. 'Except I didn't know he was a murderer, just some dude with a dope plantation. Dead set.'

I shoved him towards the Patrol. He shoved back. 'Fuck, man,' he said peevishly. 'No need to get so heavy.'

I balled my fist, seething with anger, frustration and anxiety. 'I'll get as heavy as I like, pal,' I said. 'One of those kids is my son. And if anything's happened to him, I'll have you up on so many charges you'll be meeting parole conditions for the rest of your sorry-arsed life.'

The sky was darkening, the trees groaning in the wind. I shivered, a coldness creeping through me. Finger by finger, I unballed my fist.

Douglas and Pamela had gone into whispered conference beside the Patrol. Now Pamela turned on her heel and strode towards the driver's door. 'For God's sake, Douglas,' she said. 'This is an emergency.'

I followed Mongoose into the back seat. Douglas took the front passenger slot. Pamela got behind the wheel and turned the key in the ignition.

'Seatbelts,' she commanded.

She slammed the Patrol into gear and gunned it along the rutted outline of the track. Lips tight, pearls swaying as the leviathan powered forward. She was, I knew at once, a formidable presence on the tennis club social committee.

Mongoose retreated into his corner. He smelled of sweat and fear and patchouli oil. But even in his deflated state, there was a hint of nervy charisma about him, an expectation that people would turn towards him. I could understand how his bush-warrior pose might appeal to a surly, insecure kid like Matt Prentice.

Redmond Whelan, on the other hand, should have known better.

I tried to picture the scene at Syce's camp, imagine his reaction to the sudden appearance of a stampeding herd of plant-plundering adolescents. At least, if the funked-out Mongoose was to be believed, he hadn't starting blasting away with his shotgun. On the other hand, he didn't need a gun to be lethal. A shovel would do, or even an oyster knife. I didn't want to think about it. Drop my bundle now and I'd be no use to anyone.

Pamela was boring ahead like a three-time veteran of the Paris–Dakar. I leaned into the gap between the seats and gave them a thumbnail of the situation. A police operation was in progress, I told them, but this was a new development. I said I was worried the police might get there too late. Didn't mention the doings of the previous night. Fudged the reasons for my involvement. Clear as mud, but it covered the ground.

'Dreadful,' said Pamela above the grunt and thrash of the engine.

'You're a member of parliament, you say?' Douglas sounded sceptical.

'Labor,' I explained.

'Ah.'

The track divided. The right-hand fork, better-defined, ran uphill. Douglas fussed with the map.

'Go right,' said Mongoose. He shot a furtive glance down the side track.

'Stop the car,' I said.

Pamela hit the anchors and hoisted the handbrake. We propped precariously, bullbar angled upwards.

I loomed over Mongoose like a cobra. 'It's down there, isn't it?'

'I'm not going back, man. Not without…'

'Yeah, yeah,' I cut him off. 'At least give me directions.'

'Surely you're not thinking of going alone?' said Douglas.

'How would you feel if it was Verity?' said Pamela.

Douglas said nothing, but if I wanted to get myself shot, it was fine with Mongoose. 'Track ends at a fallen tree,' he said. 'Somebody's had a go at it with a chainsaw. Slope drops away, totally steep. Creek's at the bottom. Follow it downstream, ten, fifteen minutes.'

I repeated the instructions to myself and opened the door.

'What's your shoe size?' said Pamela.

'Nine,' I said. 'Why?'

'Give him your shoes, Douglas,' she said. 'And socks. He can't go tramping through the bush in those sandals.'

Douglas unlaced his Timberlake hikers. A Christmas present, judging by their mint condition. He peeled off his cream cotton socks and handed them over. Socks and boots both were a perfect fit.

'Take care,' Pamela said, laying a motherly hand on my shoulder. 'Good luck.'

The Patrol grunted upwards. I jogged down the left fork in my brand new seven-league boots, plastic bottle in hand. I ached in some parts and chafed in others, but the exhaustion had evaporated. I was hyper. Dark possibilities coursed through my brain.

The faint ruts, the barest figment of a track, sank deeper and deeper into the swaying grey-green immensity of the ranges. After ten minutes of thudding footfalls and heaving lungs, they were just a gap in the vegetation, a narrow seam weaving through the trees.

The trunk of a long-dead stringybark blocked my way, a decaying giant notched with incisions. Once upon a time, an optimist had tried to clear the path, given up. I vaulted the log and traversed the shoulder of a ridge. The ground dropped away to one side. Like, totally steep, man.

This looked like the place. Unless Mongoose had been winding me up. He wouldn't dare, I told myself.

It was nearly three o'clock. Jake Martyn was expected mid-afternoon. Any time now. The cops, I assumed, had already established some sort of perimeter. With luck I'd connect with them or the fish dogs as I approached the camp. I half expected to see a hovering helicopter, squaddies abseiling down ropes into the tree canopy.

I plunged down the incline, skidding though clumps of parrot-pea and careening off grey-gums. The drop was almost vertical. Hurtling headlong, I snatched at anything in reach. Thorns and blades of native grass ripped my skin, wiry, like frayed cable ends. I fell on my arse and rode the seat of my pants to the bottom, steering with my feet.

The creek was a chain of tea-coloured puddles, midges swarming. I caught my breath, examined my abrasions, took an abstemious slug of my bottled water and started to work my way downstream.

The watercourse meandered through a tangle of rotting logs and moss-covered rocks, its fern-crowded banks never more than three or four metres apart. The air smelled peaty and primeval. Bellbirds pinged. The air was almost still, the wind a distant moan.

The slopes on either side gradually became less steep. Dry, undergrowth-choked gullies converged with the creek bed. At the mouth of one, I found footprints in a spill of quartz-speckled sand. Mine, I concluded. My lost-at-sea loafers. I spent half my political life going round in circles, but this was beyond a joke.

Nerve-ends tingling, I began to move more cautiously, half-recognising features of the terrain from the previous night. The wind picked up again, sighing and whistling in the treetops. The creek bank became a redoubt of weathered, lichen-colonised granite. Edging around it, I caught a glimpse of the sandbagged dam, hose running up to Syce's camp.

I turned and crept back the way I had come, assessing the lie of the land. A hundred metres upstream I scrambled up the bank. I began to circle the camp, dreading what I might discover.

Where were the police, I kept asking myself? Surely they were somewhere nearby, monitoring the comings and goings. Surely they were up to speed on the desperately changed situation by now. My old lack of confidence in the constabulary was back with a vengeance.

The cloud was breaking apart, the light flickering and shifting as it fell through the swaying leaf canopy. I approached the camp from high ground, duck and dart, bent in a half-crouch.

I spotted the Hilux, caught a fishy smell on a gust of wind. The abalone kitchen was a camouflage-dappled cube in the dusty green. The screen-wall tent was gone, struck.

Nothing moving. Nobody talking, weeping, groaning.

No barking. Not yet, anyway. I changed position, keeping well back. Now I could see the whacky-backy patch, a deeper green, half of it uprooted. And Syce. I could see Syce.

He was standing beside a tree, the one Tony Melina had been chained to. He was staring at its trunk, very close, his back to me, his hands moving at the sides of his head as though batting at his ears.

Jesus, I thought. He's wigged out, gone Lady Macbeth.

My blood ran cold. His nerves were fine when he was torturing and murdering Tony Melina. It must have taken a far worse atrocity to whip him into such a psychotic lather. Far, far worse.

I got down on my belly with the snakes and the lizards and slithered through the leaf-litter.

'I need to pee,' pleaded a girl's voice.

'Shuddup,' grunted Syce. 'You peed already.'

The voice came from inside the shed. It had to be Jodie Prentice. And she wasn't too terrified to speak. And Syce was not too deranged to respond. These were good signs, I told myself. A minuscule ripple of relief ran through me.

I manoeuvred until I could see the doorway of the shed. It was a black rectangle, the interior obscure. I now also had a profile view of Syce. He wasn't flipping out. He was snipping his hair with a small pair of scissors, checking his reflection in a shaving mirror hooked on a nail hammered into the tree.

A fine drizzle descended, a momentary sun-shower, bathing the scene in a brief, sugar-sprinkled incandescence. In the sudden flash of light, a cluster of figures took shape in the shed. They were sitting on the earth floor, hugging their knees, blindfolded. One, two, five. Jodie, Red, Matt, two boys I didn't know. The mongrel dog lay on its sack in the doorway, scratching.

Relief again. A small tsunami this time.

But where were the frigging cops? And did they know yet that Syce was not alone? That abalone shed was just a tin box. If push came to gunplay, the kids could get caught in the crossfire.

I backed up the slope, hunkered down in the shrubbery and did the trigonometry. It was the police plan, last I'd heard, to wait until Jake Martyn arrived at the camp before making their move. Until then, they were probably holding back, wary of spooking Syce. Martyn would come up the creek bed. So, in all likelihood, would the main force of plods.

I needed to connect with them before things started happening, give them the low-down on the set-up.

As I started toward the creek, the dog began to bark. Syce said something brisk, the word inaudible. The woof-woofing ceased immediately. I crouched, frozen, hearing nothing but the creak and rustle of the bush, the buzz of bugs. Syce spoke again, the words lost, the tone instructional.

Instant replay of the previous night. Martyn was arriving. Syce was telling the kids to behave themselves.

Skirting the shed, I navigated for the creek bed. But a vehicle was already emerging from the tunnel of vegetation. I pulled up short and took cover behind a thick stringybark.

The car was a dark green Range Rover. Syce was watching it, too. He was standing in the lee of a towering bluegum, double-barrel shotgun in the crook of his arm. He'd whittled his full beard down to a rough stubble, thicker at the chin. Likewise the front of his scalp. Got a head start on the big make-over. Charles Manson meets Fu Manchu, the rough-cut.

The Range Rover laboured onto the slew of sand below the camp and stopped. Jake Martyn got out. Big shirt, comfortable pants. Syce came down the slope to meet him, shotgun angled to the ground. Martyn toted a sports bag. That'd be the money. Tony's passport, the airline ticket, the salon accessories. Avon calling.

They walked back up towards the shed, Syce doing the talking. Explaining. Persuasive hand gestures. The shed doorway was out of sight, around the corner. The dog padded out to meet them, metronome tail, sociable as a parish priest in a public bar.

The guard has deserted its post, I thought. Syce must have realised the same thing. He increased his pace, still pitching his line. Jake Martyn was asking curt questions, not liking the answers.

The cops, the cops. Where, sweet Jesus, were the cops?

Then the dog was woofing again. This time, Syce didn't silence it. He turned towards the shed, the shotgun swinging around with him, rising as it came. Martyn reached out and grabbed the barrel. The gun went off. Boom. Astonishingly loud.

224

Birds erupted from the trees, an explosion of screeching feathers. Jake Martyn went down, keening like an air-raid siren, blood gushing from his thigh. As if responding to a starter's pistol, figures bolted from the shed and scattered into the bush. The kids were breaking out. The dog took off in hot pursuit, barking and snapping.

Syce recoiled from the accidental discharge. Even from thirty metres away, I could tell that he was losing it. The best laid plans were turning to shit, coming apart at the seams. He swept the shotgun in a jerky, erratic arc. Then, snatching up Jake Martyn's tote bag, he bolted for the Range Rover.

Just as he reached the creek bed, a stick figure in hipsters and a halter-top burst out of the undergrowth and skidded down the bank. Jodie Prentice. The dog had its fangs in the hem of her jeans, slathering and thrashing. She kicked out, trying to shake it loose.

Syce swung around, dropped the sports bag and brought up the shotgun.

Then Red appeared, sprinting, an upraised stick in hand.

Jodie was yelling and swearing, dragging the dog behind her. 'Fuck off, shit-bastard animal.'

Jake Martyn was back upright, one hand clutching his wound, mouth opening and closing.

Screaming girl, rabid dog, rushing boy, desperate maniac, ruined plan, pointed shotgun. I didn't like the way the dominoes were falling. Not with one barrel to go and Syce's history in tight corners.

And where were the pinhead pigs?

I stuck my head out from behind cover. 'Hey, you,' I shouted. 'Up here.'

My words were lost in the cacophony. Windwhip,

dogsnarl, birdscreech. Jake Martyn's gunshot yabbering and Jodie Prentice's industrial-strength cursing.

I stepped into plain sight and thundered down the slope, weaving through the saplings, a bellowing buffalo. 'Syce,' I screamed. 'Over here, arsehole.'

He spun around and I dived behind a tree. The shotgun came up to his shoulder and the barrel swept the hillside.

Red started belting the dog. It turned on him, sabre-toothed. Syce swung the shotgun around at the sound.

He'd run out of rope. I could see it in the way he was tensing, his grip whitening on the stock of the shotgun, finger crooked at the trigger.

Again, I stepped from cover and yelled. The shotgun came around again. The business end was pointed directly at my chest. I was maybe ten metres away.

Red and Jodie were in retreat, Red beating at the dog with all his rower's strength. Snarl, snap.

A thunderclap rang in my ears and a blow struck my chest, powerful as a runaway bus. I felt myself lifted off my feet, thrown backwards through the air.

Everything went black.

A heavenly chorus filled my ears.

'Drop it.'

'Police.'

'Don't move, police.'

'POLICE!'

My shoulder slammed into the ground with a lung-flattening *womph*. The runaway bus landed on top of me, pressing my face into the earth. The hubbub of voices swelled. Two shots rang out in rapid succession. In their echo came the unremitting battle-cry of the dog. A voice started yelling, 'Don't shoot, I'm not armed. Don't shoot.'

Over and over, a mantra.

I spat gumleaf crud and unscrewed my eyelids. A body was straddling mine, a black-clad blur, pinning me flat. It shifted aside to let me breathe but maintained the pressure between my shoulder blades. I twisted my head and registered the black as a coverall uniform. Special Operations Group. The Sons of God.

Heavy footfalls drummed past my head. Jake Martyn stopped his shouting. A shrill whistle pierced the bush and the hubbub abated a little. The weight on my spine eased. I was being helped to my feet.

The soggie hauling me upright had a boxer's nose and Tartar cheekbones. He squinted into my face and spoke, his voice beamed from a distant planet.

'Yoke, eh?'

My hearing was MIA, still ringing with the din of the gunshots and my impact with the forest floor.

'R. U. O. K.?' he repeated.

I nodded stupidly. Okay enough, I guessed. Nothing a month in traction and a bionic ear wouldn't fix. A blood-curdling snarl pierced the fug. I spun around, searching for the source of the sound.

The dog was still on the job, fangs bared as it snapped at Red's groin. My boy was engaged in a desperate holding action. His stick was no more than a shredded stump. Tight-lipped, he was fighting a losing battle.

As I launched myself towards him a soggie appeared, cocking his leg. He sank a high-laced boot into the slathering beast's belly. With a startled yip, the dog rose high off the ground and flew ten metres though the air. Straight through the middle of two tall saplings. It hit the embankment, gave a terminal yap and was finally silent.

Red's head turned to follow the trajectory of the punted pooch. The goal-kicking copper grabbed him by the arm, steadying him, and said something. The kid's shell-shocked grimace dissolved into a tension-draining laugh. Then the anxiety flooded back and he looked around urgently.

I raised an arm. He spotted me and took the salute, his relief evident. Then he buckled at the knees. The cop supported his weight.

Between us, on the broken slope of creek bank, Jake Martyn was lying face-down in the forest debris. Two soggies with pump-action shotguns loomed over him while a third cuffed his hands behind his back.

Nearby, Rodney Syce was flat on his back, motionless. His neck was twisted at an unnatural angle, about 328 degrees at a guess. His arms were flung out from his torso. A swarm of soggies surrounded him, pump-actions converging at point-blank range. One of the troopers nudged the double-barrel shotgun from Syce's limp grasp. Another dropped to a crouch and pressed his fingers to the prostrate felon's neck.

Up the hillside, a line of dark shapes was advancing through the trees. Two police four-wheel-drives roared from the canopy of vegetation over the creek bed and pulled up behind Jake Martyn's Range Rover. The doors flew open and cops piled out, DS Meakes among them. Jodie Prentice was limping across the gravel towards Red, escorted by a uniformed officer in short sleeves and a bullet-proof vest.

'This way, sir,' said the squaddie at my side. He put a hand on my shoulder and steered me down the slope.

'You saved my life,' I said.

He shrugged. 'We get time and a half on public holidays.'

'Taxpayers' money well spent,' I said. For once.

Jake Martyn was whimpering, not so full of zest now. The soggies rolled him onto his back and one of them clamped a wad of bandage to his wounded thigh.

The cop with his fingertips on Syce's carotid shook his head and stood up.

For a clearing in a forest wilderness, the place was busier than the federal tally room on election night. Cops were pouring in from all points of the compass. Matt Prentice and his mates straggled out of the mulga, each with an attendant officer. Jodie and Red stood in the creek bed, watching me approach. She was hanging onto his arm, stroking it like it was a pedigree Siamese. When I got to the bottom of the bank, Red detached himself and ran to meet me.

We clung to each other for dear life, hearts pounding together.

'I was so scared,' he said.

Me too. I pressed his head to my chest and buried my face in the glutinous spikes of his hair.

'I'm sorry, Dad,' he said. 'I'm so sorry.'

'You are so fucking grounded,' I said. 'You'll spend the rest of the holidays locked in your bedroom.'

Over the top of his head, I could see Jodie Prentice laying into her big brother with balled fists, kicking him in the shins. He was copping it, making no attempt to defend himself.

Our manly embrace ran its course. Red started to speak. One question now, I knew, would quickly become a torrent of explanation and justification.

'Later,' I said, raising my hand. It was trembling. 'The main thing is, you're okay and I'm okay. Only the bad guys got hurt. Go stop Jodie killing her brother while I have a word with the police.'

'I'll kill him myself,' muttered Red. 'Bloody idiot.'

'Let's wait until there aren't so many cops around.'

I looked back up the slope towards Syce's body. Two cops

stood beside it. Damian Meakes in his light brown summer-weight suit, and a nuggety man with a bony forehead and close-cut iron-grey hair. A homicide cop called Kevin Hayes. One of the many jacks I'd met that morning at the Lorne cop shop.

A uniform blocked my path. I called Meakes' name. He turned and stared at me from behind the rimless ovals of his green-tinted sunglasses. After a long moment, he nodded.

The uniform stepped aside and I trudged up the incline. The wind had dropped away and the clouds were breaking up, but the air still had a damp feel to it. I rubbed the bare skin of my arms and shivered.

I'd wanted to see Syce lying dead on the ground, no denying it. I'd lived with the want aching in the marrow of my bones for almost two years. From the instant the gutless prick did what he did to Lyndal. I'd felt it burst into a raging fury when he pointed his shotgun at my son. But now the moment had arrived, I felt only an unexpected emptiness.

The two cops moved apart, wordless. I stared down at the corpse.

He was dead, all right. No doubt about it. His shirt was unbuttoned, the bullet wounds clearly visible. Two in the side, one where his neck joined his shoulder. Very little blood, a quick death. Flies were already buzzing at the dark-rimmed punctures. My gaze moved up to his face. There were flies there, too. They crawled across the rough remnants of his beard and swarmed at his lips. His skin was the colour of putty, the lividity already draining away.

For the first time I looked at the man properly. Close up. Broad daylight. When my gaze reached his lifeless green eyes, a shudder started deep in my body. My stomach clenched and my mouth filled with a bitter taste.

The fruit of knowledge.

I stared until the silence grew unbearable, then turned to Meakes. His face, too, was motionless. He looked back at me, hands clasped in the small of his back, eyes invisible behind the lenses of his sunglasses. He was waiting for me to speak. But speech, at that moment, was not within my power.

It was Hayes who broke the silence, his tone conversational. 'Your second message didn't get through until events were already in progress, Mr Whelan. Your presence here came as something of a surprise to the officers on the ground.'

'It's been a big day for surprises,' I said stiffly, looking at Meakes. 'Sorry for the inconvenience.'

I turned and walked back down the incline. Gutted. Meakes fell into step beside me.

I'd been overly harsh on DS Meakes. Maybe it was the fashion-plate suits. Or the Heinrich Himmler eyewear, or the cold-fish personality. But that was all water under the pier now. When it came to the crunch, the detective sergeant acquitted himself well. Did his legwork. Came out of his box like a greyhound. Crack of dawn, New Year's Day. I couldn't fault that.

Meakes waited until we reached the creek before speaking.

'I'm heading back to Melbourne,' he said. 'Homicide will be handling things here from now on.'

'Better luck next time, eh?'

I extended my hand. Meakes accepted it. We shook, a moment of silent communion.

'We'll get him,' he said. 'No matter how long it takes.'

'I know,' I nodded sombrely. 'I know.'

The action sequence was over. The wash-up was beginning. Uniformed cops were running crime-scene tape around the area, tying yellow ribbons round the old gum trees. Jake Martyn's bulk was being manoeuvred onto a stretcher. Intermittent squeaks and gasps indicated that his condition was painful but not critical.

Kevin Hayes took charge of me. He said the parents of the other teenagers had been informed that their children were safe. Everything else would be sorted out back in town.

A police four-wheel-drive ferried us along the creek bed to a dirt track and a row of cars. The kids were subdued but physically none the worse. If there was other damage, it was not yet evident.

Red and I had the back seat of a prowl car to ourselves for the trip down to Lorne. His tee-shirt was streaked with sweat and dirt.

He looked so young and vulnerable and brave that it almost broke my heart.

'What a maniac,' he said, stroking his jaw like a war veteran at a reunion. 'And how about you, charging through the trees, going ballistic?'

'I thought he was going to kill you,' I said.

While a uniformed constable steered us along dirt tracks to the asphalt hardtop, Red told me all about it.

Mongoose had sucked them in, he said. He kept leading them deeper and deeper into the bush, their destination always just a little further ahead. He told them the crop probably belonged to some hippie surfer who only visited it occasionally to water the plants. It'd just be walk in, walk back out with the smoke.

'We wanted to turn back, Dad,' he said. 'Me and Jodie. But Matt and the others…' he shrugged. 'And after a while, we knew we'd get lost if we didn't stick together.'

They reached the camp about eleven. Mongoose scouted ahead and reported. The dog was out and about, the surfer asleep in a tent. Mongoose's plan was to distract the dog while the others crept into the dope patch, grabbed a couple of plants each and scattered into the bush.

It went fine until, mid-harvest, the plantation owner appeared. Not a spaced-out seaweed sucker but a bearded redneck brandishing a shotgun and screaming questions.

He calmed down when they said they were just hikers, lost in the bush. Told them he'd let them go in a while if they did what he said. Then he herded them into the shed and blindfolded them.

'We were scared,' Red said. 'But he didn't hurt us, so we sort of believed him.'

In the rear-view mirror, I saw the cop at the wheel of the prowl car tilt his head, the better to hear.

'And we thought Mongoose was maybe out there somewhere, getting help or figuring out a way to spring us. That's why we didn't say anything about him first up.'

'You did the right thing,' I reassured him. 'Exactly the right thing.'

It was past four o'clock when we reached Deans Marsh Road and began our descent to the sea. Thirty hours since I'd risen from my bed. Red, too, looked buggered. We yawned simultaneously. When he started up the questions again, I fended him off with the minimum. There were things it was better he didn't know, too much that I didn't yet understand.

'Tell me something,' I said. 'When that cop booted the dog, what did he say to you?'

He grinned. 'He said not to dob him in to the RSPCA.'

My boy, I sensed, would get though his experience intact.

A small crowd was milling on the street outside the Lorne cop shop. The other kids had arrived a few minutes ahead of us and family reunions were taking place. Barbara Prentice was huddled with Jodie and Matt, her sunglasses pushed back on her head. Her expression was a mixture of relief and admonishment, both kids talking at once. Across the street, Faye and Leo Curnow leaned against their Volvo wagon. Tarquin sat in the front passenger seat, door open, elbows on his knees, thumbs working his Gameboy. His sister Chloe combed through a *Who Weekly*. Our driver continued past and deposited us at the back door.

Proceedings inside were brisk, almost perfunctory. With my permission, Red was taken away to give a brief preliminary statement. I was parked in Sergeant Pendergast's office with a cup of tea and a Tim Tam. An officer would be with me in due course.

I sat there and counted the number of ways a man can be a fool. A slat of sunlight inched its way across the wall map. My tea went cold. And then Hayes of Homicide was dropping a wallet on the desk in front of me.

'Yours,' he said. 'We found it among Surovic's stuff up there at his camp.'

'Surovic?' I said. 'That his name?'

Hayes looked down at me, hands sunk deep in his pockets. 'Michael Surovic,' he said. 'According to items found at the camp.'

I thumbed through my wallet. Credit cards and whatnot were still there. The Polaroid. I took it out and looked at it.

'For what it's worth,' Hayes said, 'in my opinion he does look a bit like Rodney Syce.'

Perhaps that was supposed to make me feel better. I waited for the shard of ice to melt, then put the photo away.

'And Jake Martyn?' I said. 'Enlighten me.'

Hayes rubbed his nose thoughtfully. 'A superficial wound, but painful. And there was an awful long wait for the ambulance.'

'Terrible delays, apparently,' I said. 'Since the privatisation.'

'We did our best to make him comfortable. He was very grateful. Opened his heart to us. Told us about his run of bad luck at the blackjack table.'

'High roller?' I said.

'Deep shit,' nodded Hayes. 'Spiralling debts and a business partner impatient to be paid out. Desperate frame of mind.'

'And an easy mark in Tony Melina,' I said. 'Did he

really think he'd get away with it?'

Hayes shrugged, a man who'd seen it all. 'He still might. What he told us back up there in the hills isn't admissible evidence. The actual killer is dead. And Tony Melina's body is somewhere on the bottom of Bass Strait. A lot will hang on your testimony, Mr Whelan.'

I lowered my head and groaned.

'All in good time,' said Hayes. 'Right now, I suggest you get some shut-eye. We'll talk again when you're rested up. Your son's waiting outside.'

So was Barbara Prentice.

As I stepped into the glare of the late afternoon, she came forward to meet me.

I must have looked like an insurance assessor's nightmare. But there was understanding in her eyes, and gratitude, and the promise of consolation. Before I knew it, her arms were reaching to enfold me.

She drew me close and held me tight, my head cradled in the hollow of her hand. The short blond hairs behind her ear gleamed in the afternoon sun.

A long time had passed since I'd felt the warmth of a woman's arms, the press of a woman's body. A small sigh escaped me. A dam burst.

I began to cry.

Not just a sob and a sniffle. Not just a quiet weep. Great shudders racked my body. Tears gushed from my eyes. I blubbered, whimpered and gasped.

Barbara rocked me, soothing me with strokes and sympathetic murmurs.

Women say they appreciate vulnerability in a man. Admire it, even. So they say. But nothing can convince me they find it sexy. Not the full waterworks. Not the pathetic bawling that dribbles gooey strings of snot onto the downy hairs at the back of their necks.

You've blown it, sport, I told myself. And I didn't mean my nose.

'You're a good man, Murray Whelan,' said Barbara.

That sealed it. I drew a shaky breath, extricated myself and firmed my upper lip.

'Better be going,' I snuffled.

It never would have worked anyway. A potential minefield. That son of hers, for a start. What a ratbag. And Velcro Girl, the daughter. And when it came to the clinch, as it just had, she was a bit too skinny for my taste.

'You okay, Dad?' said Red, stepping deftly into the gap.

They say that time is a great healer.

So is pursuing your personal demon to the heart of the labyrinth. Confronting him one on one, and seeing his fly-blown carcass in the dirt.

Okay, so it was Mick Surovic, not Rodney Syce. But as far as I was concerned, the rage was spent. The evil spirit was exorcised.

We went back to the holiday house and I slept like a felled tree, twelve hours straight, Red on a blow-up mattress on the floor beside me.

'Just in case you need anything in the night,' he said. Also because he had no choice in the matter. He and Tark had ripped a hole in the tent at the Falls, so they had to find sleeping space in the house. The ban on the Docs remained.

Early next morning, I went down to the beach.

There was a secluded spot not far from where I'd staggered ashore. I walked barefoot into the lapping foam and stood for a moment, watching the fall of the waves. Then I laid the photograph of my never-born little girl on the gently ebbing tide and watched it float away.

Lyndal, I felt sure, would have approved.

A few days later, back in Melbourne for a meeting with the coppers, I tossed the Syce file into the garbage. Didn't even open it. Lyndal was beyond caring about Rodney Syce and so was I. He lived a crappy life and he'd die a crappy death. I had better things to think about than the form it might take.

That was six months ago. There's been plenty to keep me busy since then.

The federal election has come and gone, with all its attendant demands on the party faithful. We lost, of course. Routed. The Labor Party is now in the wilderness at national, state and municipal level. And you know how I feel about wilderness.

Jake Martyn is languishing in the Remand Centre, awaiting trial for murder. Not conspiracy, not delegation of a messy unpleasant chore, not possession of illegal abalone. Certainly not oops.

As predicted, he reneged on his forest-floor fess-up. Went the clam. The Director of Public Prosecutions is concentrating on the paper trail, working to buttress my eyewitness testimony. Visibility from that aluminium dinghy wasn't too hot, after all, and the absence of a body in a homicide case is always problematic.

Gusto has gone into receivership. One of the creditors is Prentice & Associates, Architects. Another reason I haven't returned Barbara's calls.

Red still sees Jodie, but only in passing at school. For the moment at least, he has forsworn romantic entanglements. Girls are more trouble than they're worth, he tells me, although I suspect he's got his eye on one of the munchkins in the Year Eleven production of *The Wizard of Oz*.

The big loser among the living is poor Rita Melina. The Black Widow of Melbourne Upper, as Ayisha calls her.

What with the tax office and the fish dogs and the overseas bank accounts, Tony's estate still hasn't passed probate. The way things are looking, Rita will be lucky if she ends up with enough dough for a decent root perm. Worse still, she has to live with the fact that she ratted out a husband whose infidelity was limited to feeling up the hired help. And did it while he was chained naked to a tree, pleading to be allowed to call her.

The bodacious waitress, Tony's supposed elopee, had in fact upped tits without notice to accept a lucrative job offer as a hostess in a Tokyo nightclub.

Out of concern for Rita's finer feelings, the business with Tony's ear has not been divulged.

Likewise, I've never disclosed the promise I made to blow the Premier's bugle in public if the man in the shadows wasn't Rodney Syce. There was nobody there to witness my pledge, after all. And anyway, that particular service is more expertly and frequently provided by the organs of the mass media.

Nor have I yet found an appropriate use for the videotape that was waiting in a plain envelope on my desk at Parliament House when I returned from the summer break. It was unlabelled and the first few seconds of vision were so jumpy and jerky that I thought it must have been a misdirected submission to the film funding commission.

Then the focus sharpened, the camera steadied and I found myself watching crystal clear footage of Dudley Wilson chucking his chunks over Alan Bunting on the deck of a Natural Resources launch near Cape Patterson.

I think I'll wait until Dudley's Coastal Whatsit Panel submits its draft recommendations to the government. If he proposes further reductions in DNR staffing levels, I'll slip a copy to every parliamentary member of the National Party. It might not affect the final outcome but it should sow some acrimony in the ranks of the enemy.

Parliament is currently in recess for the winter and I'm spending my working hours at the electorate office. Detective Sergeant Meakes called me here a few days ago. It was the first time we'd spoken since New Year's Day.

'I thought you should know,' he said. 'A man's body was found yesterday morning.'

It was discovered in an old storm-water drain during excavation work on the new freeway tunnel under the Yarra at Richmond. It had been lodged there for a fair while and there wasn't much of it left. There was enough, however, to get some partial fingerprints.

It was Rodney Syce.

The way Meakes figured it, Syce ditched the Kawasaki in Richmond after the shoot-out, then went to ground down a manhole cover. Perhaps he was injured from his spill off the bike, perhaps he got lost in the maze, perhaps he had an accident in the subterranean darkness. Whatever the case, however he died, his body was swept into an ancient section of piping.

As to the other aspect of closure, I won't say too much. Suffice to mention that I've met someone who shows signs of playing a significant role in that regard.

We live in hope.

What else can we do?

BOBBY GOLD

ANTHONY BOURDAIN

Meet Bobby Gold, by night the security chief of a New York City night-club, by day a reluctant bonebreaker and enforcer. Graduating from the "gladiator school" environment of an upstate prison, he views the grim work of coercion, assault and murder as jobs to be done with a crafts-man's work ethic.

"Sharp and funny . . . if it's gangster rap you want to read then Bourdain is your man."

Daily Express

£6.99

1 84195 327 X (10-digit ISBN); 978 1 84195 327 4 (13-digit ISBN)

BONE IN THE THROAT

ANTHONY BOURDAIN

Sous-chef Tommy just wants to perfect his seafood chowder. But his kitchen is being used for more than food preparation – with his mobster relatives finding imaginative applications for a meat cleaver you won't find in *The Naked Chef*.

"A superb tale of violence and back-biting set in the seething testosterone-heavy company of a crew of New York cooks." GQ

"Raw and cooking. Rare and well-done." A.A. Gill

£6.99

1 84195 287 7 (10-digit ISBN); 978 1 84195 287 1 (13-digit ISBN)

www.canongate.net

GONE BAMBOO

ANTHONY BOURDAIN

Welcome to the retirement home of Henry and Frances, ex-New Yorkers and professional assassins. A luxury hotel suite in an idyllic, tequila-drenched Caribbean hideaway. But when a job icing a Mafioso godfather goes awry, trouble hits paradise . . .

"Reads like Carl Hiaasen on holiday with Elmore Leonard and goes out with a bang like a tequila slammer." The Times

£6.99

1 84195 367 9 (10-digit ISBN); 978 1 84195 367 0 (13-digit ISBN)

MISSING

KARIN ALVTEGEN

In the Grand Hotel, a homeless woman charms a businessman into paying for dinner and a room. When his dead body is discovered the following morning she becomes the prime suspect. When a second person is killed, she becomes the most wanted person in Sweden.

"Relentless and frightening . . . compassionate and gritty . . . Alvtegen is a name to watch." Guardian

£6.99

1 84195 498 5 (10-digit ISBN); 978 1 84195 498 1 (13-digit ISBN)

www.canongate.net

MIDNIGHT CAB

Winner of the CCWA Award

JAMES W. NICHOL

A three-year-old boy is abandoned at the side of a country road. His mother whispers to him to hold on to a wire fence. She never returns. Sixteen years later, Walker Devereaux sets out to discover the truth about his early life. In pursuit of answers he uncovers his family's dark secrets. . .

"Takes the reader on a wild ride through the past, and into the mind of a madman. Utterly gripping." Kathy Reichs

"One of the most sinister and unforgettable villains crime fiction has drawn in a long time."
Maxim Jakubowski

£6.99

1 84195 567 1 (10-digit ISBN); 978 1 84195 567 4 (13-digit ISBN)

BETRAYAL

KARIN ALVTEGEN

When Eva discovers her husband's been having an affair, her grief and rage drive her into vengeful action. Reminiscent of the work of Patricia Highsmith and Henning Mankell, *Betrayal* exposes the pain of deception and the destruction it leaves behind.

"Alvtegen gets under the skin of a lovely obsessive." Independent

£6.99

1 84195 709 7 (10-digit ISBN); 978 1 84195 709 8 (13-digit ISBN)

www.canongate.net

More Murray Whelan Mysteries

THE BIG ASK

SHANE MALONEY

With an election looming, a homicide cop on his heels, adultery in the air and a gun buried in his backyard, political minder and spin-meister Murray Whelan is in for a frenzied few days. The two murky worlds of politics and crime are about to collide . . .

"Whelan is like an Aussie Rebus, he is cynical but smart, punch-drunk but dogged."
Sunday Herald

£6.99

1 84195 476 4 (10-digit ISBN); 978 1 84195 476 9 (13-digit ISBN)

THE BRUSH-OFF

SHANE MALONEY

Summer in the city. Murray Whelan is in the undergrowth of Melbourne's Botanic Gardens having a romantic encounter with the delicious Salina Fleet. Meanwhile, across the park, the body of a disgruntled artist is being fished out of the public art gallery's ornamental moat. Whelan, political spin doctor and artless lover, goes looking for the big picture.

"An engaging read, with our hero displaying an all-too-human mix of brains and stupidity. Peppered throughout with deft and amusing one-liners." Big Issue

£6.99

1 84195 356 3 (10-digit ISBN); 978 1 84195 356 4 (13-digit ISBN)

www.canongate.net

NICE TRY

SHANE MALONEY

When Murray Whelan, lovelorn political minder and part-time fitness fanatic, is recruited to massage Australia's bid for the Olympics, he has no idea how tough the going will get. Not even the sight of the gorgeous Holly Deloite in her taut blue leotard at the City Club can stop him diving head first into trouble.

"There's no doubting the brilliance of the writing." Ian Rankin

"Nice Try *gets a big tick."* The Australian

£6.99

1 84195 809 3 (10-digit ISBN) ; 978 1 84195 809 5 (13-digit ISBN)

STIFF

SHANE MALONEY

The fiddle at the Pacific Pastoral meat-packing works was a nice little earner for all concerned until Herb Gardiner reported finding a body in Number 3 chiller. An accident, of course, but just the excuse a devious political operator might grab to stir up trouble with the unions. It's all in a day's work for Murray. Then the aqua Falcon turns up and it gets personal. Because don't you just hate it when somebody tries to kill you and you don't know who or why?

"Brilliantly mixes the comic and the tragic." Rolling Stone

£6.99

1 84195 531 0 (10-digit ISBN); 978 1 84195 531 5 (13-digit ISBN)

www.canongate.net